JV-18

GHOST OF A GAMBLE

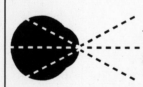

A GHOST OF GRANNY APPLES MYSTERY

GHOST OF A GAMBLE

SUE ANN JAFFARIAN

THORNDIKE PRESS
A part of Gale, Cengage Learning

GALE
CENGAGE Learning·

Farmington Hills, Mich • San Francisco • New York • Waterville, Maine
Meriden, Conn • Mason, Ohio • Chicago

GALE
CENGAGE Learning®

LIBRARY OF CONGRESS CATALOGING-IN-PUBLICATION DATA

Jaffarian, Sue Ann, 1952–
  Ghost of a gamble / by Sue Ann Jaffarian. — Large print edition.
    pages ; cm. — (Thorndike Press large print mystery)
  ISBN-13: 978-1-4104-7172-7 (hardcover)
  ISBN-10: 1-4104-7172-1 (hardcover)
  1. Mediums—Fiction. 2. Apparitions—Fiction. 3. Grandmothers—Fiction.
4. Gangsters—Fiction. 5. Las Vegas (Nev.)—Fiction. 6. Large type books.
  I. Title.
PS3610.A359G487 2014
813'.6—dc23   2014021147

Published in 2014 by arrangement with The Berkley Publishing Group, a member of Penguin Group (USA) LLC, a Penguin Random House Company

Printed in Mexico
1 2 3 4 5 6 7 18 17 16 15 14

ACKNOWLEDGMENTS

Although this is not my first Ghost of Granny Apples book, it is my first full-length novel with the Penguin publishing family, so I'm feeling a lot of special gratitude.

A big shout-out of thanks to Whitney Lee, the agent of light, who found Granny her new home at Berkley Prime Crime. To Emily Rapoport, my first editor at Berkley who bought the Granny Apples franchise, and to Faith Black, my current editor, who picked up the Granny banner from Emily and gives me great guidance.

Ladies, this book is for you!

CHAPTER ONE

The light fixture was as common as a rock. A simple white metal cylinder recessed into a textured, plain white kitchen ceiling, it beamed soft light down onto the counter below without fanfare or embellishment, like the billions of light fixtures like it around the world.

Emma Whitecastle peered up at it and saw nothing unusual. The baby, however, thought it the greatest attraction since peekaboo. His face blossomed with joy and he dissolved into a fit of giggles each time he looked up. From his seat in the bouncer, the child waved his pudgy arms and legs like a turtle trying to right itself and jabbered happily at the ceiling. His laughter was infectious and Emma couldn't help giggling along with him.

If you didn't count Oscar, her ex-husband's midlife crises son from his midlife crises bimbo second wife, it had been a long time since Emma had seen a baby up close and personal. Even with Oscar, she'd kept her distance, given the family dynamics. Emma looked down at the little boy in the bouncer and thought about her own child, Kelly, and how she'd been a sweet, good-natured baby like this. Kelly was now in her third year at Harvard.

"He's sure a happy little fella." The comment came from Granny Apples, who watched the child from a few feet away.

Emma nodded without acknowledging the presence of the ghost of her great-great-great-grandmother, instead keeping her eyes on the little boy dressed in pint-size jeans and a green T-shirt covered in orange giraffes.

"What's his name again?"

The question was not aimed at Granny, but at the woman standing behind the counter on which the baby's seat rested. The counter jutted out from the wall like an arm, separating the cluttered but cheerful kitchen from the eating area that housed a well-used wooden kitchen table.

"Nicholas," the woman replied. "He's about seven months old."

Nicholas giggled again and bent in half, grabbing his feet in his little hands in a form of infant calisthenics. When he let go, his face beamed upward, as if searching for approval. He still wasn't looking at Emma. Nicholas only had eyes for the overhead light, communicating to it with smiles and baby babble.

Emma looked up. "You're right, Dolly. There is something odd about that light fixture."

"I call it Lenny the Lightbulb."

"You gave the light a name?"

"Why not? His stuffed animals have names."

Dolly Meskiel moved closer to the counter. She was in her mid-seventies but moved with the lightness of a much younger woman. A multicolored scarf held her long silver hair back from her still attractive face. Her flouncy Indian print skirt was paired with a long-sleeved peasant blouse of creamy cotton, divided at the waist by a cord of burgundy velvet with silver embellishments. On her feet were hot pink Crocs. Hanging heavily around her neck was an impressive squash blossom necklace. Dolly was not afraid of color.

Emma felt Dolly's eyes on her, studying her through wire-rimmed glasses perched on the end of her slender nose. Behind the lenses sat sharp blue eyes that matched the color of her thick eye shadow.

"At first it was a silly joke," Dolly explained. "I started calling the light Lenny when I noticed Nicholas talking to it all the time." Dolly gently stroked the baby's fine dark hair with a thin hand. "When his fixation continued, I wondered if there was more to it, especially since Nicholas doesn't obsess on any other lights, just this one."

"You think there might be a ghost haunting your house?" Emma looked up at the light again. She couldn't feel the presence of any spirits, save Granny, and she presently couldn't see any except for Granny. With Dolly's air-conditioning running, it was also difficult for Emma to gauge any unusual pockets of cool air, often a sign that spirits were nearby.

"Not my house, just that light." With a protective hand still on the child's head, Dolly also peered up at the fixture. "Can ghosts inhabit lights? I've never heard of such a thing, but thought if anyone would know, it would be you."

The comment gave Emma a start. Dolly's only child was Milo Ravenscroft, Emma's mentor, friend, and world-famous medium. Emma had driven to Las Vegas as a favor to Milo, though she was still puzzled as to why he needed her help. He was far superior to her in communicating with the other side.

Milo was in Las Vegas with Tracy Bass, his fiancée and Emma's closest friend, but although the couple was staying with Dolly, neither was currently at Dolly's townhouse in a quiet neighborhood that seemed light-years away from the glitz and glamor of the famous Strip. Once Emma had arrived and introductions had been made, Milo and Tracy had left, saying they had an appointment at the university. Emma knew it was an excuse to let her interact with Dolly without distraction. Before leaving, Milo had said he and Tracy would meet up with Emma later at her hotel. In her head, Emma was working on a list of questions to ask Milo when she saw him.

Emma had left her home in Pasadena shortly after six that morning, just ahead of Tuesday rush hour traffic. She'd covered the two hundred sixty miles to Vegas in a little over four hours, stopping once, in Baker, to grab a bagel and a cup of coffee at the Mad Greek. Eager to find out what was going on, she'd driven straight to Dolly's from there. Granny had been excited to tag along to Las Vegas. She loved the place and she loved long car trips. During the drive Emma had listened to a book on tape, something she enjoyed doing and something Granny liked a great deal.

"I may not be able to read very well," Granny had said, excited as the trip began, "or hold a book, but I sure can listen."

Emma glanced quickly at Granny, then flashed her eyes upward, indicating she wanted to know what the ghost thought about the light fixture. She did not want Dolly to know about Granny, at least not yet.

Granny moved into Emma's line of sight and shrugged, letting her know she hadn't picked up on any spirits either.

"Why Lenny?" Emma asked Dolly.

Dolly hesitated before answering. "I don't really know. It just seemed to fit."

Dolly's hand went from the baby's head to her own hair. A long lock had fallen across her shoulder. She twisted it while she gave the question more thought. It was a gesture Emma expected from a very young woman, not from someone her parents' age. She watched Dolly more carefully, wondering if the hair twisting was a sign of nervousness or simply an unconscious habit.

"It was the oddest thing," Dolly explained. "One morning the name just sort of popped out of my mouth, rather like a hiccup." She stopped playing with her hair, tossing the long gray strand back over her left shoulder. "Sounds good, though, doesn't it? Lenny the Lightbulb. Sounds a lot better than Jack the Lightbulb or Maurice the Lightbulb."

"She's got a point," added Granny, who floated closer to the baby, stopping next to Emma.

Emma wiggled the baby's foot with its blue sock and cooed at him. Still laughing at the light, Nicholas responded by letting his eyes drift down to her. He smiled, showing off two bottom front teeth. When his gaze drifted to Emma's right, where Granny stood, he wiggled in his seat and grinned in that direction.

"I think the little tyke can see me," Granny told Emma. Granny slowly moved away from Emma. With his eyes, Nicholas followed Granny's movement. When she got several feet away, he frowned with confusion and twisted his head to see her better. Granny started to move back toward him. When she got close, Nicholas's face lit up. "Now I'm sure of it."

Emma took note of Granny's experiment, but said nothing. She turned her attention back to Dolly, "What do his parents think?"

"His parents think Lenny the Lightbulb is a funny, cute game I play with their son. I haven't said anything to them about ghosts."

"Probably a good idea, at least for the time being. Do you know where they stand on the paranormal?"

"Not really. I've been watching Nicholas for nearly two months now, but haven't spent much time with the Fosters. Usually John drops the baby off every weekday morning between seven thirty and eight. He's a cop here in town. Suzanne works part-time in a doctor's office and picks him up around one or one thirty in the afternoon. They live in this complex, but a few buildings over. It's convenient for them and a good way for me to supplement my income. Plus I enjoy it. It makes me feel less of an old lady."

Dolly went to the refrigerator and pulled out some baby food. "I didn't want to scare them, or make them think twice about letting me take care of Nicholas. John already thinks I'm a bit of an eccentric, what with the fortune telling and all, but I was referred to them by people they trust."

"You tell fortunes?" asked Emma with surprise.

"Yes, didn't Milo tell you that?"

Emma searched her memory until she found the answer. Milo had never said a thing to her about it, but Tracy had. In a phone call to Emma after her first meeting with her future mother-in-law, Tracy had announced to Emma with amusement that

14

Dolly was a fortune-teller right out of central casting, and a former showgirl.

"No," Emma said, "but I do recall now that Tracy mentioned it. She also said you were once a showgirl."

Dolly straightened her posture and smiled. "That's right, in one of the best shows of its kind. Of course, that was when I was in my twenties. Both Vegas and I were fresh and sassy back then."

Emma gave the woman a big smile in return. Behind the heavy makeup and loose clothing, Dolly was still a very attractive woman and maintained a trim figure.

"I have a little shop downtown on Fremont Street where I read fortunes," Dolly said with the same pride she held for her showgirl days. "Been there quite a long time."

Emma looked around the townhouse, understanding now some of the decor. Even though the complex was modern, Dolly's home looked like an explosion of a gypsy wagon. While the ceilings were a plain creamy white, the walls were painted different bold colors, and brightly patterned rugs and cushions were scattered across the wood floor. The furnishings were solid and old and also brightly colored. Nothing seemed to match. Books and candles were

15

everywhere. Dolly's home definitely was not the norm for desert décor.

Knowing Milo and his quirky ways, Emma didn't expect his mother to be a June Cleaver knockoff, but she wasn't quite expecting Dolly. So far, she liked the woman. According to Tracy, she also liked and got along well with Dolly. There was something whimsical about Milo's mother — a rare combination of daffy and wise under the hippy-dippy clothes and electric eye makeup. But Emma still wondered why Dolly hadn't asked her son to check out Lenny.

"May I?" Emma asked, indicating she wanted to pick up Nicholas.

Dolly smiled. "He loves to be held and cuddled."

Emma scooped up the solid baby boy and held him so he was facing her. He wiggled and cooed and touched her face, but his eyes never left Granny. They moved as she moved. Emma walked around Dolly's dining area and living room with him, but Nicholas was determined to keep eye contact with Granny Apples. It wasn't until Granny disappeared that he concentrated on Emma, changing his focus to her chunky necklace. When she walked back to the kitchen counter, the bold jewelry was

16

quickly forgotten as the baby held out his arms — not to Dolly, but toward the overhead light.

"See what I mean?" Dolly held out her arms and Emma transferred the baby into them. "There's something in that light. Something only Nicholas can see."

Although she was in agreement, Emma kept her own counsel. She wanted to talk it over with Milo and see what he thought about the little boy's behavior. Although Emma knew it was not uncommon for very young children to see or sense spirits, she'd never encountered one personally.

"It is odd, but let me think on this a bit, Dolly, and I'd like to discuss it with Milo. He's really the expert."

At Emma's words, Dolly pursed her lips in disapproval. Or was it disappointment? Emma couldn't tell.

"I'll be in town for a few days. Do you mind if I drop by again?"

"Not at all. It would be a pleasure, Emma. I'm usually home until about four each day. After that you can find me at my shop, The Raven's Craft. Milo has the address, but it's easy to find. It's located on Fremont Street almost across from The Golden Nugget. I usually arrive between five and six and stay quite late, depending on business." She made a funny face at Nicholas as she wiped away a bit of drool with a napkin, but he still only had eyes for the light fixture.

Emma walked over to the wall next to the counter and flicked a light switch. Instantly the light overhead went out. She watched the baby, expecting him to lose interest in the now dark fixture. He didn't.

Dolly bounced the baby. "I've tried that many times. It doesn't matter if it's on or not."

"And he stares at it all the time?" Emma glanced up and thought she saw a hint of sparkle in the dark orb, but it quickly disappeared.

After some thought, Dolly answered, "Not all the time, no, but most of the time. Sometimes Nicholas giggles and plays like today. Other times he just stares up at it, as if he's waiting for something."

Emma turned to retrieve her purse from a nearby chair where she'd left it.

"Did Nemo's boys send you?"

She whipped around. Dolly was again occupied with making faces at Nicholas.

"Did you say something?" she asked Dolly.

"I was just telling my little man here I had some yummy strained peaches for him. He loves peaches."

"You didn't say anything about Nemo?"

"Nemo?" Dolly stopped playing with Nicholas. "Where did you hear that?"

"Just now. I thought I heard you say something to me about Nemo."

"No." Dolly shook her head back and forth with quick jerks. "I didn't. You must have heard me say *num num num.*" She looked the baby in the face and repeated the words. He giggled.

Emma would have bought the explanation, except for catching Dolly giving Lenny the Lightbulb a furtive glance.

CHAPTER TWO

"Vegas reminds me of a twenty-dollar prostitute dressed in couture." Emma looked out the large window of her suite at the Venetian Hotel, her arms crossed in front of her. Beyond her was a fabulous view of the Strip. Her words weren't said in judgment, but a simple statement of her opinion.

Milo Ravenscroft got up and went to the window to stand next to her. The city of Las Vegas lay before them — an odd collection of fake landmarks and bogus palaces from around the world dropped in the Nevada desert like flashy shoes flung from a passing car. Between the humongous hotels and casinos, bars, restaurants, and cheap souvenir shops clung like tooth plaque, vying for overflow dollars. The sun was high. Once it went down, the buildings before them would be ablaze in color and lights.

"It's always been a twenty-dollar whore," Milo added, "but at least in the old days it was an honest whore without pretention."

Emma looked at Milo with interest. "That's right, you grew up here."

"Yes, born and raised. Never liked the place. Then or now." He stretched an arm out as if presenting a prize in a game show. "Where else in the world could you find the Eiffel Tower, an Egyptian pyramid, and a medieval castle in the same place?"

"Disneyland offers the Mississippi River, a Swiss mountain, and an African jungle all within walking distance of each other," offered Tracy from her seat on the sofa. "And they both have pirate ships. Of course, Disneyland doesn't offer gambling and nude revues."

"I don't know," Emma chuckled. "I hear those cartoon characters can get quite racy after hours."

She took a seat on the opposite end of the large L-shaped sofa and propped a foot up on the large glass coffee table. She'd just filled Milo and Tracy in on what had happened at Dolly's. "I have a few housekeeping questions before we get to the business of the ghost."

Tracy glanced over at Milo. "I told you to tell her."

"If it's about Dolly being a fortune-teller," Emma told Milo, "Tracy had already mentioned it to me. But why didn't you? And why did you call me here to do something you can do much better?"

Milo took off his glasses and inspected the cleanliness of the lenses. "What can I say, Dolly is an original." He shook his head. "She's one of those fortune-tellers you see in bad movies, complete with potions on display."

"Wait a minute," interrupted Emma. "You call your mother Dolly?"

"Everyone calls his mother Dolly," added Tracy.

"Even when I was a kid," Milo added, "she hated to be called Mom or Mother, probably because she was so young when she had me. She's been Dolly to me since I was old enough to talk."

Emma couldn't imagine calling her mother Elizabeth. More to the point, she couldn't imagine her mother wanting or tolerating it. Nor would Emma want her own daughter calling her Emma. But to each their own. If you discounted Granny Apples, her family was fairly traditional and Emma liked it that way.

Emma squared her shoulders, readying herself to ask a very personal question. "Milo, are you ashamed of your mother and what she does?"

Milo took a full minute before answering. "*Ashamed* is a strong word, Emma." He paused, sucking on one end of his glasses. "Okay, maybe I'm a bit embarrassed by her business. Though why should I be? Right? To most people, what I do is no different, just on a bigger scale. But I'm also concerned for Dolly." Milo put his glasses back on. "As you can see, she can be quite colorful and unconventional. As for her skills, even after all these years, I've never seen anything concrete beyond her ability to convince people of the things she's telling them. She can be quite persuasive, especially when someone's willing to pay more. The local authorities have been cracking down on scams against tourists. I'm always afraid she'll get in trouble. All it would take is one unhappy customer to complain to start trouble."

Emma rubbed the soft gold brocade on the arm of the sofa. "Okay, but why did you call me here? It's not that I'm not happy to help out anytime you need it," she rushed to clarify. "But it seems strange you'd ask me to Las Vegas to check on a ghost."

Tracy cleared her throat. "The ghost is not the problem, Em."

Looking from Tracy to Milo without getting an answer, Emma pushed, "Is it because it's in your mother's home?"

Emma could tell by the way Tracy twisted her mouth from side to side, she was dying to tell her, but was restraining herself. Something quite difficult for Tracy's natural exuberance. She looked up at Milo with encouragement.

After a deep sigh, Milo said, "Yes, it is because it's at Dolly's, and because she specifically asked if I could convince you to come to Las Vegas to investigate."

Emma pointed a finger at herself. "Me? Why me when she has you here?"

Milo got up and went to the window again. "Dolly is convinced it's something only you can do."

Tracy closed her eyes for a second. When she opened them, she said with kindness, "Please don't take it personally, darling. You said yourself your communication with spirits goes awry around Dolly."

"I'm not going to lie." He looked from Tracy to Emma. "I do take it personally. Dolly has always thought my skills were nothing more than a con, a scam like hers." A strangled half laugh followed his words. "She claims she got the idea for her palm-reading setup indirectly from me."

Emma sat forward in her seat, trying to get a handle on what Milo was trying to say. "But she doesn't think I'm a scam?"

"Not at all. She records your show and watches it faithfully. She says it gives her ideas for her own business."

Emma cringed inwardly at the idea, but admitted to herself that, like Milo, many thought her medium abilities were nothing more than tricks and scams and she had the mail back at the studio evidencing those opinions, along with mail supporting her and the show.

"Dolly doesn't understand that Milo is your mentor," added Tracy. "I've tried to explain that to her, but she won't listen."

"When I was a small kid, my mother was a showgirl." With a slow, deliberate gait, Milo paced across the room. "Not in one of the big extravaganza productions, but it was still very popular. She slept during the day while I was in school. At night I'd sit in a corner of her dressing room. I'd stay out of the way and do my homework or read until I fell asleep. The other dancers didn't mind as long as I behaved." Milo laughed. "Believe me, I saw my share of naked women as a young boy and was the envy of a lot of my school friends. When I was older, Dolly let me stay home in our apartment by myself. That's when I first started seeing spirits."

He looked up at Emma. "Do you have some water? I'm a bit parched. A Coke would be even better, if you have it."

Emma got up and opened the minifridge, retrieving a can of Coke. She filled a glass with ice from the bucket on the counter and poured the soft drink over it. The sound of carbonation and the tinkling of ice filled the room like bees hitting wind chimes.

"At first I was scared," Milo continued, "then the spirits became my friends and kept me company."

Emma handed Milo the glass and retook her seat on the sofa. "You must have spent a lot of time alone."

He nodded and took a big drink from his glass. "Yes, but I didn't really mind. I buried myself in my schoolwork. By the time I was thirteen, I'd skipped two grades." He took another gulp of soda. "That's when I went from being a cool kid surrounded by show-girls to a target for bullies."

"You never told me this," said Tracy, leaning forward.

"I know, my love, and I'm sorry." Milo took another drink before continuing. "Most of the time Dolly came straight home after her last show. Sometimes she went out with friends for drinks afterward. But almost always she stayed up to make sure I

26

got off to school on time, and she even made me breakfast and packed my lunch." Milo smiled into his glass. "We'd talk over eggs and toast about school and who came into the club the night before and what we were going to do together on her night off. It really wasn't so bad. She was really a good mother and I never doubted she loved me."

"Sounds very lonely, Milo." The comment didn't come from Emma, but from the ghost of Granny Apples, who had just appeared.

"Did you tell Dolly about the spirits?" Emma asked.

"Not at first, but as they visited me more, I did." With his index finger, Milo poked at the ice in his glass. "She always thought they were simply imaginary friends cooked up by a lonely kid with too much time on his hands. Over time, I studied the paranormal as much as possible and developed my communications with the other side. After I graduated from high school, I went to college here in Las Vegas and graduated at twenty. I put myself through college giving readings and conducting private séances, much as I do now, but on a smaller scale and with less experience."

He sighed and took another drink. "Dolly always thought her smart baby boy had come up with a slick way to make money. I don't think she's ever believed I could really see and speak to spirits."

"But what about your reputation?" asked Emma. "You've written several bestselling books on the subject. Doesn't she know that?"

"Yes, she does, and she's quite proud of my success. She just about ruptured with excitement when I bought her that town-home with my royalties. But considering I can't do a lick of anything spiritual when I'm around her, why should she believe it's real?"

Milo drained his glass, placed it on the table, and poured in the rest of the soda from the can that Emma had left in front of him. "My mother can be a real piece of work, Emma, but she has a good heart, and fortunately, she seems to have taken a shine to Tracy."

Tracy shrugged. "What can I say? We're two peas in an eccentric pod who happen to love the same goofy guy. But," Tracy said, pointing a finger at Milo, "I draw the line at getting married by Elvis."

"Elvis?" asked Emma.

"Yes," Tracy told her. "Dolly wants us to get married here in Vegas by a justice of the peace who is also an Elvis impersonator.

Apparently, he's a friend of hers."

Emma chuckled and shook her head. "I can just see your stuffy family going for that."

"Her parents are just as bad," added Milo. "Just in a different direction. They want us to have this big wedding and reception with two hundred of their closest friends, none of which we know."

Emma got up and went to the window and looked out over the Strip. Granny floated over and hovered by her side.

"I love Vegas!" the ghost said with enthusiasm. "They didn't have fancy places like this when I was alive. People gambled in the back of beer halls." Granny had lived during the late 1800s in Julian, California, a gold rush town in the mountains north of San Diego.

Emma could take or leave Las Vegas. When she was married to Grant White-castle, the famous bad boy of television talk shows, they'd come here often. He'd gamble in the high roller rooms while she shopped or lounged by the pool. He loved Caesars Palace. She preferred the Venetian. Neither had cared for the newer hotels. She'd returned to the city a couple of times since their divorce, but that had been with Phil Bowers, the man she was currently seeing.

She had much more fun with Phil, who loved the shows and spending time together more than the gaming tables.

Phil couldn't make this trip. He was tied up with work at his law firm in San Diego. When she'd called him to let him know she'd arrived safely, he'd said if he could, he'd try to get away from the office and fly up for at least a day or two.

Emma wouldn't be here now herself if not for Tracy and Milo. She could hardly say no to Milo's request, not after everything he'd done for her since she first learned she could speak to and see spirits. Without him, she wouldn't have *The Whitecastle Report,* her cable TV show on the paranormal, or be able to help the ghosts and people who came to her for assistance. Milo had mentored and schooled her in the way of the other side. She owed him big-time. As for Tracy, she was like a sister to Emma. She wasn't due back in Los Angeles for a couple of weeks when they were scheduled to shoot the next few segments of *The Whitecastle Report.* That should give her more than enough time to take care of any ghost Milo's mother thought was visiting her, if there was one, and get in some R and R with Phil.

Next to her, Granny was nearly bouncing with excitement. "Maybe this visit we'll see some of those *CSI* folks, or maybe a dead body in a casino. That's what happened last week on TV. This man was stabbed by a broken beer bottle just as he hit a big jackpot."

Milo started to say something to Granny, but Emma signaled to him to leave it be. "Don't encourage her."

CHAPTER THREE

"So you have no channeling or spiritual abilities around your mother?" Emma asked the question while walking from the window back to the sofa. "Or do you simply choose not to use them around her?"

Tracy turned to Emma. "Milo goes blank around Dolly."

"Blank?" Confusion danced across Emma's face.

"Dolly is Milo's kryptonite," Tracy explained. "Around her, he seems to lose his paranormal powers."

"Completely?" Emma looked at Milo, her confusion turning into disbelief.

Milo, a slight man of fifty-three with thick glasses and serious nerdy overtones, stared down at his hands like a child being chastised. Until recently, Milo had kept to himself, writing books on the afterlife and communication with it. He also saw private clients and conducted group séances. Emma knew he and Tracy had come to Las Vegas because Milo had been invited to give a talk at UNLV — the University of Nevada, Las Vegas. The latter had been something Tracy had set up through her own contacts as a college professor. Since falling in love with Tracy, Milo had started coming out of his shell and was doing more public appearances with her encouragement. He had always been confident with his clients and in his abilities, but speaking before people had made him shake with fear — a problem he was overcoming with Tracy's help. His public appearances were a huge success and demands for his time on the rise.

"Yes, it's true," admitted Milo. "It's like my spirit radar goes on the fritz." He ran a hand over his head, mussing his sparse brown and gray hair. "A lot of people have mother issues. I guess that's mine."

"And probably why you don't live near her?" ventured Emma.

Milo nodded at Emma's accurate perception. "It's difficult to earn a living as a medium when your gifts have the plug pulled."

"Did you try to reach out to the spirit in Dolly's home at all?"

"I did when we first arrived, but got nowhere with it."

"Lenny ignored him," added Tracy with a grin.

"Yes, Lenny." Milo laughed. "Lenny could have been dancing on my head for all I knew."

"Have you had a chance to see Nicholas interact with the light?"

Milo nodded. "We arrived Friday about an hour before his mother picked him up. Whenever Dolly took him into the kitchen, he did seem preoccupied with that particular light fixture, but he only stared at it. Same thing this morning when he was dropped off by his father before you arrived. Nicholas watched the light, but he didn't get animated like he did when you were there. All weekend I kept checking, trying to sense something, even when Dolly wasn't home, but got nothing at all but a stiff neck from looking up."

Emma thought about that. "Do you think the baby is the connection?"

"You mean," asked Tracy, "that the ghost is visiting Nicholas and not necessarily Dolly?"

"It's possible, isn't it?" Emma turned to Milo.

Milo nodded in agreement. "Could be Lenny is a dead relative visiting the boy. Maybe we should ask the parents."

34

"Dolly told me she doesn't want to alarm them or make them think she's strange." Emma got up and retrieved a bottle of water from a cluster of them lined up on the credenza. "She likes taking care of Nicholas and doesn't want to lose that. Although I'd like to meet them, especially at Dolly's to see if there is any change in how the baby reacts to the light when they're present." She held the water bottle out to her friends. They both declined.

"Your mother obviously believes in spirits," Emma said to Milo as she opened her water and sat back down on the sofa. "Are you sure she doesn't have any special talents in connection with them?"

"Not that I've ever seen." Milo crossed over to the sofa and perched on the arm next to Tracy, putting his arm around her shoulders. "But who knows, maybe she does possess some paranormal gifts. Maybe I received mine from her."

"Kind of like you and your mom, Emma," Tracy pointed out.

It was true, Elizabeth Miller could hear Granny, but could not see her. Emma's daughter could both see and hear Granny, and recently Emma learned that Kelly could interact with other spirits, though that didn't happen often. Emma wasn't sure if that was a decision made by Kelly herself or if the spirits were leaving Kelly alone. Either way, Emma was pleased. She didn't want any distractions from Kelly's education.

"The talent does seem to be genetic, at least in my family," Emma admitted. "And you give readings, Milo, so maybe Dolly being a fortune-teller isn't that far off the mark. She might be more accurate than you think." She thought about something else. "What about your father?"

"I have no idea who he is. Dolly was barely twenty when she had me. I always figured it was some guy who'd passed through Vegas. She's never spoken about him and refused to answer my questions." Milo's face darkened like sunlight turning to dusk as he spoke. "I've never met any of my mother's family either. I only know what Dolly has told me, that she's originally from somewhere in New York and that her family disowned her when she came to Las Vegas to be a dancer. Apparently, they were quite religious."

Aching with curiosity, Emma asked, "How did she get from dancer to fortune-teller?" It was one of the many questions on her mental list she could now cross off.

Milo gave a weary shrug. "She danced until they felt she was too old to be attractive. From there she got a job in a casino as a cocktail waitress, then as a dealer. She didn't start up with The Raven's Craft until she was in her late fifties and standing at the tables all day started to bother her. She doesn't make as much money as in the casino, but it's her own business and seems to make her happy. Like I said, she claims she got the idea from my readings."

"Which came first," Emma asked Milo. "The Raven's Craft or Ravenscroft?"

Milo chuckled. "My last name actually. When I was fifteen, Dolly asked me if I wanted a different last name. She said I could keep Milo Meskiel if I wanted, but that it sounded like a bug-eyed accountant instead of someone who would one day be famous and important." He laughed again.

"See," said Tracy, pointing a finger at him, "your mother might very well be clairvoyant. You are famous and important."

Milo snorted and pushed his thick glasses up the bridge of his nose. "And still bug-eyed, my love."

Turning his attention back to Emma, he continued, "Dolly said to take my time and find a name I'd be happy with for the rest of my life. During my senior year in high school, I came across *Ravenscroft* in a book and instantly glommed on to it. Dolly liked it, too, so she had my last name legally changed to it. I entered high school as Milo Meskiel and graduated as Milo Ravenscroft. When she started her shop, she asked if I'd mind her using a version of it. Which I didn't, of course."

Tracy leaned forward with eagerness. "So do you think Dolly really knows there's a spirit in her house?"

Emma took a drink of water. "I think there is a good possibility she senses something."

Remembering the comment she'd heard just before she left Dolly's, Emma asked, "Tell me, what does the name *Nemo* mean to you?"

Tracy piped up first. "That cute fish in *Finding Nemo*?"

Emma turned to Milo. "And what about you?"

Tracy leaned toward Emma and said in a loud whisper, "I'll bet five dollars he says Captain Nemo from Jules Verne's *Twenty Thousand Leagues Under the Sea.*"

Milo got up from the sofa and paced, his hands jammed into the pockets of his slacks, as he gave the question consideration. "Normally," he said to Tracy, "you would be right. That was one of my favorite books as a youth. However, given we're in Vegas, another thought came to mind."

He sat again on the arm of the sofa and focused all his attention on Emma. "Tell me, Emma, why are you asking?"

"Shortly before I left Dolly's, I could have sworn I heard someone say, 'Did Nemo's boys send you?' " She paused to let the words sink in. "I'm pretty sure that's what I heard." Emma ran a hand through her cropped blond hair. "I wish Granny hadn't left before that."

"I wish I hadn't, too." The ghost left the window and floated over to the sofa. "Sounds like something Edward G. Robinson would say."

Milo nodded. "Granny's right." Quickly, he passed along to Tracy what the ghost had said.

Tracy looked at the empty air by Emma. "How do you know about Edward G. Robinson, Granny?"

"You forget," Emma answered instead, "she watches a lot of TV." She glanced at the ghost. "Too much, in my opinion."

"And that's all it is," Granny snapped, "your opinion, not the law."

"She's now hooked on old movies," continued Emma, "especially black-and-white crime films. She and my father have been watching them together."

"Yeah, but when Dr. Miller snores, I can't

39

hear." Granny crossed her arms. "I gotta figure out a way to work the clicker on my own."

Emma sighed, thinking that if Granny could work the TV remote and the DVD player on her own, the TV would be going day and night.

"Granny might not be too far off," Milo said, returning to the subject at hand. "Back when I was a kid here in Vegas, there was a well-known hood named Nemo."

The two live women and the dead one turned their attention fully on Milo. "Really?" asked Emma, the first to find her voice.

"Yes. He was a local guy named Nelson Morehouse, but everyone called him Nemo. I don't think he was officially Mob, but he had connections to them. He was in the news a lot. As I recall, he was suspected of running drugs from Mexico and operating gambling scams. I think he was even connected once to a casino robbery."

"So if there is a spirit in the light, it might be him?" Tracy put a hand on Milo's knee. He covered it with one of his own hands.

"The voice asked if Nemo's boys sent me," Emma said, "so whoever was speaking was probably not Nemo."

"What about the light fixture?" asked

Milo. "Do you really think there's a spirit inhabiting it, and that's who spoke to you? Or could it have been another spirit lingering nearby?"

Tracy snorted in laughter. "Lenny the Lightbulb. How funny would that be for a gangster name?"

"I kind of like it," said Granny with enthusiasm.

Emma played with her water bottle as she dug through her memory for exactly what she'd felt at Dolly's. "At first I wasn't sure there was a ghost haunting the light, but it was obvious that Nicholas could see Granny, and he is fixated on that particular light."

"Isn't it odd," asked Tracy, "that the baby could see Lenny the Lightbulb and you couldn't?"

"Not really," Milo answered. "If the ghost specifically didn't want Emma to see him, she wouldn't."

"But he definitely wanted me to hear him," Emma pointed out. "At least at the end of my visit."

Remembering the way Dolly had glanced at the light, Emma asked Milo, "Do you recall if Dolly had any friends named Lenny?"

Milo looked surprised. "Do you think my

mother knows the ghost in the light?"

"I don't know," Emma admitted. "It's just that when I asked how she came to give him the name *Lenny,* she seemed a bit nervous when she answered. And when I mentioned the name *Nemo,* I caught her glancing up at the light in an odd way."

Milo tapped his left foot on the carpet as he tried to think. "I really don't recall her having any friends named Lenny. Then again, she did her best to keep our life together separate from her life at the casinos, especially after I was old enough to be left alone."

"Could have been nothing," Emma said with a shrug. "She just might have been nervous about the light."

Putting her water bottle down on the coffee table, Emma got up and went to the desk in front of the large window. On the desk was her iPad. She turned it on and brought it back to the sofa and sat down.

"Milo," she asked as she waited for the iPad to connect to the hotel's Wi-Fi, "how about the Nemo guy? Do you remember if Dolly knew him?"

He shook his head. "I just remember him from the news."

"What did you say his name was again?" Emma pulled up a search engine.

42

Milo and Tracy settled in on either side of Emma so they could see what she was searching. "Nelson Morehouse," replied Milo. Granny hovered nearby.

Emma typed the name into the search engine. Up popped many references. Scanning down the list, Emma saw entries that had nothing to do with a Vegas criminal. There was a doctor in Des Moines and an artist in Florida with the same name. Another, a lawyer from Seattle, wrote novels on the side.

"There." Milo tapped the screen at a listing. "I'll bet that's him."

She clicked on the link and found herself reading a Wikipedia entry on a Nelson Morehouse, a Las Vegas gangster also known as *Nemo*. Emma scanned the information.

"According to this," Emma told them, "Nemo was purported to be a local front man for some Mafia activities in Las Vegas. In 1979 he was caught up in the sweep the FBI conducted on the Tropicana on Valentine's Day. He was charged with fraud and conspiracy, but never convicted."

"Look at this." With excitement, Tracy pointed to an entry in Nemo's bio. "It says here that Nelson Morehouse was a prime suspect in the Lucky Buck Casino robbery in the sixties, along with someone named Leonard Speidel."

Emma read the rest of the entry aloud. " 'Speidel disappeared shortly after the robbery and the money, thought to be in excess of a million dollars, was never recovered. Charges against Morehouse were eventually dropped for lack of evidence.' "

"Could Lenny the Lightbulb be Leonard Speidel?" asked Tracy. *"Lenny* is a nickname for *Leonard."*

"If they are the same, we know he's dead," said Granny. "How about that Nemo guy?"

"He must still be alive," answered Milo. "It says here he was born in 1928, but it doesn't give a date of death."

A small grainy photo showed a man in a suit, with a round face, almost pug nose, and little hair. The scowl he wore made him look like a piglet with an attitude. Emma studied it, wondering what the man might look like today. "That would put him in his eighties," she noted. "I wonder if he's still involved with criminal activities or even in the area?"

"Hard to say." Milo took a deep breath. "But I'm dying to know what my mother has to do with this, if anything. Or if it is Nicholas who's the draw. That's my first concern. Secondly, I want to know why this

44

Lenny guy popped up suddenly. There's often a specific reason why spirits return when they do."

"Oh, I hope that Nemo guy's alive," Granny said, clapping her hands together in excitement. "Then we can interrogate him. Bet I could make him talk."

In unison, Milo and Emma turned to look at the ghost. Milo looked worried. Emma shook her head slowly.

"What?" asked Tracy, looking to the spot where they had their eyes trained. "What did Granny say? I just know it was something good."

CHAPTER FOUR

Emma took off her sweater and placed it and her purse on the passenger's side of her Lexus hybrid SUV. Before going to lunch with Milo and Tracy, she'd changed from the heavy jeans and shirt she'd worn during the drive to crisp navy slacks and a pale green and white lightweight silk sweater worn over a white tank top. It was early May. The weather was warm, but not yet oppressive like it would become in another month. The sweater had been needed to fend off the air-conditioning in the restaurant.

"Nice duds," Granny commented, joining Emma next to the car. "That sweater new?"

"Yes, Mother bought it for me."

Granny looked down at her long, home-spun skirt and long-sleeved blouse. "Wish I could wear something like that. It gets tiring wearing the same old thing for a hundred years." With a sigh, the ghost looked up. "At least Kelly lets me tag along when she goes shopping. I don't think you shop enough."

Emma looked over at Tracy and Milo. They were on the phone with Dolly. She turned her attention back to Granny. "Is that where you've been lately, Granny? Visiting Kelly?"

The ghost nodded. "I wanted to make sure she was settled in after her recent visit home."

"Thank you for looking in on her. I spoke to her yesterday and she sounded fine, but she still went through a difficult time trying to help that friend of hers when she was home." Emma sighed, thinking about how her grown daughter made her feel both proud and older. "Hard to believe she'll be starting her last year at Harvard soon." She turned to Granny. "How's that new boyfriend of hers? What's he really like?"

Granny scowled and crossed her arms. "I don't visit Kelly to spy on her for you. You'll have to ask her about him yourself."

"I do ask, but she doesn't say much. That worries me. Besides, you just told me about her shopping."

"Shopping is one thing. Boyfriend's another." Granny gave Emma a wise wink. "What happens in Boston stays in Boston.

Isn't that how the saying goes?"

Emma narrowed her eyes at Granny. "That's supposed to be what happens in Vegas stays in Vegas, and you know that. Boston and my daughter are entirely different."

Granny put her hands on her narrow hips, facing off with Emma. "And what about what happens in Pennsylvania stays in Pennsylvania?"

Emma flinched at the words. While investigating a ghost in Jim Thorpe, Pennsylvania, at the beginning of last summer, Emma had encountered mixed romantic feelings for Dr. Quinn Keenan, a dashing archeologist and Pennsylvania native who had been helping her.

"I told Phil all about Quinn."

"Even about kissing him?" Granny challenged.

"Yes. Even about that. Satisfied?"

Granny pursed her lips to think about it. "How'd the cowboy take it?"

"You mean you didn't eavesdrop?" Emma hated the defensive tone in her voice, but couldn't help herself. Telling Phil about Quinn had not been easy for either of them and had nearly broken them apart. She also knew Granny hadn't been present during the discussion. Quinn had been a topic

Emma hadn't discussed with anyone but Phil and briefly with Tracy, and had discussed with no one since.

"No need to get all snippy on me." Granny moved closer to Emma. "This was one time I kept my nose out of things. And it was difficult, I can tell ya that."

"Phil wasn't happy, to say the least," Emma told the ghost, who had become a close, albeit an often annoying, companion. "But we got through it. I told him it was over, and it is. I haven't spoken to or heard from Quinn since I returned from that trip to Australia in the fall. Last I heard, he'd gone to South America to check out a new dig."

What Emma left out was that Quinn had asked her to go with him to South America to meet some tribal spiritual leaders. It had been a difficult decision. She'd wanted to go and do research for her show. When he'd asked her to Australia, it had been to spend time at a dig and to learn about the Aborigines. In spite of her attraction to Quinn, the trip had been offered and accepted only on a professional level. Partway through it, Phil had flown down to join her. There had been definite tension between the two men. It wasn't obvious but ran like an underground current whenever the three of them were together until Quinn left for another assignment near the end of Emma's stay. Emma was attracted to Quinn, but it wasn't the same thing as the deep love she felt for Phil. By the end of the trip, she was sure Phil finally understood that Quinn was just a friend, and as a globe-trotting archeologist, he was a wonderful resource for information about ghosts and spiritual beliefs of other cultures.

Granny, sensing the downturn in Emma's mood, tried to put a hand on her great-great-great-granddaughter's shoulder, but it just fell through Emma's solid presence like a warm knife through butter. "Kelly's new boyfriend seems to be a nice young man," she offered in place of physical comfort. "He's polite and smart and quite smitten with her."

When Emma looked up with a mother's eager eyes, Granny pointed a hazy finger in her face. "But that's all I'm telling you, you hear?"

"It's enough." Emma gave the ghost a smile. "For now."

"I'm guessing you're chatting with Granny." Tracy had stepped over to join Emma. Milo was still on the phone. "Or else you're impersonating a crazy person."

Emma shot a look at the ghost. "Granny

makes me crazy."

Granny stuck her tongue out at Emma like a petulant child. Although Granny appeared older, in truth the tiny ghost had been a few years younger than Emma when she'd been wrongly accused of killing her husband and murdered by vigilantes. Emma liked to tease Granny about being her elder.

"So what's the verdict with Dolly?" asked Emma, ignoring Granny.

"Milo has convinced her to attend his lecture this afternoon before she goes down to her shop." Tracy held out a key on a simple leather fob to Emma. "Here's Milo's key to the townhouse."

Emma took the key. "Don't you think Dolly would be upset if she found out I'd been snooping around while she was gone?"

Tracy shrugged. "I think she'd be okay with you checking out the ghost while she's not there, and it's not like you're ransacking her house. If anyone sees you and asks who you are, just say you're picking up something for us while we're at the university." Tracy paused. "What exactly are you hoping to find?"

"I'm not sure," Emma answered honestly. "If Lenny is only visiting Nicholas, he's probably not there now. Even if it's Dolly he's interested in, he may not be there if she's gone. I just want to see if I can coax him out while we're alone. Ghosts often have a favorite spot they like to hover around. I'm hoping Lenny's spot is that light. It's encouraging that he spoke to me once."

Tracy laughed. "Too bad he wasn't a dog. You could use a treat to do it."

Emma grinned. "If it were only that easy."

Tracy waved to Milo and pointed at her watch, letting him know it was time for them to get moving. He ended the call and joined them at Emma's car. "Dolly is going to meet us there a little before three," he told them. "After my lecture and the meet and greet after, we'll take her out for an early dinner, then she'll go on down to her shop. She said since it's Tuesday, it should be very quiet so there's no need for her to rush to Fremont Street."

"So she should be there around six?" Emma asked.

"I'd say that's about right," he confirmed. "Are you going to go down to The Raven's Craft?"

"I'd like to see it," Emma told him. "She invited me down."

Milo smiled. "She asked if you were going to help me at the lecture. I told her I'd be fine on my own and that you were going to rest after your long drive."

"I've told you, she doesn't mean anything by that, darling." Tracy stroked his arm.

"I know she doesn't," Milo assured her. "But it still stings a bit, even after all these years."

"What about the lecture?" Emma asked. "Won't having her there upset your presentation?"

"Not really," he assured her. "This is a lecture based on my latest book, not a demonstration. I won't do demonstrations. Spirits shouldn't be used as circus animals. They were once people like us and should be respected as such."

"I totally agree," chimed in Granny. "People are either afraid of us or think we're some sort of entertainment. There would be a lot more communication between us and the living if they would just learn to chillax."

Milo and Emma whipped their heads around to stare at the ghost. Tracy vibrated with frustration. "What did she say?"

"Granny just used the word *chillax*," Emma told her friend. "What's more amazing, she used it correctly."

The spunky old ghost crossed her arms in front of her. "Seems to me, you three need to chillax."

Milo shook his head with amusement. "Granny, you never cease to amaze me. Where in the world did you pick that term up?"

"She's been hanging around Kelly and her friends a lot lately," Emma explained.

"Some of those classes are pretty interesting," Granny noted. "I even understand some of them."

"You're attending classes at Harvard?" Milo asked with surprise.

"I'm simply expanding my education," Granny sniffed. "You'd be surprised how many spirits are floating about the hallways of that place."

"Actually, I wouldn't," answered Milo as he rubbed an earlobe. "I did some research on it several years ago, but never heard of any spirits auditing classes. You taking the exams, too?" He laughed and translated the conversation to Tracy so she could join in on the fun.

"If you're going to make fun of me," Granny said, getting peeved, "I'm leaving."

"I'm not making fun of you, Granny," Milo assured her. "I just find it really fascinating."

Granny began to fade. "Later, dudes."

Emma turned from looking at the empty air where Granny had just been to Milo.

"Some days it's like I have two children, and one of them is overly sensitive."

"I heard that!" came a disembodied voice.

Milo fought back laughter long enough to translate Granny's latest comment to Tracy.

"Then hear this," Emma called up into the sky. "Meet me at Dolly's."

There was a moment of dead air, followed by a faint, "Gotcha, Chief."

CHAPTER FIVE

Key or no key, entering someone's home without their knowledge made Emma feel like an interloper snooping in someone's private world, which she was. There was no sign of Granny, just the silence of a place waiting patiently for someone to return and make it a home again.

Emma immediately went into the kitchen and stared up at Nicholas's favorite light, looking for the telltale sign of a faint but flickering sparkle that often accompanied spirits. She saw nothing. With deliberation, she moved through the spacious townhouse, keeping an eye out for any signs, small or large, that she was not alone.

Dolly's home was all on one level with the living room joining with the kitchen and dining area to form an open great room. A large picture window faced the small front yard and beyond that the street. The drapes were open. Off the dining area, sliding glass doors opened onto a sizable covered patio with a patio table, chairs, and a chaise lounge. Beyond the concrete apron a small patch of desert landscaping covered the few yards between the patio and the block fence shared with the next building. The few decorative plants in the back were of the low-water type typically found in desert communities.

Going back through the living room area, Emma entered a hallway. Off the hallway was a large master bedroom and bath and a nice-size second bedroom with a guest bath across the hall. Like the rest of the house, these rooms had been decorated in a kaleidoscope of colors and fabrics. Emma stopped to inspect a display of photos hung on the hallway wall. The hallway was long and dark, so she snapped on the hall light to get a better look.

The photos were mostly older ones. There was a grouping dedicated to Milo's school pictures. Emma studied each one. As a child, Milo didn't look that different from how he looked now, just younger and with more hair. His face was studious and solemn, the type of bookish loner other kids would pick on for generations, whether or not he had the distinction of hanging out with half-naked dancers.

Other photos on the wall included several with Dolly and Milo together at various stages in Milo's life, including both his high school and college graduations and various celebrations. Except for a few with him surrounded by spangled and feathered dancers, none of the photos of Milo had anyone other than Dolly in them. There were none of the budding medium with other children at any age. A gush of sadness for her friend coursed through Emma like warm water. Milo had definitely been a lonely child. No wonder he had discovered his talents at such an early age and that it had taken someone like Tracy to draw him out of his shell socially.

Alongside the photos of Dolly and Milo were many photos of Dolly in dance costumes, both covered and skimpy, alone and with other dancers. In some photos, she posed with other people. Emma recognized celebrities, major and minor, from decades ago in a few of the photos. Dolly had been stunning in full makeup and plumage, standing on long legs encased in fishnet hose. There were also some photos of Dolly in street clothes sitting around tables drinking with friends, both men and women, having a good time, and a few with people in standard outdoor poses. Unlike her son,

Dolly Meskiel did not seem to be plagued with shyness.

Putting on a recently acquired pair of reading glasses, Emma took a closer look at the photos. One man showed up in several, both in a group and alone with Dolly, making Emma wonder if he had been Dolly's boyfriend at the time. She would have to ask Milo.

She was almost ready to move on and check the rest of the house when a particular photo caught her eye. It was of Dolly and another dancer in full showgirl regalia posing with men in tuxedos. One of the men standing to the side looked a lot like a young Nemo Morehouse. One man was older but Emma didn't recognize him. The third made her do a double and triple take. She pulled her iPad out of her bag and started up the search engine. When she got the results she expected, she checked the time. The event at the university wasn't due to start for another thirty minutes. She punched one of the speed dials on her phone.

"Hi there," answered Tracy. "I didn't expect to hear from you yet. Did you talk to Lenny?"

"No sign of him. Is Milo around or is he already tied up?"

"He's right here. We're in the green room waiting."

"Can I ask him a quick question?"

"Sure. Hang on."

"What's up?" asked Milo when he came on the line.

"Milo, did your mother know Jimmy Hoffa?"

Milo let out a big laugh. "So you're checking out her rogues' gallery, huh?"

"Yes. That is Hoffa, isn't it?"

"Yes, it is. That photo was taken at the opening of Caesars Palace in 1966. Mom and some other dancers were hired to mingle with the guests for color. That photo is one of her prize possessions, second only to the one taken with Sinatra."

"Yes, I saw that one. Dolly met some interesting people when she was dancing." She paused. "Do you recall the other men standing with her in that photo with Hoffa?"

Milo hummed a low tune while he thought about it. "It's been a while since I've taken notice of those photos, but I believe one of the men is Moe Dalitz, a mobster known as the Father of Las Vegas."

"Would that be the older gentleman in the photo?"

"Yes."

"There's a third one in the photo that I

believe is Nemo Morehouse."

"Really?"

"I think so. He's much younger than in the photo I found online."

Milo paused. "Dolly took tons of PR photos like that. It doesn't mean she knew Nemo."

"True, but maybe Lenny thinks she's connected to him somehow. Anyway, curiosity was killing me so I just had to call and ask. You have a great presentation. Is Dolly there?"

"She's sitting in the front row, but I'm going to pretend she's not there." Milo gave another laugh, this one laced with nerves.

"You'll be great, as always. I'll talk to you later, after I visit The Raven's Craft."

After ending the call, Emma continued moving through the house slowly, being sensitive to any shifts in air currents or light that might indicate a spirit. She felt nothing, not even the presence of Granny.

Returning to the kitchen, she sat on one of the stools at the counter and looked up at the dark overhead light. "I know you're up there. I'm a friend and I'm here to help." She waited. Nothing happened. The house remained still and lifeless. "It's safe to show yourself," she continued.

"Got anything?"

Emma nearly jumped out of her skin at the voice so close to her ear. "Dammit, Granny," she scolded the ghost once she'd composed herself. "You know I hate you sneaking up on me like that."

Granny looked pleased, not chastised. "For someone used to dealing with the dead, you sure spook easy."

Granny started to say something else, but Emma held up a hand to stop her. *"Shhh."* They both stopped and listened.

"Do you hear that, Granny?" Emma whispered.

"Sounds like someone chuckling, or maybe clearing their throat."

"Sure does," Emma agreed.

Looking up at the light, Emma thought she saw a few tiny sparkles of light, like a small scattering of spilled glitter.

"See," said Granny, "I'm not the only one who finds it peculiar that you scare so easily."

"Granny, please," Emma said to her. "I'm trying to listen."

Again a faint chuckle was heard above them.

"If you have any manners," said Granny to the light, "you'll show yourself instead of laughing at us."

While the tiny shimmers remained, the

faint sound of amusement stopped.

"That's a start," snapped Granny.

"Granny, please," Emma said without taking her eyes off the light fixture. "We want him to stay, not get mad and leave."

In a calm voice, Emma asked the light, "Are you Leonard Speidel?" The sparkly haze in the light intensified for a brief instant, but remained silent.

"You think that was a yes?" Granny asked Emma.

"If it wasn't," Emma responded, "I think the spirit at least recognized the name."

Not satisfied, Granny looked up at the light. "Are you Lenny Speidel?" she asked. "Blink one time for yes. Two times for no."

Instead of responding to the request, a faint voice asked, "Did Nemo's boys send you?"

Granny and Emma looked at each other, both with raised eyebrows. "Do you mean Nelson Morehouse?" Emma asked.

Instead of responding, the spirit repeated the question. "Did Nemo's boys send you?"

"No, they didn't. And neither did Nemo," said Granny with growing impatience. "We're here to help you. Do you need help going over to the other side?"

The glittery light went dark for several seconds, then flashed twice.

"Looks like a no to me," Granny said to Emma, who nodded in agreement.

"Are you Leonard or Lenny Speidel?" Emma asked again. After a long pause, the hazy light above went dark, then sparkled again. Emma sighed with relief. At least now she knew who she was speaking with.

Before either she or Granny could ask another question, Lenny the Lightbulb said, "Tell Nemo I know his time is near." Then the light disappeared.

Emma and Granny hung around Dolly's home for about thirty more minutes hoping Lenny would return, but he never did.

"Granny," Emma said to the ghost. "I'm going to head down to Fremont Street and check out the area and maybe do some more research on this Nemo guy before I meet up with Dolly at her shop. You look like you're fading. Why don't you get some rest in the meantime."

"I'm dead," the ghost quipped. "I'm eternally resting, or did you forget that?"

Emma shook her head at the sarcasm. "Sometimes I do forget. But you are fading, so why don't you go recharge your energy and meet me later?"

"Sounds like a plan," Granny agreed. "Do you think Lenny will turn up at Dolly's shop?"

"I have no idea. I did find a photo in the hallway in which Dolly and Nemo are shown together, so maybe Dolly is the connection and maybe Lenny's trying to send Nemo a message through her."

"But why does he keep asking if Nemo's boys sent you? It's like he thinks you're the connection."

"Who knows? Maybe he's confused. You know how sometimes spirits who don't often visit from the other side get confused about times, places, and people. To Lenny, it might still be the 1960s."

"Do you think that's when he died?" Granny was starting to fade even as she asked the question.

Emma thought about the photo on the wall with Dolly and the two known criminals. Milo had said it was taken in 1966. "Could be. It was in the sixties when he and Nemo supposedly robbed the Lucky Buck Casino." Emma sighed. "I have a lot of questions to ask Dolly when I see her. If I don't scare her off."

"She's a fortune-teller, Emma," came Granny's disembodied voice. "And she believes in ghosts, even if she doesn't believe in Milo's abilities. Do you really think for one instant when she named the ghost Lenny the Lightbulb that she didn't have an inkling that it might be the ghost of Leonard Speidel? That's simply too much of a coincidence, to my thinking."

"Mine, too, Granny. But why did she ask for me to come here?"

"Maybe to confirm it's him and to ask him to leave?"

Emma wasn't sure. "More like to find out what he wants."

Emma was about to get into her SUV when she noticed a woman dressed in shorts and a tank top pushing a baby stroller down the sidewalk in front of Dolly's home. Even though the little boy was wearing a cap against the sun, Emma recognized him. She waved to the woman and approached.

"Hi," Emma said. "Are you Nicholas's mother?"

"Yes," the young woman answered with some wariness.

"I'm Emma, a friend of Dolly's son, Milo. I was visiting Dolly this morning and met Nicholas." Emma bent down toward the stroller. "Hey, handsome boy, nice to see you again." The baby rewarded her with a big smile.

Emma stood up and smiled at the woman. "He's such a good-natured little guy. My daughter, Kelly, was like that when she was a baby."

The young mother melted noticeably. "Yes, he is. And he really likes Dolly. She's wonderful with him." She paused, then stuck out her hand. "I'm Suzanne Foster."

Emma shook the offered hand. "Emma Whitecastle."

"Nice to meet you, Emma," said Suzanne. She hesitated, thinking for a moment before adding, "Aren't you the lady with that talk show on TV about the paranormal stuff?"

"Yes," Emma said, pleased always to be known for that instead of as Grant Whitecastle's ex-wife.

"I guess it figures Dolly would know you, her being a fortune-teller and her son a famous psychic."

"I've known her son, Milo, for several years, but today was the first time I've met Dolly. She's quite a character, isn't she? And she sure does love your son."

Suzanne gave off a nervous laugh and looked away for a moment. "My husband thinks she's very odd. I had to convince him to let her watch Nicholas. He's still not sure about her, but he sees how happy Nicholas is with her and her schedule is very convenient with ours."

"Yes, Dolly mentioned that your husband is a police officer here in Las Vegas."

"He's actually a detective," Suzanne said with obvious pride. "He's one of the youngest they have."

"I just love the little game Dolly plays with Nicholas." Emma smiled. "You know, the one with Lenny the Lightbulb."

Suzanne also laughed. "Yes, how funny is that, huh?"

"Nicholas must also be fascinated with the lights at your house. Kids do that. They latch on to something and hold on for dear life. For Kelly it was keys of any kind. The bigger and more jingly, the better."

Suzanne thought about the comment. "That's the odd thing. At home he could care less about the light above the kitchen counter, or any of the others. Our house is set up just like Dolly's but he never gives our kitchen lights a second thought."

"Maybe it's because they don't have a name," Emma suggested with a wink. "Maybe if you called the light Rover or Kitty, he'd fall in love with it like he did with Lenny."

Suzanne laughed and bent down to straighten Nicholas's cap. "Now there's a thought."

CHAPTER SIX

As ambivalent as Emma was about Las Vegas, she'd never cared for Fremont Street. It was old school Vegas, which was exactly why many tourists loved it. The casinos were louder and smokier. The stores were schlockier and the inhabitants gaudier. It was a mecca for hard-drinking, hard-partying patrons with its cheaper drinks and food. At night it wasn't uncommon to see go-go dancers outside clubs and street performers that looked right out of a circus side show.

In the 1990s, in a bid to attract more tourists to downtown from the fancier Strip, a roof or canopy had been constructed over several blocks of Fremont Street that had been closed to traffic. Every night a spectacular light show was displayed on the underside of the canopy. Emma, in all the times she'd been to Las Vegas, had never seen it. Usually when she visited Fremont

Street, which was rare, it was for a short time and during daylight. Phil, upon learning that, had insisted they take in the show the last time they were in town. It had been fun and the light show well worth seeing, but both preferred the Strip with its glamour, big-name shows, and fine restaurants.

Emma parked in a nearby parking structure and made her way to Fremont Street. Dolly had said The Raven's Craft was directly across from The Golden Nugget. Above Emma came giggles, shouts, and screams of delight. She looked up to see people flying — fairies dressed in shorts and sneakers. They were traveling along the zip line nestled under the canopy. She'd wanted to do the zip line when she and Phil were here, but Phil, with his fear of heights, just couldn't muster up the courage to do it. Maybe this trip she'd do it, even if she had to experience it alone.

She located The Raven's Craft exactly where Dolly had said it would be. The sign above the door had two shop names: *The Raven's Craft* and *Crafty Beads.* It was a storefront with a slightly split personality. In the store window was a large placard advertising fortune-telling services by Madam Dolly with posted rates for fifteen-minute, thirty-minute, and sixty-minute sessions.

Stepping inside, Emma found herself in a cheerful shop that sold handmade jewelry, as well as beads, stones, and supplies for those wanting to make their own trinkets. Along the walls were locked display cases of jewelry with a small photo pinned near each grouping. At the main counter a young woman with multicolored hair and a nose ring was sorting beads on a tray. She looked up and greeted Emma with a smile through lips slicked dark purple. She appeared to be the only one in the shop.

"Can I help you?" the girl asked.

"I'm looking for The Raven's Craft," Emma said, approaching the counter. She glanced around. In spite of the sign outside, the bead shop was evident, but the fortune-telling business was not. "Is Dolly here?"

"Are you Emma?"

Emma looked at her with surprise, wondering if the girl was a psychic herself. "Yes, I am."

"Dolly called a few minutes ago and said you might be in. She said to tell you she was running late and to apologize for her."

"Did she say when she might arrive?"

The girl stopped pawing at the beads in the tray and consulted a scrap of paper. "Maybe around six thirty. She said if you have other plans, she'd understand and you could meet her tomorrow at her place."

"Thanks," Emma said, thinking things must have gone well with Milo's presentation and Dolly's interest in it. They were probably still at dinner

Emma walked around the store looking at the various jewelry. Some of it was lovely. Some of it kitschy. The store itself wasn't very wide, but it was deep. In the back was a door painted red and marked *The Raven's Craft* in bold, black Gothic lettering. Next to the door was a large rectangular window. Emma peered through the glass to see a small room set up with a couple of chairs, a small table, and several shelves with books and bottles. Around the room were brightly scattered pillows and fabrics. It was a mini version of Dolly's home. Just outside the door were a couple of plastic chairs, probably for waiting clients. On the door was a small sign decorated with brightly colored beads. In the center was a clock face. The sign informed people that Madam Dolly would be back around six thirty.

Emma returned to the counter. "I take it through that door is where Dolly sees clients."

"Yes," the girl answered without looking up from her work. "She closes the drapes on the window when she's with someone."

"Does Dolly also work for the bead store?" Emma asked, thinking that The Raven's Craft must rent space from the bead store, and maybe Dolly also worked in the store in exchange for her space.

"She owns it," the girl answered after writing something down on a slip of paper. "The whole place, both businesses."

"I'm sorry," Emma said, apologizing. "I didn't realize you were taking inventory."

"That's okay," the girl said without a hint of annoyance. "I'm just counting beads and I have all night to do it. It's slow on Tuesday nights. Now what was it you asked?"

"Does Dolly work for the bead store, too?" Emma repeated. "You know, on slow nights."

The girl noted where she'd stopped her counting and pushed the tray aside. "Madeline actually runs the jewelry end of things while Dolly does the fortune-telling stuff. They're partners in the place, sharing the profits from both ends, but Dolly's usually too busy with clients to pitch in behind the counter."

A partner, thought Emma. Neither Milo nor Dolly had said anything about Dolly having a partner in her business. "Is Madeline here?"

"She's not feeling well today. She's my

aunt. Well, actually my great-aunt. I work here with a couple of other girls who go to UNLV."

"Looks like it would be a good part-time job for a college student. My own daughter is in college back East. She's a junior."

The girl brightened and gave Emma a wide smile. "Me, too! I'm studying earth and environmental science. My name's Megan, by the way."

"Nice to meet you, Megan." Emma indicated the locked wall displays. "Do you and some of the other girls also make the jewelry? One of those photos looks like you."

"Yeah, that's me before I colored my hair. Some of us make stuff to sell. Other things come in from local artisans. Madeline sells the jewelry on consignment for us. If you see something you like, let me know. It's not fine jewelry, but if we don't keep it locked up, it gets stolen."

Emma went back to the display with Megan's photo. She liked the girl's work. It was very creative. Youthful and trendy without being cheesy and cheap looking. "I'd like to see those two pairs of earrings, if you don't mind."

Megan came from behind the counter and unlocked the case. She pulled out the earrings Emma had chosen and handed them to her. One pair was made of a blue stone with veins of gold and lavender. The other was more dangly with stones in striking earth tones. Both hung on sturdy silver wire.

"You do very nice work," Emma told her after examining the jewelry. "I'll take them. I think my daughter will like the blue ones and the other pair is perfect for her friend Tanisha."

When Megan returned to the counter to ring up the sale, Emma's eyes caught several framed photos on the wall behind the girl. They were photos of old-time Vegas show-girls similar to the photos back at Dolly's.

"Is that Dolly?" She pointed at one of the photos she recognized as a duplicate of one back at Dolly's house.

"Yes, and that's Aunt Madeline with her." Megan pointed to a statuesque brunette standing next to Dolly. "They've known each other forever. They were both show-girls back in the sixties." Megan laughed. "Although Aunt Madeline is very roly-poly these days while Dolly has pretty much kept her figure."

"I'm a friend of Dolly's son, Milo. Does Madeline have any children?"

Megan shook her head. "No. Aunt Madeline never married." She looked at Emma with curiosity. "So you know Dolly's son,

75

the famous psychic?"

"Yes, quite well. In fact, he's engaged to my best friend."

"Dolly talks about him sometimes. She claims he can see and talk to ghosts. Is that true?"

Emma smiled. First Suzanne Foster, now Megan. Dolly believed in Milo more than Milo knew. "Yes, it is true. He's amazing. Do you believe in the paranormal, Megan?"

Megan blew out some air and twisted her mouth in a thoughtful knot before answering. "I'm not sure. I know a lot of the people that come in here to see Dolly do and they believe she can see their future. Madeline's told me that The Raven's Craft pulls in more money than the bead shop does."

Almost as if she'd conjured up proof of her words, two young women walked into the store. One was dressed in a strapless sundress. The other in shorts and a low-cut knit top. Both wore high-heeled sandals, heavy makeup, and were holding large plastic cups.

"May I help you?" asked Megan.

The one in the dress answered, "We were told there's a pretty good fortune-teller here."

"Yes," Megan replied. "But Madam Dolly won't be in until about six thirty. Would you like to make an appointment?" She picked up a small calendar from the counter behind her. "That way you won't have to wait."

The two women consulted each other with raised eyebrows and whispers before the one who'd spoken earlier answered, "No thanks. We'll check out the other one." Without another word, they left.

"The other one?" Emma asked.

"Yeah." Megan rolled her eyes. "She came in about a year ago with a fancy painted wagon. It's parked at the other end of Fremont in front of an Indian souvenir shop." She knitted her brows. "Fremont Street didn't need two fortune-tellers, but Laura convinced the powers that be it did and got her business license."

"Her name is Laura?"

"She bills herself as Lady Laura, but her full name is Laura Crawford. She's young for a fortune-teller, not much older than I am. I think that was part of her pitch. She probably told them Dolly was getting too old and didn't attract the younger tourists."

"Has her presence impacted Dolly's business much?"

Megan shrugged. "I'm not sure. Dolly has her regulars, mostly locals, and she does get a lot of tourists, but Laura gets a lot of hype with that wagon and she works longer hours. Personally, I think she's kind of weird."

Suddenly, Emma wanted to see the Lady Laura.

She smiled at Megan. "Thanks for your help, Megan. When Dolly comes in, tell her I'll be back later tonight. I'm going to walk around a bit and get something to drink."

"Okay, I will. And thanks for the purchase. I hope your daughter and her friend enjoy the earrings."

CHAPTER SEVEN

As soon as Emma left the store, Granny Apples popped up, startling her. Collecting herself, Emma inserted her cell phone earpiece. She always did that in public so people passing by would think she was speaking on the phone instead of into thin air, or to a spirit. "She's not in yet, Granny. Dinner with Milo and Tracy must have run later than planned."

"No, it didn't." Granny told her with a raised eyebrow. "I went to Milo's presentation. He did an excellent job, by the way, but Dolly made some excuse to wiggle out of dinner and took off right after."

"Really?"

Granny nodded as her eyes scanned the people milling about the gaudy street of casinos, food vendors, and shops. Overhead a couple more people flew by dangling from the zip line. "That looks like fun," the ghost said, pointing up. "Wish I could do that."

Emma was concerned about Dolly. "I hope she's feeling okay. Maybe I should call her or check in with Milo."

"Dolly's hunky-dory," Granny said, returning her attention to Emma.

"How do you know?"

"I followed her. As soon as she left Milo's thing, she went to some place filled with old people to visit someone. She's probably still there."

"Some place? You mean like a rest home or hospital?"

"Yeah, but I don't think it was a hospital."

"And who did she visit?"

"I don't know, but it was a man — a very old man. He didn't look too well neither. He was in a wheelchair and using oxygen. I'd say he has one foot in the grave."

"But you don't know who it was?"

"If I did, I'd tell ya, wouldn't I?" the ghost snapped. "Dolly and the man were off in the corner of some sort of public sitting room talking. It looked pretty serious, too, not idle chitchat about the weather. I tried to listen, but there was one old lady there who I think could see me. She kept pointing at me and shrieking, saying things like 'Death has come for me' over and over. It was pretty disturbing, I can tell ya that."

Granny ran her hands down the front of

her long skirt, as if wiping off the memory. "So I left."

Emma stepped onto a narrow side street, not much more than an alley. As she moved farther down it, her nose wrinkled at the tangy odor of urine. She backtracked until she was out of its reach and jabbed at an entry on her phone. When the call was answered, she said, "Milo, it's Emma."

"How's your visit with my mother going?"

"She's not here yet. Granny told me she ditched your dinner plans."

"Yeah, she said she had something to do before meeting you, but I got the feeling it wouldn't take long."

"Do you have any idea who she might know in a rest home or retirement home? An older man who might not be doing very well."

There was a pause on the other end. "No, I can't think of anyone, but I'm sure Dolly has a lot of friends I'm not aware of, especially from the old days, and most would be elderly."

"Yes, I just met Megan, Madeline's great-niece, at the shop. I didn't know Dolly had a partner in her business."

"I should have mentioned that but forgot. Sorry. Madeline Kurtz deals solely with the bead store. She and Dolly have been best friends forever, even going back before I was born. She's like an aunt to me. I really should stop by the shop before I leave and see her."

"Megan said Madeline is out ill today. I saw several photos of Madeline and Dolly as showgirls. I'll bet if Dolly knew Nemo Morehouse and Lenny Speidel, Madeline did, too."

"I'm sure of it. Those two did everything together. I'm embarrassed I didn't think of that myself. If one won't talk, maybe the other will. Do you want me to call Madeline? I have her home number. She's my mother's local emergency contact. I could make it seem like a social call."

Emma hesitated, wondering how smooth Milo would be in a questioning situation, but it would save time and Madeline wouldn't be suspicious if he called. "Sure, why don't you give her a ring."

"I'll do it right now before dinner."

"I thought you guys were having an early dinner."

"We were when Dolly was going with us, but when she bailed, I promised Tracy we'd go out for a romantic evening. We haven't had much time to ourselves this trip."

Granny had drifted back to where the side street met Fremont. The ghost was hovering, her head tilted up, watching more people fly by on the zip line. Granny really did want to experience a lot of the things modern people took for granted and Emma wished she could.

"Milo," Emma said into the phone, returning to the task at hand. "Do you know of a Las Vegas clairvoyant named Laura Crawford? She also uses the name *Lady Laura.*"

Milo laughed. "All I know is that Dolly claims she's an upstart and is stealing her clients."

"I think I'm going to pay her a visit. I'm not sure why, but I have this gut feeling I should. Does the name give you any vibes?"

There was a full minute of silence from the other end of the phone, then Milo said, "All I'm getting is that you should proceed with caution."

"You mean Lady Laura might hurt me?"

"I'm not sure if it pertains to Laura or to physical danger or even tonight in general. I'm just getting the feeling something or someone is going to endanger you in some way."

Emma glanced over to where Granny was still watching the people on the zip line. "Well, I was considering riding the zip line tonight. Maybe I shouldn't." She laughed.

Done with the call, Emma started back

down Fremont Street.

"So where are we going?" asked Granny after she caught up with her.

"To see a psychic named Lady Laura."

CHAPTER EIGHT

It wasn't difficult to find Laura Crawford's place of business. Unlike The Raven's Craft, Lady Laura conducted her fortune telling out of a small gypsy wagon parked at a jaunty angle in front of the souvenir shop Megan mentioned. The wagon sat high up from the street, supported by four wheels with large wooden spokes. The wheels were painted school bus yellow. The rest of the wagon was painted in a geometric pattern of purple, blue, and green. The roof was curved downward. There were two small windows on either side, both covered with curtains. Along both sides was painted in a fancy script: *Lady Laura, Clairvoyant.* A soft light glowed from within.

Emma walked entirely around the wagon before coming to a stop in the front of it, where several people were waiting, some sitting on folding chairs. On the side by the door was a sign posting Lady Laura's rates.

They were similar to Dolly's. The back door of the wagon was a Dutch door painted dark purple. Steep wooden steps led up from the ground to the entrance. On the door was hung a sign: *Session in Progress.*

Emma saw the two women who had entered Crafty Beads earlier and approached them. "Is this where you wait for Lady Laura?"

One of them nodded. "The end of the line is right after us."

Mentally, Emma counted the people waiting in front of her. If each took the minimum fifteen-minute session, her wait would be at least an hour and fifteen minutes. She looked at her watch. It was five thirty now. If she waited for Lady Laura, Dolly should be at The Raven's Craft by the time she was done. She had nothing else to do, but she was thirsty. Just steps away was a snack bar selling drinks and quick snacks.

The women in front of her were engrossed in conversation so Emma turned to the man who'd entered the line right behind her. He was kind of dumpy, wearing loose jeans and a faded T-shirt sporting an old rock band logo. "Would you mind holding my place in line while I grab something to drink?"

He glanced up from the comic book he was reading. "Sure, go ahead. Got nuthin' else to do."

Emma thanked him and covered the distance to the food place with quick steps. Less than two minutes later she returned holding a large fruit smoothie.

"I would have held your place," Granny said to Emma when she returned, "but who'd notice."

By the time the door to the back of the wagon opened, Emma was slurping down the last of her smoothie. A young man with red hair came out, bounced down the stairs, and closed the door behind him. A minute later the door opened again and a woman came out and looked at the line of people. By now there were two others lined up behind Emma.

"This gal's popular," noted Granny.

Emma studied the woman at the door to the wagon. She was small in both stature and frame with very long medium brown hair that hung loose around her like a cape. She was dressed in jeans and a man's white dress shirt that hung almost to her knees.

Instead of waving the next person in line up to the wagon, the woman locked eyes on Emma and stared at her. "I'm glad you made it. I was worried you wouldn't."

Emma pointed an index finger at herself.

"Yes, I mean you," Laura said. "Now

come along so we don't keep these other folks waiting any longer than necessary." She indicated for Emma to approach.

After tossing her empty drink cup into a nearby trash bin, Emma started for the wagon.

"Hey," said a woman sitting on one of the folding chairs. "We were here first."

Murmurs of protest came from the others, but Lady Laura stopped them with a simple wave of her hand and a gracious smile. "Yes, but Emma made an appointment, and she's right on time."

Before anything more could be said, Emma scooted up the steps past Laura Crawford and entered the wagon. The door closed behind them.

"Please take a seat there," Laura said, directing her to a wooden chair in front of a small table on which sat a burning thick white candle and a deck of tarot cards. Emma obediently sat, pulled out her earpiece, and stuck it in her bag, which she put on the extra chair next to her.

The inside of the wagon was sparsely decorated and tidy. There was the table and chairs — two chairs on one side and one on the other. Opposite the table was a counter on which sat an electric teapot, a few mugs and jars with an assortment of loose teas, and several small burning votive candles. Under the counter was a minifridge. There was a small bookcase next to the counter filled with books and odd-looking knick-knacks. Like the outside of the wagon, everything was painted in colorful hues.

"How did you know my name?" asked Emma. "I never made an appointment."

Laura's lips formed a slow, slight smile as she took the single chair opposite Emma. "Yes, you did, Emma Whitecastle. You just didn't know it. You came to me in a dream last week."

"Last week I didn't even know I'd be coming to Las Vegas."

"Maybe not, but here you are. I wasn't sure when myself, but I knew I'd know you when I saw you."

Laura swung her head, making her long hair flip back away from her face. Emma clamped her lips tight before a gasp could escape. Laura Crawford's face was disfigured. The left side was pretty and unblemished, but the right side was pulled tight and the eye drooped with a half-closed lid. Scars ran along her jawline and in front of her ear. Emma wondered if her face had been surgically reconstructed after a horrible accident.

"Would you like some tea, Emma?"

"No, thank you." Emma shifted in her seat and silently told herself to get a grip. She was hardly a stranger to physic phenomenon. She'd sat in on many of Milo's sessions, not to mention her own experiences.

Laura looked up, away from Emma and toward the closed door. "And welcome to you, friendly spirit."

"She can see me?" asked Granny, coming closer.

"Who are you speaking to?" Emma asked Laura.

Laura gave her Mona Lisa smile again. "To the spirit with you. It's female, is it not?"

"Yes," answered Emma, deciding to be honest about Granny. "It's the ghost of my great-great-great-grandmother. We call her Granny. Can you see her?"

"Not clearly. It's more like I can sense her presence." Laura turned her attention back to Emma. "I've seen your television show. It's interesting and well-done."

"So you recognized me from TV when you saw me out front?" Inside, Emma relaxed. That would explain how Laura knew her name.

Laura shook her head slowly. "I'd never seen it until last week. Your name came to me in the dream so I looked you up, which

90

led me to your show. I watched a couple of old episodes on my computer."

Emma didn't know whether to believe her or not, but decided not to push the point. "So in your dream, why did I seek you out?"

"That wasn't revealed, but I get the sense you are looking for someone, someone already deceased who is lingering or visiting on this side."

Emma leaned forward. She wasn't sure she fully trusted Laura's abilities, but the girl was impressive. "Can you help me with that?"

Laura was still for a long while before answering. "I don't really know who the spirit is, only that he has a purpose for being here."

"That's true of most spirits. In my experience," Emma told her, "most spirits want to go to the other side and stay there as soon as they pass, except for those like Granny, who enjoy walking among us. Others stay for a specific reason, then leave when it's accomplished."

"Shortly," continued Laura, "a conflict between two spirits, this and another, will rise up and you will be caught in the middle, trying to protect the living in their path."

A chill ran up and down Emma's spine like an electrical current.

"Two ghosts?" asked Granny, hovering nearby. "Ask her if one of them is that Speidel character. You know, Lenny the Lightbulb."

"Is one of the spirits named Leonard or Lenny?" asked Emma.

Laura closed her left eye. Her right remained in a half-open droop. When she opened her eye, she said, "I'm not getting a name, but as we speak, the other is crossing over from life to death."

Emma hugged herself against the chill in the wagon. "You mean the other ghost is dying right this minute? Or rather the person is?"

"Yes. His life is oozing out of him as we sit here." Laura's voice turned almost tinny and mechanical. "I can feel it." Laura opened her eyes wide and starred into Emma's face. "He is being murdered."

"Holy crap!" shouted Granny, using a phrase she'd picked up from Phil Bowers.

Granny moved to stand by Laura. She looked her up and down, then turned to Emma. "This girl is the genuine article, Emma. I can feel it."

"I think you're right, Granny." Emma spoke the words to Granny aloud, not caring if Laura heard them.

Even though Laura's eyes were open, she

appeared in a trance. She continued to stare at Emma, but with an unsettling vacancy in her eye. "Nemo's boys will come for you, too."

Emma sucked in her breath and scooted backward, her chair scratching the worn wooden floor of the wagon. She wanted to pick up her bag and flee, but couldn't. She needed to learn more. Instead, she said to Laura, "Lenny, are you in there? Are you using Laura's body?"

Laura didn't move. She continued to stare, unblinking, at Emma, but now her face shimmered like gauze catching sunlight.

"Come on out," Granny demanded to the spirit inhabiting Laura. "Show yourself and leave that poor girl alone. We're here to help you."

Granny and Emma watched as the haze left Laura's face, but the spirit didn't materialize to them. The chill in the wagon diminished as Laura shook her head, cleared it, and returned to herself.

"Like I said, Emma," the medium continued, picking up the conversation where she'd left off. "I sense someone has been murdered. His spirit has unfinished business with the spirit you seek."

Emma leaned across the table and took Laura's hands. "Who was the spirit who just inhabited you?"

The girl looked genuinely puzzled, but didn't pull back. "No spirit visited here except for your Granny."

"No spirit took over your body to speak with me just now?"

"No," Laura said in earnest. "Channeling is not one of my gifts, though I wish it were."

"Well, I'll be," said Granny, bending down to get another close look at Laura. "She has no idea how gifted she is. She's like Milo, just not as developed."

"I agree, Granny." Emma let go of Laura's hands and leaned back in her chair, mentally exhausted.

Emma looked at Laura. "Have you ever heard of Milo Ravenscroft?"

"Yes, of course. He's a famous psychic and medium."

"He's also a close friend of mine, and he's the son of Dolly Meskiel, your colleague down the street."

Laura looked surprised. "You mean the old woman who tells fortunes out of the bead store?"

"Yes."

"I had no idea." Laura's face changed. Her mysterious mask dropped and she became a simple young woman just a few years older than Kelly. "I thought she was just a batty old lady. I tried to tell her when I set up my wagon that there was enough business for both of us, but she didn't want to listen."

"No matter, but I believe you need to get in touch with Milo and talk to him. He's in Las Vegas right now." Emma reached inside her bag and pulled out one of her business cards. She jotted down Milo's cell phone and her cell phone numbers on the back and handed the card to Laura. "Call Milo tomorrow. That will give me time to talk to him about you first."

"You'd do that for me?"

"Yes. I think you have more gifts than you realize. Milo can help with that. He mentored me."

"I'd really like that." Laura smiled. This time it wasn't tight and shadowy, but wide with excitement.

Emma pulled out her wallet and plucked a couple of twenties out. She looked at the bills, then plucked out two more. She put them on the table and pushed them toward Laura. "Is that enough?"

"That's way too much, Emma. And you are hardly one of my touristy customers." Laura pushed the money back toward her.

"Keep it, Laura. You earned it." Emma got up. She was about to open the door when Laura stopped her.

"Emma, one more thing. And this is for you personally."

Emma turned back, waiting.

"A door is about to open," Laura said, her face serious and determined. "It's up to you if you open it and enter, but the presence of the door itself will challenge and change your life."

"A new business opportunity?" Emma asked.

Laura shrugged. "I don't know. But consider the consequences before you act on anything."

Getting up from the table, Laura held out her hand. "It was a real pleasure to meet you, Emma." After the two women shook, Laura turned her attention just to the right of Emma. "It was also nice to meet you, Granny. Emma is lucky to have you in her life. Take care of her."

The ghost looked from Laura to Emma, her brows knitted in concern. "That's the plan, Stan," she said, not caring if the medium could hear her or not.

CHAPTER NINE

"Boy, that was spooky." Granny floated next to Emma as she made her way back to the snack bar she'd visited earlier and bought herself a bottle of water. Then Emma found a bench, sat down, and reinserted her ear-piece.

"Yes, it was, Granny. It was very unsettling for many reasons."

Her time with Laura had given Emma a lot to digest, and most of it was disturbing. She opened her water and took a long drink. Around her, Fremont Street was starting to liven up with evening foot traffic, busy even for a Tuesday night. Emma consulted her watch. She'd spent thirty minutes with Laura, but it had felt more like an hour. By jumping to the head of the line, she also had a little more time before Dolly would arrive at her shop.

She took another drink of water and thought about the dichotomy that was

Laura. One minute she displayed a maturity beyond her years, the next, as when she was speaking about Dolly, she seemed like any ordinary twentysomething. Emma wanted to know more about the girl. How did she become a psychic? How did her face become disfigured? Where was she from? She hoped Laura would call Milo. If the girl was to continue with her fortune telling and maybe even advance her skills, she needed to learn how to use her gifts properly.

It had been the same with Kelly's friend Tanisha in Boston. When Emma learned Tanisha could communicate with spirits, she'd insisted Tanisha be mentored, just as Emma had done with Kelly. Emma had invited Tanisha to visit them in California when Kelly came home over her last Christmas break. At first wary, Tanisha agreed and came for the visit the week between Christmas and New Year's. She and Kelly divided their time between the Los Angeles area and Julian, the small mountain town where Granny was from and where Emma maintained a vacation home across from Phil's ranch. Granny and Emma also spent a lot of time with Tanisha, and included some time with Milo. By the time Tanisha headed home, she was more comfortable with her abilities and they had determined that for now Tanisha seemed only to be able to see faint images and hear some audio from the spirits. Whether that would increase in time, they would just have to wait and see.

Emma had liked Tanisha Costello immediately. The daughter of a famous crime novelist and a college professor who died when she was young, Tanisha was a budding journalist, tough on the outside and as soft and vulnerable inside as a high-end caramel. Emma had taken her under her wing like an abandoned chick. Something Kelly accused her of doing with many of her friends, but Emma noticed Kelly's accusation came with a sense of pride and amusement.

Emma's maternal instincts and observation told her Laura was very different from Tanisha and Kelly. Judging from her language and appearance, she was probably less educated than both and most likely from humbler beginnings, but she had the same independence and fire. She also had the early signs of advanced medium and clairvoyant skills. Skills that went far beyond the telling of fortunes to eager tourists.

"So which part are we tackling first?" asked Granny, who perched on the bench next to Emma. "The murder, finding out why Lenny's here, or that secret door that's supposed to open for you?"

Emma fiddled with the label on the water bottle, picking at a loose edge. "We can't do anything about what she said to me personally until it presents itself, and right now only a headache is making itself known." Emma dug into her bag until she located a small container of aspirin. She shook two into her hand and tossed them into her mouth, followed by another pull on the water bottle.

"As for the murder," Emma continued in a low voice after a few seconds, "who knows if Laura's vision was literal."

The ghost shivered. "She said it was happening right then, while we were with her."

"Yes, but you know sometimes psychics aren't always on schedule with visions. If there was a murder, it could have been in the past, or in the future."

"But she also said the spirit of whoever was murdered is going to be locking heads with Lenny the Lightbulb."

"Again," Emma noted, being cautious, "if she was literal in her prediction."

Granny got up and faced Emma, her hands on her hips. At that moment a couple walked by, hand in hand, heads together, laughing. They went right through the ghost without a second thought. Granny stomped her foot. "Boy, I hate that!"

Emma could only shake her head and hope the aspirin would do its magic in short order.

Granny stomped her foot again. This time at Emma. "Aren't you forgetting the most important part of our time with Laura?"

Emma knew what Granny was getting at, but chose instead to look up and watch the current batch of people fly by on the zip line.

"Lenny was there," Granny went on, a deep scowl on her face. "He said Nemo's boys were coming after you. I would think you'd be focused a little more on that, don't ya think?"

Emma picked again at the label, this time until she had it half off the plastic bottle. "I'm not sure Lenny, Spirit of the Light-bulb, can really be considered an oracle of doom. Do you?"

Granny leaned in closer. "And denial is just a river in Egypt."

Emma yanked the label off the bottle and shot a look at Granny. "And where in the world did you hear that phrase?" She sighed and held up a hand. "Wait, don't tell me. It was Phil. He says that sometimes, especially to his boys."

"Phil's a smart man," Granny said with a

determined jerk of her chin. "I learn a lot from him."

"I'm not in denial, Granny. I heard what Lenny said, although we haven't determined yet if that ghost is Lenny Speidel."

"Well, the spirit who entered Laura is the same one as back at Dolly's house. We know that by the voice. It was identical."

"Yes," Emma agreed. "It was." She looked at her watch again. It was almost time to start back to The Raven's Craft. "But we still need to determine why he's here and who the spirit is he's supposedly having a conflict with."

"You mean the spirit from the new dead guy." Granny rubbed a hand over her chin. "Maybe it's Nemo himself."

"I've been wondering that myself, Granny. We know if Nemo Morehouse is still alive, he's pretty old. Maybe he's the one passing away who is going to cause trouble for Lenny."

"You mean Nemo is the fresh murder victim, don't you?"

Emma took another drink of her water, screwed the cap back on the now naked bottle, and got up. "I'm not sure what I mean anymore. This is certainly becoming more complicated than a spirit haunting a household light fixture." She started walking back down Fremont Street. "One thing is for sure, Dolly needs to start fessing up about stuff if she expects my help."

They weren't moving fast down Fremont, but taking their time, letting the noise of the casinos, the crowd, and the smell of fast food wash over them in waves. Emma was lost in her thoughts about what Laura had said and what Lenny had meant by his comment. She was sorting all the pieces and trying to put them into neat piles like freshly folded laundry. She was also mentally preparing what she was going to say to Dolly. Granny floated beside Emma, happily taking in the loud sounds and garish sights of the famous gambling street.

They were almost to The Raven's Craft when they heard, "Emma?"

Emma looked up, still lost in her thoughts. It took her a minute to focus to see who had called her name.

"Emma Whitecastle, is that really you? Here on Fremont Street?" The voice was male, deep, and confident.

Both Emma and Granny turned to see the tall, dashing figure of Dr. Quinn Keenan standing not more than ten feet away. He was staring at Emma with amused disbelief. She stared back at him, her mouth slightly open. A group of people passed between them. Quinn threaded through the crowd of pedestrians to make his way to her, a wide smile on his handsome face.

"Uh-oh," whispered Granny in Emma's ear. "Don't look now, but I believe that door Laura mentioned is coming your way."

Quinn scooped Emma in his arms and gave her a hearty hug. "I can't believe it's you. What are you doing here?"

Caught off guard, Emma blurted out the truth. "Granny and I are here helping Milo with a ghost problem." Quinn knew about her skills and about Granny, but ordinarily Emma would not have said something like that out loud in public. Fortunately, with the noise, lights, and action, no one walking near them noticed or gave it a second thought.

Quinn looked to Emma's right. "Hi, Granny. Nice to not see you again."

Emma pointed to her left. "She's there."

Quinn adjusted his eyes to Emma's left. "Hi, Granny."

"Hi back at ya, handsome," the ghost said with delight.

"Granny says hi back," Emma reported.

Granny shot Emma a dirty look. "You forgot the handsome part."

Ignoring the ghost, Emma asked Quinn, "And what are you doing here? Don't tell me there's a famous archeological dig under these old casinos."

Quinn laughed. "I'm here with a few buddies for a bachelor party. We flew in on Friday night. Most took off Monday morning but two of us stayed on to get in some more golf."

"There you are," a tall man said, approaching them.

"Hey, Bob," Quinn said to the guy. "I want you to meet Emma Whitecastle." He turned to Emma. "Emma, this is my mate Bob Emmons, the groom-to-be and a fellow dirt digger."

Emma shook hands with the man. "Congratulations on your upcoming marriage. When's the happy day?"

"In three weeks." He gave Emma a wide grin. "So you're the famous Emma Whitecastle. I've heard a lot about you."

Next to Emma, Granny said, "He's almost at cute as Quinn. What is it about these archeologists? They're all as dashing as Indiana Jones. Is that a requirement?"

Ignoring Granny's remark, even though she agreed with it at the moment, Emma smiled at Bob. "Well, don't believe half of it."

Bob laughed. "One thing for sure, old Quinn here wasn't exaggerating about your beauty, fair ghost chaser." He gave her an exaggerated bow. "So I'm sure he was on point about your brains."

Emma felt the blush traveling up her neck and was helpless in stopping it. She looked at Quinn, who seemed to be taking delight in her discomfort.

"You here for work or play, Emma?" asked Bob.

"Emma's working," Quinn answered for her. "Ghost stuff."

"Yes," Emma said, finding her voice. "And I'm about to meet someone, so I'll be off and won't hold up your fun."

"Actually," Bob said, "I'm shoving off tonight. I'm off to grab my bag from our hotel and head to the airport, but Quinn here isn't leaving until tomorrow." He nudged Quinn with an elbow. "Maybe you could help out the lady before you go."

"I am available until tomorrow afternoon," Quinn commented, looking at Emma. "And I believe I proved to be a valuable sidekick on one of your other adventures." He paused and looked around. "Unless, of course, Phil's here to watch your back."

"Phil didn't come with me," Emma answered. "At least not this time."

Granny tried to get Emma's attention. When she wasn't successful, she got between Emma and Quinn and faced Emma. "Be careful here, Emma," the ghost warned. "Just because the door presented itself doesn't mean you have to open it and walk in. Remember that."

"I know, Granny."

Bob's mouth dropped and he turned to Quinn. "Is she actually talking to a ghost right now?"

"Yeah, Bob, she is," Quinn answered with amusement. "The ghost of Granny Apples is her almost constant sidekick." He moved his eyes away from Emma to his friend. "But isn't it time for you to head to the airport?"

Bob looked from Quinn to Emma and back to Quinn. "Yeah, it is." He slapped Quinn on the shoulder and laughed. "Thanks for reminding me."

Quinn embraced his friend. "I'll catch you at the wedding."

Bob held out a hand to Emma, extending it through the determined Granny, who bristled and moved out of the way. "It was a real pleasure, Emma. And I mean that."

"Same here, Bob," she said, shaking his hand. "And again, congratulations on your upcoming marriage."

After Bob left them, Quinn turned to Emma. "So where are we off to tonight?"

"I don't know about *we,* Quinn, but Granny and I are meeting someone." She consulted her watch. "In fact, we're running a little late, so if you'll excuse me."

"Us," Granny corrected. "Excuse us."

"Let me come with you. I don't have anything else to do tonight with Bob gone. I'll be quiet as a mouse unless you need me."

Emma was torn. Quinn did believe in ghosts and had a good head on his shoulders for facts and piecing them together. It couldn't hurt to have someone else, someone objective, to run ideas past. As Granny had said, just because the door is there, it didn't mean she had to walk through it, and having Quinn's company didn't mean she was entering his door. Then again, maybe Quinn wasn't the door Laura mentioned. Laura could have been way off on everything, including the new murder and the ghosts doing battle. Then she remembered the voice coming from Laura's lips. It hadn't been Laura's voice. It had sounded like Lenny the Lightbulb, and he was warning her. But Lenny wasn't warning her about doors and choices for her personal life.

"A ghost, not Granny but the ghost of a former Vegas hood, told me just minutes ago that someone is coming for me. It could be dangerous."

Quinn didn't hesitate. "I'm in."

CHAPTER TEN

With Quinn by her side, Emma stepped into the bead store. Megan was still there, waiting on a couple. The woman was eyeing some of the baubles in one of the glass cases while Megan expertly described the stones and the artist who made the jewelry. The man was slouched against the next cabinet looking bored. There was no sign of Dolly. Two older ladies came in right after Emma and Quinn. They went straight to Dolly's office and eyed the clock. It still said Dolly would return at six thirty, but it was now past that time.

Megan cast an eye at Emma, then at the ladies standing by Dolly's door. "I'm sorry," she said to them all, "but Dolly isn't in yet and hasn't called. You might want to try back a little later."

The ladies, looking genuinely disappointed, left saying something about returning after they had dinner. Megan smiled at them before going back to helping her customer, who was deciding between a bracelet and earrings. The man with her looked at Quinn and rolled his eyes, looking for manly sympathy. Quinn chuckled and shrugged in response.

"Looks like Dolly isn't back yet," Emma said to Quinn. She turned to him, but aimed her next words at Granny in a low tone. "Granny, would you be able to check on Dolly? See if she's on her way or still at that rest home."

"Will do." The ghost disappeared.

When Quinn and Emma stepped back outside, he turned to her with a grin. "That's pretty handy, sending Granny to check on people whenever you want. It's like you have a private and portable surveillance camera. Ever check up on Phil like that?"

Emma was not amused. "No, I don't, and even if I wanted to, I don't think Granny would go along with it. She's pretty close-mouthed about things like that. She visits my daughter regularly and won't say a peep about Kelly's life at Harvard."

Emma looked around, trying to decide what to do next. "Besides," she continued, "Granny can't always zero in on people she's not close to and can't do it at all with people she's never met. She followed Dolly earlier today. That's the only way she knew she had visited a rest home. If Dolly's left there, Granny might not be able to reestablish a connection since she and Dolly have had very little contact." She looked at Quinn. "If there is something I've learned, it's that working with spirits is not an exact science."

Quinn gently took her arm. "Since we seem to be in a holding pattern, why don't we grab some dinner and you can tell me what this is all about. There's a really good restaurant here with a great view of Fremont Street. It's primarily a steak house but they also have a nice choice of seafood for you, m'lady."

Quinn started gently guiding her down Fremont Street, but Emma hesitated.

"You okay?" he asked.

Was she? Emma wasn't sure. She did need to eat dinner, but would a meal with Quinn mean something else to him, or to their relationship? If he was the "door" Laura spoke of, was she about to open that door with its consequences? Had Laura not said a word, Emma knew she wouldn't have given it a second thought. Quinn knew she was in a serious relationship with Phil and dinner would simply be just that — dinner with a good friend. But would Phil think otherwise? He was very jealous of Quinn. As far as Emma could see, Quinn was the only man Phil had concerns about. She'd told him about her attraction to Quinn in Pennsylvania and even about the kiss, but assured him that it was just a passing fling with uncertainty and that she was now dead sure she loved him and wanted to be with no one but him.

Still, the words of the young psychic rattled in her head like a snake about to strike. With a brush of her hand through her hair, she dismissed them and with a smile followed Quinn to the restaurant.

The restaurant did have a spectacular view of Fremont Street and of the light show. They were seated by a window just as it began and watched in silence while enjoying a glass of wine. When it was over and they were eating their salads, Emma told Quinn about Lenny and Dolly and everything else she'd uncovered since coming to Las Vegas.

"Wow," Quinn said, putting his fork down. "All that has happened just since this morning?"

Emma took a bite of artichoke heart and nodded. After she swallowed, she said, "I have a whole list of questions to ask Dolly as soon as I find her."

"And you think she knows the ghost in her light?"

"I think she at least knows who he is. I also want to question Madeline. That's her partner in the shop we just left. They were showgirls together years ago and most likely hung around the same people, but she's out ill today according to her great-niece Megan."

"Was that the girl in the shop?"

Emma nodded and took a sip of her wine. Her attention had been captured by the people now zooming along on the zip line after the show was over.

"You ever do that?" Quinn asked.

"A zip line? No, never, but I've always wanted to." She looked back at Quinn. "There's one in Catalina I'd like to do, but haven't yet."

"Why not? It's not far from you."

"I know and I visit Catalina at least once a year. I love it over there." She smiled to herself. "It's just that Phil has a fear of heights." She looked back at the zip line. "I wanted to take Kelly when she was home visiting in March, but we never got the chance."

Quinn laughed. "That big gruff guy is afraid of heights?"

"It's true. He can stare a rattlesnake in the eye and tackle the wildest bronco, but take him off the ground and he's a mess."

"But he flew to Australia to be with you last year."

"And had to be sedated for the flight." She smiled again, and warmth filled her heart. "One time Phil took one of those tiny private helicopters to Catalina because he thought I was in danger. He did it cold-turkey, without drugs or even a drink. He put my well-being before his biggest fear. My ex-husband would never have done that. That's when I knew for certain Phil really loved me."

After their meals were served, Emma started eating her seafood entrée with enthusiasm. Quinn didn't start eating, but instead took two slow sips of his wine, pausing between each as he studied Emma. "I really don't have a chance with you, do I?"

Emma stopped eating. She studied the smart, rugged, and handsome man across the table from her. The door had been opened. The choice to walk through it or not was hers. She knew the answer. "Romantically? No, Quinn. My heart belongs to Phil and only him. I'm sorry."

"Don't be," he told her. "I kind of knew it when he came to see you in Australia. You two are good together and he's a great guy. I'd like him a hell of a lot if he wasn't my competition."

Emma laughed and put her lips to her own wineglass.

"What's so funny?" he asked her.

After swallowing some wine and dabbing at her lips with her napkin, Emma picked up her fork. "Phil said exactly the same thing about you when he was in Australia."

When they were finished with their meal, Quinn pointed out the window. "Let's say we take a ride down the zip line when we leave here. At least we'll always have that."

"I have to get back to the store to see if Dolly's in."

"Call Megan and see if she's arrived yet."

While Quinn paid the check, Emma stepped into the hallway by the restrooms and called the store. Megan answered and said Dolly still had not come in or called. Emma then called Milo but only got his voice mail. She left a message saying Dolly had not shown up yet and asking did he know where she was? Granny hadn't popped back in with information either.

"No Dolly yet," she reported when she rejoined Quinn. "And Milo isn't answering his phone. He did say he and Tracy were going out for a romantic dinner tonight so maybe he shut his phone off."

"I really hope I get to meet Milo."

"I know both he and Tracy would like to meet you. But if you're leaving tomorrow, there might not be time, unless you're leaving later in the day."

"I don't have to leave tomorrow at all," he suggested as they got up to leave. When Emma raised her eyebrows, he added, "No strings, I promise. But I don't have to be anywhere in particular and you might need some help if this turns crazy."

Emma thought about what Phil might think of Quinn spending more time with her. "I don't know, Quinn. It might not be the wisest thing to do."

"Because of Phil?"

"Yes. Both he and I had spouses that cheated on us. I wouldn't want him to think he has to worry about my faithfulness."

"Would he have to know I'm here in Las Vegas?"

"Yes," Emma answered with no thought to doing otherwise. "He would. I plan to tell him tonight when he calls."

"See, Emma," Quinn told her with a wry half smile. "It's exactly that kind of loyalty and confidence that makes men want you even more." He opened the door of the restaurant for her to exit.

She shook her head and laughed as they left the restaurant and headed for the zip line.

"I was just thinking," Quinn said after they climbed the stairs to the zip line platform to wait their turn, "maybe you should text Milo. If he has the phone's ringer off, he might see a text sooner than notice your voice mail."

"Good point," Emma agreed. While they waited, she took out her phone and quickly sent Milo a text with the same message as her voice mail.

Emma loved the zip line. After being strapped into the harness and receiving instructions on how to secure her purse, she took off, speeding down the high line at a slight angle toward the other end of Fremont Street. Wind streaked through her hair as she looked down at the people and colorful signs and activities below her. It was exhilarating and made her want to do the one in Catalina all the more. On the line parallel to hers flew Quinn. She looked over at him and laughed, letting him know she was glad she'd taken him up on his offer of the attraction.

The ride was over in a matter of seconds. At the platform at the other end, Emma's happy smile dropped from her face as she flew through the scowling figure of Granny Apples and landed.

After Emma and Quinn were unharnessed, they walked down the stairs to the street level.

"I take it you enjoyed that?" Quinn asked once they were on the ground.

Instead of answering, Emma walked to a doorway of a closed business, signaling for Quinn to follow. When they got there, she said, "Granny's back and she's not too happy."

"You bet I'm not happy," the ghost said with her arms crossed. "I'm off working and you're pretending to fly. And you know I hate it when people go through me."

"Then, Granny," Emma told her with frustration, "you shouldn't have been standing at the edge of the platform in my way. It's not like I had anywhere else to go." She quickly gave Quinn a rundown of the conversation, which he found hilarious.

"Laugh it up, Indiana," Granny snapped. Emma didn't relay that message.

"Granny," Emma said, trying to get down to business and diffuse the ghost's annoyance, "Dolly still hasn't shown up here. Did you locate her?"

"No," the ghost answered, still testy. "She wasn't at that place anymore, but I do have something to report."

"And what's that?"

"You know how Laura said someone was being murdered at the moment we were talking to her."

Emma nodded.

"Well, the man Dolly visited is now dead."

Emma leaned back against the wall of the building. "He's dead?"

"What's going on?" asked Quinn.

Emma held up a hand, signaling for him to give her a minute, then to Granny asked, "Are you sure?"

"I know death when I see it, Emma. Trust me." Granny sniffed in the air. "He was alive when I saw Dolly with him earlier. Now he's dead."

"Did you see his spirit?"

Granny shook her head. "No. It might have left his body already. But I saw several others."

"What others?"

"Just spirits hanging around their loved ones. Looked to me to be mostly husbands and wives."

"Any ghosts hanging around the man that died??"

"None that I could see."

Slowly, Emma inhaled and exhaled several times to steady herself. "But you said before he was pretty old. Maybe he just died of old age or illness. Maybe Dolly was there to say good-bye to an old friend, knowing his end was near."

Granny considered that option. "Could be. But I will say, no one at the place seemed too upset or saddened by his death, not even the guy taking care of him. You know, his nurse. That was kind of sad to me. I mean, to die and no one cares." Granny shook her head at the thought.

Emma brought Quinn up-to-date.

"Maybe," he suggested, "that wasn't the person the fortune-teller was referencing."

"He's got a point," Granny agreed.

Emma stepped out of the shadow of the doorway, Quinn and Granny in tow. "Let's go back to Dolly's shop and see if she's turned up yet."

CHAPTER ELEVEN

This time when they entered the bead store, Megan was alone, her back to the door. Emma immediately picked up the sound of crying.

"Megan," Emma said softly, approaching the girl.

Megan held up a hand without turning around. "Sorry, we're closed." Her words were thick and wet.

Emma repeated her name, "Megan. It's me, Emma Whitecastle. What's wrong?"

Megan turned around. Her face was swollen from crying, and her eye makeup tracked down her face like dripping ink. Crumpled in her hand was a sodden wad of tissue.

Granny moved forward. "The poor child is beside herself."

"I need to close the store and go home," Megan said, her puffy eyes darting from Emma to Quinn and back to Emma. "Madeline's . . ." She choked and couldn't continue. After blowing her nose, she blurted out, "Madeline's dead. My mother found her when she went over to check on her."

A couple of people walked into the store, but quick-thinking Quinn stopped them before they got too far across the threshold. "I'm sorry, but there's been a family emergency and the store is closed for the night."

"Even the old fortune-teller?" a woman with a bad dye job and thick glasses asked.

"Yes," Quinn answered. "The whole shop is closed for the night. Please come back another day." He ushered them out and closed the door behind them, turning the closed sign outward as he did.

"Madeline was Megan's great-aunt," Emma explained. "And Dolly's best friend."

"Maybe Dolly knows and that's why she's not here?" suggested Granny.

That sounded plausible to Emma. "Megan, is Dolly over there now? Is that why she's not here?"

Megan shrugged. "My mother thinks Madeline died in her sleep. She didn't say anything about Dolly." She wiped her face and hopped off the short stool she was sitting on. "I need to go home."

"We'll stay until you lock up," Emma said.

"And we'll walk you to your car," Quinn added.

Emma reached out and stroked the girl's arm with tenderness. "Maybe I should drive you home since you're so upset. Quinn here can follow and drive me back."

Megan shook her head. "No. I'll be okay, but thanks." She got out a piece of paper and a pen and jotted down a note, then stuck it to Dolly's office door. "Just in case Dolly comes in," she explained. "She'll want to know as soon as possible."

Emma, Quinn, and Granny saw Megan to her car in a back parking lot. Before she left, Emma gave Megan a quick hug and promised to tell Milo about Madeline and to find Dolly and tell her.

Granny said, "I didn't want to say anything in front of the girl, but something's fishy."

"It wouldn't have mattered, Granny," Emma replied. "She couldn't hear you."

"I realize that," the ghost answered, her face sad as she watched Megan's car exit the parking lot, "but it still didn't seem fitting to talk about it in front of her."

"Why do you think something's fishy, Granny?" Emma asked. Next to her, Quinn went on alert.

The ghost shrugged. "Two people con-

124

nected to Dolly dying in the same night."

Emma conveyed Granny's comments to Quinn, then returned her attention back to the ghost. "But they were both ill and elderly."

"Maybe," Quinn said, rubbing a hand over his chin, "this Madeline was the death Lady Laura was foretelling and not the old guy at the rest home."

"But Laura specifically said *he* when speaking to Emma," Granny said.

"True, Granny," Emma answered, "but just because Laura used a male pronoun, it doesn't mean specifically a man." Emma looked to Quinn.

"Don't worry," he told her, "I followed that from your comment." He glanced to both sides of Emma to cover his bases, then said, "Granny, Emma's right, people use *he* and *him* and *his* all the time when they're not being gender specific. And from what I've seen of psychics and fortune-tellers in my travels, they can't always pinpoint gender or age, just generalizations."

Granny wasn't mollified. "But you don't think it's peculiar that two people close to Dolly died tonight within hours of each other. Maybe even at the same time?"

Emma translated to Quinn.

"I do think," he answered the ghost, "that

it definitely bears looking into."

"Maybe," said Granny as she paced a small area of the parking lot, "Dolly killed the old guy, then went to Madeline's and knocked her off."

Emma conveyed the comment to Quinn, then said to both of them, "I don't know about the man Dolly went to visit tonight, but she and Madeline were like sisters. And even though I just met her once, I can't see Dolly murdering anyone, let alone her best and longest friend."

"I think Emma's right, Granny," added Quinn. "Did you by any chance catch the name of the guy who died tonight?"

"No, I didn't," the ghost answered. Emma turned to Quinn and shook her head.

Before anyone could come up with any other theories, Emma's phone rang. She pulled it out of her purse and looked at the display. "It's Milo," she told them with a down-turned mouth.

"Milo," she said into the phone. "I'm glad you called."

"I'm sorry I didn't get back to you sooner," Milo told her, "but we were at dinner and I just now got your messages." He spoke quickly with a slightly higher pitch to his voice. "I'm starting to get worried about my mother. I can't reach her. Please say

126

she's there with you now."

"I'm sorry, Milo, but she's not." Emma paused, not sure how to pose her next question. "Um, did you ever get in touch with Madeline Kurtz?"

"Why yes. I called her right after I last spoke to you. She sounded awful, but said it was just a cold and that she would soon be on the mend. I offered to drop by but she said she didn't want to infect me and Tracy."

"Milo," Emma began, then stopped to clear her throat. "I have something awful to tell you. Megan just told us that Madeline died tonight."

"What? That can't be. I spoke to her just two hours ago!" Milo's anguish came through the phone so loud, Emma pulled the phone from her ear. Quinn and Granny could both hear his questions of when and how pouring from the phone in a flood.

"I don't know what happened," Emma told him after putting the phone back to her ear. "Megan's on her way home now. She said her mother found Madeline and thinks she died in her sleep. It must have been right after she spoke to you."

"This is going to break my mother's heart," Milo said, his voice cracking. He paused and Emma could hear Tracy's voice in the background. "We're going back to the house this minute," Milo said, speaking to Emma again. "If you find Dolly, please tell her to come home immediately. In the meantime, I'll try to find out more about Madeline."

"Will do, Milo," Emma told him. "And I'm so very sorry for your loss. I know you said you were close to Madeline."

Emma wondered if she should tell Milo about the man at the rest home when he segued into the topic on his own. "I wonder," he said to Emma, "if my mother is still visiting that friend of hers you told me about earlier. I wish I knew where that place was and who she was seeing."

Emma took a deep breath before answering. "Well, here's another bit of bad news. According to Granny, the man Dolly was visiting passed away tonight, too."

"What?" Milo said again in a high pitch. "Are you sure?"

"I haven't confirmed it myself," said Emma, "but Granny's pretty sure it was the same person. And Lady Laura told me when I saw her that someone was passing, specifically being murdered, while I was with her." Emma started to tell him what Laura had told her when he stopped her.

"I'm sorry, Emma," Milo said, cutting her

off, "but this is just too much to take in all at once. Do you mind meeting us at my mother's? I know you're tired from your long drive this morning, but I'd rather hear this in person than over the phone."

"Don't worry about that," Emma told him. "I'm on my way."

When she ended the call, she said to Granny and Quinn, "Milo wants me to meet him at his mother's."

"Can I tag along?" asked Quinn, who'd just finished a call of his own.

"If you want, but it might be a long night. And aren't you supposed to leave tomorrow?"

"I just called my hotel," he told her. "They said it was okay if I extended my stay."

"What about your flight?"

"My ticket is transferrable. I'll just have to pay a change fee." He gave her a determined look. "Small price to pay to make sure you're okay."

After studying Quinn nearly a full minute, Emma started walking back to Fremont Street. "My SUV is parked on the other side of Fremont."

Granny floated next to Emma. "I'll meet you at Dolly's. I gotta charge up good if we're going to discuss this properly. And I can't wait to see if Lenny shows. I have questions for him, and if he doesn't answer, I may have to punch his light out!"

CHAPTER TWELVE

When Emma and Quinn arrived at Dolly's, Tracy opened the door before they even knocked. "I'm so glad you're here," she told Emma after giving her a quick hug. She was about to say more when her eyes caught the tall, red-haired man standing behind Emma, prompting Emma to make a quick introduction.

"So you're Dr. Quinn Keenan," Tracy said with interest as she shook his hand. "Come on in. Milo's in the living room. He found Dolly's address book and is calling everyone he can about her."

As they started for the living room, Tracy held Emma back. "Where in the world did you find him?" she asked in a whisper.

"On Fremont Street at the tail end of a bachelor party," Emma answered in a hushed voice. "I'll tell you more later."

When Milo ended his current call, he greeted Emma with a hug and exchanged handshakes with Quinn.

"I'm sorry to intrude," Quinn said to Milo, "but maybe I can help should you need another pair of eyes and hands."

"Thank you," answered Milo. "Emma has told us a lot about you. I'm just sorry we had to meet under these circumstances."

"Any luck finding Dolly?" Emma asked after setting down her purse.

Milo ran a hand over his weary face. "None. I called the police but they won't look for her until she's been missing at least twenty-four hours."

"I believe that's pretty standard procedure," Quinn remarked.

"That's what they told me," said Milo. "But the officer was very understanding and said considering her age they would keep an eye out for her. He took down the description of her car. The couple of friends I've called haven't seen her, and I don't think she had many others left in the area besides Madeline." He looked down at his hands. "And now she's gone."

"Did you find out anything more about Madeline?" Emma asked.

Milo nodded slowly. "I managed to reach her nephew, Megan's father. It was his wife who found Madeline. It looks like she died in her sleep."

"That's what Megan told us," said Emma.

Tracy slipped an arm through Milo's. "Maybe, when things settle down, we should try to get Dolly to move closer to us. She doesn't have to live with us, just nearer."

Milo patted her hand. "That's very generous, my love, but I don't think Dolly will ever leave Vegas. She loves it here." He turned his attention to Emma. "So what's all this about someone else dying and Lady Laura?"

"Are you sure you want to discuss this now?" Emma asked.

"Why not?" Milo said, indicating for them to take a seat. "And who knows, it might help us locate Dolly."

Emma sat down on the sofa and filled everyone in, starting with Granny following Dolly and ending with finding Megan in tears.

"I still have no idea who that might have been in the rest home," Milo said when Emma was finished. "But it could just be a coincidence that he and Madeline died on the same night. Both were ill and old."

"Granny doesn't think it's a coincidence," Emma told him. "And the more I think about Dolly's disappearance at the same time, the less I do, too."

"Old people dying does not, but old

people who know each other and are dying or disappearing on the same night does sound very odd," Quinn agreed. "But didn't Granny say the people at the rest home weren't surprised by the old guy's death?"

"That's what she reported," Emma confirmed as she walked to the kitchen. From the living room the other three watched her as she passed the kitchen table and approached the counter.

Looking up at the light, Emma said, "We really could use your help, Lenny. Dolly's missing."

"Anything?" asked Milo, coming to her side.

Emma shook her head. "Not that I can see."

She studied Milo. "With Dolly not here, maybe you'll be able to discern something."

"It's worth a try," he agreed.

"Wait for me!" Granny popped into the kitchen, briefly startling both Emma and Milo. "I don't want to miss this."

Milo shut off the kitchen light. Emma stepped into the living room and turned off a small lamp on one of the tables. "Should we turn them all off?" she asked Milo.

He studied the effect of the lighting. "How about leaving that small one on and turning off the larger pole lamp. That will make the kitchen darker but not completely." He closed the blinds on the sliding door leading to the patio.

Emma turned the small lamp on again as Quinn stepped over to the tall pole lamp and snapped it off. The kitchen, while not dark, was cast into shadows. Milo took a seat at the kitchen table facing the counter.

"You're not going to sit under Lenny's light?" asked Granny.

"No, Granny," Milo answered. "I'll have a better viewpoint from here. No sense crowding him."

Emma closed the drapes to the front window and stepped back into the kitchen. "Do you want me here or with the others?"

Milo looked into the living room. Both Quinn and Tracy were sitting on the sofa, the best vantage point to see into the kitchen. "Here, please, Emma," he said, patting the chair to his right. "Strength in numbers."

Emma took her seat. Together she and Milo watched the kitchen in silence. Granny hovered nearby. After a couple of minutes, Milo said, "Lenny, I'm Milo, Dolly's son. We'd really like to speak with you."

Nothing.

"Please, Lenny," he tried again. "My mother is missing and I'm quite concerned about her."

Another minute passed in silence. Milo was about to speak again when Emma's eye caught a faint shimmer. She put a hand on Milo's arm as a signal and kept her face pointed in the direction of the hazy sparkle. It wasn't coming from the light fixture but from an area near the stove.

"It's show time," said Granny in a whisper.

"Welcome," said Milo to the unknown ghost.

"Is Lenny here?" Tracy called to them in a stage whisper.

"We're not sure yet who it is," Emma answered, keeping her voice low. "It's not in the light but by the stove."

The ghost said nothing but faded, then brightened, pulsating with a slow heartbeat of light.

"Is that you, Lenny?" asked Milo again, addressing the hazy light directly and not taking his eyes off it. "Are you the spirit of Leonard Speidel?"

The apparition grew slowly brighter, coming more into focus. It was a man, an elderly man. The spirit faded again, then brightened, as if struggling to stay. This time they could make out more of his image. He was a shrunken elderly man with very thin hair. He was dressed in pajamas.

"I know him," whispered Granny, barely able to contain her excitement. "That's the man Dolly was visiting tonight."

"Are you sure, Granny?" asked Emma.

"Yes, it's definitely him," Granny assured her. "He was wearing those same PJs when he died."

"He could be coming to see my mother if he was a friend of hers," said Milo. "The dead often visit those close to them right after they die."

"If he's the one in the rest home, then he's not Lenny," noted Emma.

Milo addressed the ghost, "Who are you? Can you tell us your name?"

The ghost came more into focus and moved away from the stove. He began floating slowly out of the kitchen, pausing at the kitchen table to look Emma and Milo over, especially Emma. The spirit floated into the living room and hovered near Quinn and Tracy, looking each one full in the face.

Tracy wrapped her arms around herself and shivered. "It suddenly got very cold over here. Is the ghost nearby?"

"He's right in front of you and Quinn," Milo told her, "but don't be afraid. He seems to be studying you. He did the same to Emma and me."

Granny went to the spirit, who had ignored her so far. "I saw you tonight in the place where you lived."

The ghost turned to Granny, his face coming more into focus.

"I know you passed away tonight," Granny continued. "Are you confused about going to the other side? If so, we can help."

The face of the old man softened, then broke into a wide grin framed by fleshy lips. At that moment something familiar broke through Emma's mind. It was slight and elusive, like a shy eel poking its head out from an underwater cave, then withdrawing. She tried to coax it out so she could grab hold of it and see what was itching her brain. She watched the ghost carefully, wondering why he seemed so familiar. Then it came to her.

"Where's Lenny?" the ghost asked Granny. "I was told he's here."

The question took everyone back. Emma and Milo exchanged questioning looks. Granny glanced back at them for guidance. With a nod of her head, Emma encouraged Granny to continue.

"He's not here right now," Granny told the spirit. "Is he a friend of yours?"

The ghost scoffed at the question, but replied, "You might say that."

The ghost continued to float around the

great room and the kitchen, wandering slowly back and forth, as if pacing.

"Did Dolly tell you that Lenny was here?" asked Emma.

The ghost stopped in front of Emma. "She did. Was she lying?"

"My mother does not lie," snapped Milo. "She's peculiar, but very honest."

Emma put a hand on Milo's arm. "Don't get defensive, Milo," she warned. "It might send him away before we get some answers."

"You're right, of course," Milo whispered to her. "Sorry. I'm just so worried about Dolly."

Emma patted his arm, then addressed the ghost again. "We know Dolly visited you tonight before you passed. Do you know where she is?"

The ghost shrugged. "Not my concern right now."

"Well, it is mine!" barked Milo, forgetting again to be calm.

The ghost, now fully in focus, came up to the table and hovered in front of Milo. "So you're little Milo all grown up. You still look quite the same as when you were a snot-nosed kid."

"What's going on?" called Tracy. She was sitting on the edge of the sofa, ready to leap forward to help.

Quinn was more relaxed. He sat back on the sofa next to Tracy, absorbing what he could of the conversation, filling in the blanks with possibilities offered up by his sharp intuition. Taking a lead from Emma, he put a strong hand on Tracy's shoulder. "*Sh.* It's going to be okay," he whispered to Tracy. "They're safe."

Tracy looked back at Quinn. He gave her a smile of assurance. Reluctantly, she settled back against the sofa cushions, but not before grabbing a nearby throw pillow. She crushed the pillow to her chest and kneaded it like bread dough.

"You know me?" asked Milo of the ghost.

Instead of answering, the ghost gave him a wide grin. Once again the eel poked its head out from the dark spots in Emma's memory, and this time she succeeded in grabbing it and holding on. The face wasn't as round, but the nose was the same. Getting up from the table, she disappeared down the hallway, returning a few moments later with one of the framed photos from the wall. She sat back down at the table and studied the photo, then the ghost pacing the kitchen with Granny on his heels like a guard dog. She pushed the photo over to Milo and pointed to it.

"The ghost is Jimmy Hoffa?" asked Milo

with surprise.

"Hoffa?" The question came like a short yelp from Quinn.

Emma shook her head. She pointed to a specific man in the photo. Milo studied the photo, then the ghost, still confused.

Emma got up from the table and went to stand in front of the ghost. She smiled at him. "It's nice to meet you, Mr. More-house."

CHAPTER THIRTEEN

Granny jerked a thumb in the direction of the ghost. "He's Nemo, the gangster?"

Cool and collected, the ghost of Nemo Morehouse looked Granny up and down. "The term *gangster* is rather antiquated, don't you think? Kind of like yourself."

Granny sputtered and crossed her arms in indignation, "Why the nerve!"

Ignoring Granny, Nemo turned his attention back to Emma. He bowed slightly. "It's always a pleasure to meet a beautiful woman, my dear. Too bad we didn't meet when I was alive."

Emma shook her head slightly. Old or not, dead or not, Nemo obviously still thought he was a big shot surrounded by showgirls.

"My name is Emma Whitecastle," she told him. She turned to Milo. "You know Milo Ravenscroft, Dolly Meskiel's son. Over on the sofa are our friends Tracy and Quinn. They can't see or hear you, only Milo and I can." Next she indicated Granny. "And this is Ish Reynolds, better known as Granny Apples. She's the spirit of my great-great-great-grandmother. Granny will be assisting us in helping you. So if you want help, it might serve you best to be polite to her. To all of us."

Nemo chuckled. "I always liked feisty yet refined broads. You and me, Emma, are going to get along just fine."

"Don't be so sure of that," Emma told him with the sharpness of a pinprick. "What this boils down to is, you help us and we'll help you as much as we're able."

Unable to contain herself, Tracy blurted out, "What's going on?"

Milo turned to Tracy. "It's okay, my love. But I do believe Nemo just made an advance to Emma."

Tracy's mouth fell open. "What? Is that even possible?"

Quinn, on the other hand, leaned back against the sofa and roared with laughter. "Poor Phil. Now he'll be worried about Emma and spirits. I hope he's never seen *The Ghost and Mrs. Muir.*"

Recovering quickly from her shock, Tracy joined him in laughing. "I love that movie!"

"Me, too," chimed in Granny, for the moment forgetting she was angry with Nemo.

Nemo floated over to where the kitchen met the living room area. "Your friends seem to find this very humorous."

Emma sidled up to the ghost. "Why are you here, Nemo? Why are you looking for Lenny?"

The ghost of the old man turned slowly and looked at Emma. Though not as short as Granny, Nemo's head barely cleared Emma's shoulder. "He has something that belongs to me."

"But he's dead," Granny told him, approaching. "Spirits cannot bring material things to the other side."

"Oh, I know he's dead, Granny." Nemo gave her a close-lipped smiled. "I'm the one who had him killed."

Milo got up from the table and stood near Emma. "You're admitting to the murder of Lenny Speidel?"

"Why not?" Nemo extended his arms up from his sides in an exaggerated shrug. "I'm dead. It's not like anyone is going to prosecute me now." He laughed. "And it's not like anyone missed the little weasel all these years."

"This doesn't make sense," said Emma. "If Leonard Speidel had something you wanted, why did you have him killed? That seems rather counterproductive."

"Seems downright idiotic to me," groused Granny.

Nemo shook his head, but still maintained his smile. "And you would be right, both of you. Lenny wasn't supposed to die, at least not until he gave me the information I wanted, but he tried to run and my boys got a bit rambunctious."

Boys. Nemo's boys. Emma looked straight at the ghost. "By your boys, you mean the thugs who worked for you?"

"My employees, at least at the time. Not the smartest two lugs, but I certainly thought they were smarter than Lenny Speidel. Turns out I was wrong."

The ghost of Nemo Morehouse wandered around the kitchen and great room again while Granny, Milo, and Emma kept a close eye on him. "So where is Lenny? Dolly told me tonight that he's been hanging around here."

"So you did know my mother?" asked Milo.

"Why yes," Nemo answered. "And quite well back in the day, but she hadn't been to see me in a long time until tonight."

"Why tonight?" Emma asked. "Is it because she confirmed Lenny was here?"

Nemo nodded. "She knew we had unresolved business, Lenny and I. I went to

Dolly years ago when she first set up shop as a fortune-teller. I had hoped she could put me in contact with him, or be able to tell me the information I wanted, but she didn't seem to have that ability. Pity." He looked straight at Milo. "She never told me her son did. It would have saved me a lot of time." He turned to Emma. "She only told me about you, my dear. Dolly spoke highly of you tonight."

Milo stepped forward until he was almost nose to nose with Nemo. "Do you know where Dolly is now?"

"As a matter of fact, I do. But don't worry, she's quite safe. For the time being."

Milo's eyes widened. "What do you mean by that?"

"I mean that your mother is alive and safe and under the care of my associates. If I get what I want from Lenny, you will get your mother back. If I don't, the only way you'll be seeing her is like this." With his hands, Nemo gestured up and down his hazy figure.

The sound of a cell phone ringing filled the tense air. Emma turned to Tracy. "That's Phil. Grab my phone and tell him I'll call him back. I don't want him to worry."

Tracy opened Emma's bag, retrieved the phone, and answered it. "Hey, Phil," she whispered. "It's Tracy. Emma's tied up with a ghost right now. Can she call you back?" She listened, then said, "Okay, I'll tell her."

The interruption seemed to amuse Nemo. "You're a popular gal, Emma Whitecastle. Is that a husband or a boyfriend?"

"None of your beeswax," Granny answered for Emma. "Now where's Dolly?"

Nemo brushed Granny off and concentrated on Milo, waiting for him to say something.

"What do I need to do to get my mother back?" Milo asked.

"Find Lenny and convince him to give you what I want." The ghost of Nemo Morehouse started to fade.

"And that is?"

"He'll know. And, Emma," Nemo said, addressing her with a smile, "I wouldn't go anywhere if I were you. You might come in handy in the negotiations." With that, the ghost of Nemo Morehouse disappeared.

Silence, as heavy as a wool blanket, covered the house after Nemo's departure. For several minutes no one spoke or even moved until Tracy asked, "Is he gone?"

"Yes," answered Emma.

"And good riddance," groused Granny.

Quinn got up from the sofa and snapped on the large lamp. "Wow, even without hearing his side of the conversation, that was pretty intense."

After turning on the kitchen light, Emma quickly relayed the conversation with Nemo to Tracy and Quinn.

Milo filled a teakettle with water and put it on the stove. "I don't know about you folks, but I need a cup of tea after that."

"I'd prefer a strong drink," said Tracy.

"In that bottom cupboard," said Milo, indicating one to his right.

Tracy pulled out a bottle of scotch and grabbed four glasses from a higher cupboard. She poured a healthy bit into each one and handed one to Emma and one to Quinn, who'd joined them in the kitchen. She took one for herself and pushed the last glass toward Milo. "Here, darling, you'll need this before your tea."

Milo looked at the glass of amber liquid. "You're probably quite right." He picked up the glass and took a sip, followed by a large gulp.

"So he has Dolly?" Tracy asked after taking a good long pull of her own drink.

"Yes," answered Emma. "Or rather people he knows have her."

"Don't worry, darling," Tracy said to Milo. "We'll get her back."

Quinn leaned against the counter and

sipped his drink. "Do you really think an old guy like that still has clout enough to kidnap someone? He could just be blowing smoke. After all, he's dead. Even if he gets what he wants from Lenny, what is he going to do with it?"

"That," Emma agreed, "is an excellent question." With her free hand she rubbed her eyes. "He can't pass the information along to anyone alive unless he has a medium to work through and he knows Dolly is not a medium."

"Maybe that's why Nemo's so interested in you?" suggested Tracy. "Didn't he say you might be needed as a negotiator?"

"Yes, he did, and that Dolly mentioned me to him. Funny, she mentioned me but never mentioned Milo."

"You have to remember, Emma," Milo said after taking a deep breath, "my mother doesn't believe in my abilities."

"You're wrong about that, Milo," Emma told him. "Today when I met Suzanne Foster and Megan, they both knew you were a psychic and famous. I'm sure Dolly told them."

Milo seemed surprised. "But why would she keep that from Nemo and mention you?"

Emma shrugged. "I have no idea, but if I

hadn't come along, what would she have done? Or what would Nemo do?"

"There are a lot more mediums out there than you realize," Milo said, taking out a couple of mugs and some tea bags from the cupboard. "Maybe he's working with someone else to reach Lenny but they haven't been able to do it. My mother might have scooted down to the rest home to let him know she'd found someone who could."

"What about that Lady Laura we met tonight?" asked Granny.

Emma considered it. "She definitely is a medium, but I'm not sure she knows it herself. Still, it might be worth checking to see if Nemo or any of his people have contacted her." She turned to Milo. "I gave Laura your number and asked her to call you. I think she needs mentoring in her skills."

Emma went to her bag and removed something from it and brought it to Milo. "I grabbed one of her cards on my way out. She knows who you are but didn't know you were Dolly's son. In fact, she seemed a little starstruck at the mention of your name. I'll bet if you call her, she might be off her guard enough to talk about anyone who might have approached her. Or she might be able to tell you who else in the area might be a medium."

"Good idea," answered Milo, taking the card. When the teakettle whistled, he took it off the flame and poured water into one mug. "Who'd like some tea?" he asked. "It's chamomile." Only Tracy raised her hand, so he filled two mugs.

"Maybe we should call her now," suggested Tracy.

Quinn shook his head. "If she works on Fremont Street, she's in the middle of her busiest time and probably won't answer her phone, let alone chat."

Milo sighed. "Quinn's right." He looked at his watch. "It's almost ten. Early for Vegas." He expelled a soft chuckle. "Dolly always said the best business was after ten, after people had been drinking in earnest."

"The bead store stays open that late?" asked Emma with surprise. She took another sip of her scotch, feeling its warmth spread through her body like a heating coil.

"The bead store and The Raven's Craft stay open most nights until midnight," Milo explained. "During the week, they might close around eleven if business is slow."

"Speaking of slow," said Emma, rubbing her eyes again, "I'm about to drop and the booze is making it worse."

"Emma, I'm sorry," said Milo. "I totally

forgot that you've been up since dawn just to drive here today."

"Not since dawn, but close enough," Emma said. "Vegas might be just starting, but I'm folding and fast." She took a final sip of the scotch and put the glass down on the counter. "I'm sorry, too, Milo. Sorry there's not much we can do tonight if Lenny won't show and we have no idea who has Dolly. Maybe we'd be better off starting fresh tomorrow and contacting as many people as we can to question."

"Aren't we missing something here?" asked Tracy. "We now know Dolly has been kidnapped, so why don't we call the police and tell them?"

"And tell them what, my love?" Milo tossed back the rest of his scotch while he waited for his tea to steep. "Tell them that the ghost of an old Vegas gangster who died tonight visited us and threatened to kill my mother if we don't contact another ghost on his behalf?" He sucked in a deep breath of frustration. "They'd write us off as crackpots and not give Dolly a second thought. By not telling them, they will at least keep looking for Dolly as a missing elderly person. Tomorrow we can declare her missing and they will start looking for her officially."

"Milo's right," said Quinn. "I vote for Emma's plan, that we try to get some rest and start fresh in the morning."

Emma studied Quinn. "So you've decided not to fly home tomorrow?"

He gave her a boyish grin. "After this? Not on your life. I'm here until this is resolved. Besides being fascinating to me, the more people out there hunting for clues, the faster we can get Milo's mom back safe and sound."

Milo stuck out a hand to Quinn, who took it and shook. "Thank you, Quinn. I appreciate that."

Milo finished fixing the tea and handed Tracy her mug. "I don't know how much sleep I'm going to get tonight, but I'll have to at least call the Fosters early in the morning to let them know Dolly can't watch Nicholas."

Emma was getting her purse, readying to leave, when an idea struck her. "You know, I just remembered that Nicholas's father is a detective here in Las Vegas. Maybe he can step up the search for Dolly."

"I do recall my mother saying something about him being on the police force," answered Milo with a beam of hope. He went to the refrigerator and removed a business card stuck to the front of it. "Yes, here's

153

their number. Dolly pointed it out to me last time I was here, when she first starting watching Nicholas." He turned the card over. "Their home number is on the back of John's business card. I'll talk to him about it when I call tomorrow."

"Come on," Emma said to Quinn. "I'll give you a ride back downtown."

"If you don't mind," Quinn told her, "can you take me back to the Strip. I'm staying at Treasure Island."

"Well, that's convenient," Emma said with a smile. "I'm at the Venetian, right across the street."

"Yeah," Granny said, half under her breath. "Too convenient, if ya ask me."

When Emma shot Granny a frown, Granny went to the kitchen counter and stared up at Lenny the Lightbulb. "Now might be a grand time for you to show yourself and start talking."

CHAPTER FOURTEEN

"Hi, Phil," Emma said into the phone. As soon as she was in her room with her feet up, she'd returned his call. "I hope it's not too late. Tracy said you were turning in around eleven."

"Not at all, sweetheart. I'm in bed reading, hoping you'd call."

Emma took a deep breath, almost able to smell Phil Bowers and his favorite soap through the phone. "I miss you."

"I miss ya back, but you sound exhausted. I hope you're on your way to bed and not hitting the Vegas nightlife."

"Nope, bed it is about ten minutes after this call. Maybe less if I wash my face and brush my teeth with any speed."

Phil laughed. "What's going on out there? Tracy said you were in the middle of a ghost when I called. Was that the one Milo suspected of being at his mother's place?"

"No. In fact, if the situation weren't so

serious, it would be hysterical." Emma scooted down deeper into the large sofa and thought about staying that way until morning. The scotch had definitely mellowed her out.

"The ghost I was talking to was that of an old Mafia-type gangster from the 1960s who passed away tonight. He died shortly after Milo's mother, Dolly, visited him at the rest home where he was living."

"You don't think she had anything to do with his death, do you?"

"Granny wondered that, too, but I doubt it." Emma ran a hand through her hair as if filing away the possibility for later consideration. "Anyway, Nemo, the gangster ghost, is looking for Lenny, the ghost inhabiting Dolly's kitchen light. Nemo claims he had Lenny killed way back when but that his goons didn't get the information out of Lenny before they whacked him."

Phil laughed. "You're making this up. You have to be."

"It does sound like something from a kooky TV show, doesn't it? Except this could have very serious consequences. You see, Dolly is now missing and Nemo claims he's holding her hostage until Lenny gives up the information he wants."

"Are you kidding me?" Phil's tone turned

from jovial to flat and focused. "How in the hell can a ghost hold a living person hostage?"

"Nemo says his associates have her and are willing to kill her to get the information."

"But you said this guy died just tonight."

"That's right. And unlike most spirits who pass over, he doesn't seem the least bit confused. In fact, it's just the opposite. It's almost like he died with a purpose, even though he was in his late eighties and well on his way to dying already."

"This has got to be the oddest thing you've been mixed up with yet."

"I totally agree, Phil." Emma shook off the urge to close her eyes. "All Milo and I can figure out is that this Nemo is working with another medium to communicate with his pals who are holding Dolly. Meanwhile, Lenny is MIA. On top of that, one of Dolly's oldest friends died tonight in her sleep. She'd been ill."

"I'm coming out there," Phil told her. "I don't like this one bit. It's too weird, even by your standards. Let me clear my calendar in the morning and catch a plane to Vegas tomorrow afternoon."

"A plane, Phil?" Emma's mouth broke into a tired and lazy smile. Whenever they visited Las Vegas, they drove, even though the flight was a short one.

"Yes, a plane. I gather you drove up there. No sense having two vehicles. We can drive back together."

"That's not necessary, Phil. Granny's working on finding Lenny and keeping tabs on Nemo best she can. We're looking into local mediums and doing what we can to find Dolly. Tomorrow the police will consider her officially missing and will join in the hunt."

It was about now that sleep battled with Emma's need to tell Phil about Quinn. She didn't want to hide Quinn's presence, but she also didn't want to upset Phil. She jumped in, thinking it better to tell him now than wait. "By the way, I bumped into an old friend today who is also helping out."

"Really? Who's that?"

"Quinn Keenan."

From the other end of the line came silence, long as a desert road and heavy as lead.

"You there, Phil?" Emma asked, half hoping the call had been dropped.

Phil cleared his throat. "Quinn just happened to be in Las Vegas the very day you arrived?"

"No, Phil, he didn't *just happen* to be

158

here." Emma felt herself getting defensive. "He'd been here for a few days for a bachelor party. I even met the groom when I bumped into them on Fremont Street."

"But you said Quinn is helping out with this ghost matter."

"Yes, he wants to help so he's staying around an extra day or so. You know how intrigued he is about this ghost stuff."

"Uh-huh. And is he also staying at the Venetian?"

Emma sat up, the sleep dropping from her eyes as she picked up on Phil's snarky tone. "No, Phil. Not the Venetian. For your information, he's staying at Treasure Island. You can call there if you want to check out my story."

"Emma, don't be that way. It just seems odd that he popped in like that out of nowhere and now is hell-bent on sticking around to help."

"What are you saying, Phil?"

"I'm saying maybe you let it drop that you were going to Vegas and he decided to take the opportunity to pursue you. I know the two of you stay in contact."

"We're friends, Phil. Quinn and I are *just* friends. Something I've told you many times." Emma got to her feet and paced the living room area of her suite with long strides. She was angry and tired, not a good combination, and the warm fuzzy feeling from the alcohol had disappeared. "And we're not in as much contact as you imagine in that jealous head of yours. I didn't even know myself I was heading to Las Vegas until late yesterday."

"I still don't like him mooning after you the way he does."

"Drop it, Phil. An elderly woman is missing and I'm too tired to argue about your stupid jealousy. It really is the most unattractive thing about you."

"Now, now, Fancy Pants," Phil said, using his pet name for Emma to cajole her. It only made Emma more frustrated.

"This is serious, Phil. There is nothing wrong with me having Quinn Keenan as a friend. I have lots of male friends, just as you have lots of female friends. You don't see me being jealous about them, do you?"

"This is different, Emma. My female friends are not in love with me."

"Oh no? You're a good-looking successful attorney with a ranch. Trust me, Phil, there are several who'd jump you in a hot minute if I wasn't in the picture, but I don't fuss about them because I trust you and what we have."

"Really? Who?" Phil's questions didn't

come as a challenge but more as surprised curiosity.

Out of frustration, Emma hung up and continued pacing.

Her phone rang again. It was Phil's ringtone. Instead of answering, Emma stomped through the bedroom area and into the bathroom. The bathrooms at the Venetian were Emma's favorite part of their rooms. She poured lavender bath salts she'd brought with her into the large and very deep soaking tub. While the tub filled, she washed her face, brushed her teeth, and undressed, yanking at her clothes with sharp jerks of anger. Once naked, she slipped into the deep hot water. She could hear her phone start ringing again in the other room, once more with Phil's assigned ringtone, and wished she'd shut it off, but she wasn't about to get out of the tub now to do it. It rang again, then stopped. *Good.*

A few minutes later, Emma was finally relaxing. She scooted deeper down into the tub and let her mind wander over the events of the day, trying to neatly separate them into facts and theories. She separated out what was true and what could be true, making neat mental piles. When thoughts of Phil competed for her attention, she swept them away as best she could, like debris from a rainstorm, and continued reviewing the facts surrounding Dolly's disappearance.

When she got home, she and Phil would have to have a long talk. She felt a bit guilty about ending the call the way she did. Her behavior had been fueled by exhaustion and his attitude about Quinn's presence. Grant Whitecastle had been neglectful as a husband, seeming not to care one way or another if another man was attracted to her. Phil was the opposite, although he only seemed to obsess about Quinn. Well, he'd just have to get over it because she liked being around Quinn and enjoyed his company as a friend. And she'd been telling the truth about women eyeing Phil. There were several who lived in the Julian area — two divorcees and a widow. She'd watched them fawn over Phil at festivals and town events when they were first dating, before their relationship was well known. One of them was hot on his trail even now. Emma had to admit she did get a bit jealous when she saw the woman batting her eyes at Phil or heard she'd been visiting Phil's aunt Susan at the ranch, but she kept that to herself. Yes, a long talk with Phil was in order.

Tonight when they left Dolly's, Quinn had seen how exhausted she was and offered to drive them back to the Strip. Emma had

gladly handed over her keys. They had chat-
ted about the ghosts and Dolly, but nothing
else. When they pulled up to the Venetian,
Quinn had handed the valet the keys. She'd
started to say good night when he handed
her the parking claim ticket, but Quinn had
insisted on walking Emma through the
noisy casino, his hand gently cupping her
elbow. He rode up in the elevator and
escorted her to her room, where he took his
leave like a true gentleman, saying he'd call
her in the morning. Phil would have done
the same for a female friend. Emma knew
that for sure. The two men were not that
different in how they treated women or
other people in general. Both were intel-
ligent and confident, and both were decent
and kind. Was that what Phil was afraid of?
That he recognized in Quinn the very same
characteristics she, Emma, found attractive
in him, and was worried her affections
would be turned.

Emma let out the deep breath she'd been
holding during her thoughts. Picking up the
washcloth, she finished washing herself,
then climbed out of the tub to dry off. The
bath had helped her relax after the fight
with Phil had wound her up but now she
was wide awake. After putting on her night-
gown, she crawled in bed and turned on

some late-night TV. She hoped she'd fall asleep soon since she and Quinn were going to meet at seven thirty in the morning for breakfast before going back to Dolly's to plan out the day with Milo and Tracy.

When sleep continued to elude her, Emma got up and headed for the minibar. A small bit of wine usually helped when she was restless at night. On her way to the fridge, she spied her cell phone and remembered she needed to charge it. She retrieved it from the coffee table where she'd left it after talking to Phil and retraced her steps to the bedroom area to grab her charger from her suitcase. Before plugging it in, she noticed there were two voice mails, both from Phil while she was in the tub. He'd also left her a text message apologizing for his behavior and asked her to call him in the morning.

"Nemo's boys are coming for you."

Emma whipped her head around in the direction of the voice. It was coming from the corner of the living room where the large window met the side wall by the desk. She put down the phone and took a cautious step in that direction. Then another, shuffling carefully so as not to scare off the spirit. She saw nothing, just a dark corner of the room. Then the bottom of the drape moved — slightly, as if by a small puff of air. The drape moved again, this time a foot farther away from the corner. Then another foot and another slight movement of heavy fabric. The ghost was on the move, warily coming closer. Emma stepped down from the bedroom area into the sunken living room, feeling for the shallow drop with her right foot so she wouldn't have to take her eyes off the moving drape.

"Lenny, is that you?"

At the mention of the name, the ghost started appearing. Just a shimmer at first, like a fist full of dust motes caught in a spark of random light. Then the shimmer expanded into a hazy outline.

"Lenny," Emma said, addressing the image again. "There is no need to be afraid."

The image grew sharper, filling in until Emma saw a tall, slight man with thick hair and a long angular face — a face that looked vaguely familiar. Then it occurred to her that she might have seen that face in photos on the wall at Dolly's. In several photos, if she remembered correctly.

"It's dangerous," Lenny said.

"You're in no danger here," Emma assured him.

The ghost gave her a small smile. He was plain faced, but his smile changed everything, giving him a dashing look. "Not for me, Mrs. Whitecastle. I'm dead." He moved away from the drapes. "It's dangerous for you. For all of you. Nemo is coming. His boys are coming."

"I've already met Nemo," Emma told him. She perched on the edge of the sofa's arm. "He's dead now. His spirit showed up at Dolly's place looking for you."

Lenny paced across the floor in front of Emma. "Then it has begun."

"He says his people have Dolly Meskiel. They are holding her until he gets what he wants from you."

Lenny's head whipped around to face her. "They have Doll?"

"That's what Nemo claims. Dolly was visiting him tonight before he died. She went missing right after that. He said his people will kill her if he doesn't get what he wants from you."

Lenny grabbed his head with both hands and let out a muted cry of anguish. "I tried to warn her but she couldn't see or hear me." He looked up at Emma. "But little Nicholas could. He just couldn't tell her anything. Milo also tried and failed. It wasn't until you showed up that I had any hope of protecting her, but I didn't know how. How do you tell the living that they are in danger if they're not sure you exist?"

"You could have talked to Granny, the ghost that was with me."

"I was afraid to show myself, even to another spirit. I was worried he'd enlisted other ghosts in his dirty business. I overheard him once tell Doll that he was going to get to me no matter what. He's been dogging her off and on for years, hoping she could be that contact, but she can't see or hear me. I think he finally accepted that because he hasn't been around in a long time."

"He's been sick and in a rest home. That's where Dolly visited him, and the last time she was seen."

The ghost shook his head back and forth. "Why would Doll go to Nemo on her own? She knew he was dangerous."

"She probably thought he wasn't a threat because of his age and illness."

"But his boys still are."

Emma still wanted that wine — more than ever and not for sleep. "Will you excuse me?" she said to Lenny. Getting up, she went to the minibar and extracted a small bottle of red wine. She undid the top and poured some into a nearby glass.

"Boy, that looks good," the ghost commented. "I sure miss drinking wine. And eating a nice big bowl of spaghetti with meatballs. Doll and I used to go to this little Italian place just off Fremont Street."

"Were you and Dolly good friends?"

"Much more than that." He winked at Emma and pointed the index finger of his right hand at her. "If you get my drift."

Emma laughed. "I do." She was sure now that Leonard was the man that showed up in several of Dolly's photos with her.

Lenny stopped pacing and looked at her, the smile again appearing, replacing the worry. "It's really difficult to return from the other side and not be able to enjoy all the marvelous modern things you have now. I drove a 1962 T-Bird when I was alive, but man, what I wouldn't give to get behind the wheel of one of those foreign sports cars I see going up and down the Strip like sleek rockets."

A car guy, Emma noted. She took another sip of wine before interrupting Lenny's happy thoughts with more doom and gloom.

"Lenny," she said, getting back on topic. "The men who killed you are probably very old or even dead by now. Why do you think they would come back?"

"They won't," he said simply.

"You keep saying Nemo's boys are coming. You asked me at first if they sent me, then in the fortune-teller's wagon you said

168

they would come for me? How is that possible?"

"They will hurt Doll whether you help them or not." The worry returned to the ghost's face. "It's all so confusing, even to me." He started to fade. "They've already come for her and it won't end there."

"Don't go, Lenny," Emma pleaded. She put down her wine and got to her feet. "Please. Help us get Dolly back."

The ghost's image was disappearing into a handful of dust motes again.

"Please, Lenny," Emma called after him. "What is it Nemo wants from you?"

CHAPTER FIFTEEN

Fumbling through the contacts on her phone, Emma found the one she was seeking and hit the call button. After two rings Quinn answered.

"I'm sorry to wake you," she said to him.

"You didn't. I'm actually on Fremont Street."

"What are you doing there?"

"I was too wound up to sleep so I grabbed a cab back downtown. I was hoping to see this Lady Laura myself. I figured late on a Tuesday night she might not have a line waiting to see her."

Emma was torn. She wanted to know about Quinn's visit with Laura, but she also wanted to tell him about her interaction with Lenny. Both were important. "Did you see her?"

"Not yet. When I got here, the wagon was closed up. I talked to a couple of people hanging around in the area and they said she left with two of her clients right after their session."

"Laura left with clients? That doesn't sound right." Emma's left foot jiggled with nerves.

"That's what a woman who was standing near the wagon told me when I started asking about Laura. She was pretty annoyed; said she waited forty-five minutes to see Laura, then after these two men were done with their session, Laura came out and left with them. She said it was a few hours ago. She keeps coming back hoping Laura's returned, but so far she hasn't."

"A few hours ago was right after I was there. She had a healthy line even then." Emma wondered what could have taken Laura away. "Maybe Laura decided to close up after those clients and it just looked like she left with them," Emma suggested.

"I don't know about you, Emma, but I've never heard of any of these Vegas entrepreneurs closing shop with customers waiting. That's leaving money on the table."

He had a very good point, Emma admitted to herself.

"And the woman I spoke to said she's a regular client of Laura's and never saw her do anything like it. Said Laura seemed in a daze. Didn't say a word to anyone, just walked down the steps from the wagon and left. Didn't put up the closed sign, didn't tell anyone when she would be back. Just left."

"That is odd."

"And there's more. The woman said that one of the guys was already in line waiting, but when it was his turn, he'd let the next person go ahead. He didn't take his turn until the other man came so they could go in together."

"So it was a twofer? A gay couple maybe?"

"Hard to tell. And here's something even odder. Right before you called, I tried the handle on the door to the wagon. It was unlocked. No one would leave their place of business here, not even for a bathroom break, without locking it up."

"Did you go inside?"

"No, ma'am." He laughed. "I would have if no one had been around, but not with all these witnesses."

"Now I'm concerned for Laura. Did you ask what the two men looked like?"

"Sure did. The lady I spoke to said they were an odd pair. Her words, not mine."

"Wait a minute," Emma told him. She got up and retrieved the note pad and pen next to the hotel phone on the desk. "Okay, go on."

"She said one wore a suit and was of average height. She guessed him to be in his late forties or early fifties with thinning gray hair. The other was unkempt, kind of fat, and quite a bit younger."

Emma jotted the information down. "Got it. Nice work, Quinn. Maybe they're father and son?"

Quinn chuckled. "When's the last time you saw a father and son go to a fortune-teller together? It's not even that common for men to go, is it? Isn't it usually women who seek out stuff like that?"

"Yes. At least I know Milo's clientele are mostly women." Emma sifted through her memory for a visual on the people in line at Laura's when she was there. "When I was in line at Laura's, I only saw two men. One had just come out and one was behind me." She smacked her head. "That could be him. The guy behind me was kind of unkempt and overweight. Did the woman say who was there first holding the pace in line?"

"Yes, the younger one."

"I really wished I'd paid closer attention. What I remember is exactly what that women remembers, except for the comic book. The guy standing behind me was reading a comic book. One of those with a superhero. When Laura pulled me to the head of the line, she saved me about forty-five minutes to an hour of time, so the guy I saw could have been one of the men who took off with her."

After a short silence, Quinn asked, "So what's up with you? Can't you sleep either?"

"I got a visitor tonight," she told him. "It was Leonard Speidel."

"Lenny the Lightbulb? The same Lenny that nutty Nemo is after?"

"The same. He finally materialized. He's worried about Dolly and says we're all in danger from Nemo's men. But he also seems confused. He left before I could find out what it is Nemo is after."

"Maybe he'll come back soon. Don't ghosts need to recharge?"

"They do, but he seemed disjointed. Fine one minute, fraught the next. Very unlike the cool and collected Nemo, who only died tonight."

"This is really strange."

"No kidding." In the background Emma could hear the clanging of slot machines and loud music. "And I think he was Dolly's boyfriend at the time he died."

"Didn't you say Lenny spoke through Laura when you were with her today?"

"Yes, he did," Emma confirmed. "I wonder if he's more comfortable communicating through a living person instead of with one directly."

Quinn sighed with frustration. "Now I really wish I had connected with Laura."

"Me, too. Or at least I wish we knew where she was."

CHAPTER SIXTEEN

In the morning, Quinn met Emma at one of the restaurants at her hotel. After, they took her vehicle back to Dolly's house. When they got there, two cars were parked in front — a police cruiser and a dark sedan. In the driveway was Tracy's car. Emma had learned from Milo the night before that his mother drove a silver Honda. It was nowhere in sight.

After parking her SUV at the curb in front of the house next door, Emma glanced over at Quinn. "This doesn't feel right to me."

"Maybe they're just here to take the missing person report," he suggested, but Emma could see in Quinn's eyes he was just as concerned.

When they approached the front door of Dolly's home, they were stopped by a young patrolman. After identifying themselves, they waited on the front stoop a couple of minutes before being allowed in, where they found Milo and Tracy on the sofa side by side, hands locked in support.

"What is it?" asked Emma, rushing to them. "Is Dolly okay?"

"We don't know yet," answered Milo. He introduced them to a man in a suit sitting in a chair pulled up in front of the sofa. "These are our friends Emma Whitecastle and Dr. Quinn Keenan. They were with us last night."

The man got up. He was in his mid-thirties, tall and lean with thick dark hair. "I'm Detective John Foster." He pointed to another man in a suit standing nearby, taking notes. "That's my partner, Detective Howard Garby." Garby, older and not so trim, nodded to them.

"You're Nicholas's father," Emma said to Foster with a small smile. "I met your wife yesterday." Before the detective could answer, Emma asked, "Are you gentlemen here to help us find Dolly?"

"Yes and no," answered Garby.

"They think Dolly killed someone," Tracy blurted out.

"We're just asking a few questions, ma'am," Foster corrected. He indicated for Emma and Quinn to sit and they complied, Emma taking a seat on the sofa with Milo and Tracy. Quinn dropped into a nearby upholstered chair.

"They're saying Dolly was the last person to see this man who died last night alive," Milo told Emma and Quinn. He looked like he hadn't slept a wink all night. "They're *suggesting* she might have killed him."

"It was a man by the name of Nelson Morehouse," Garby told Emma. "He went by the nickname *Nemo.* You know, like the little fish in that Disney cartoon."

Emma looked over at Milo and Tracy, wondering how much they had already told the detective. Had they mentioned anything about Nemo's visit last night? Or were they keeping mum on the subject of paranormal visitations? She wished she knew before she said something that might shed a bad light on the situation. But it was a good indication that Milo hadn't mentioned Nemo by name.

"As I told Detective Foster," Milo said to her as if reading her mind, "we've been trying to find Dolly after she didn't show up at her shop last night and none of us were successful."

On the coffee table was the photo of Dolly with Nemo Morehouse that Emma had brought into the kitchen the night before. She'd left it on the counter. Foster tapped Nemo's face. "Seems odd that your mother was reminiscing about old times with this Nemo the night he died and she disappeared. Was she looking at this before or after she visited him at the rest home?"

"Neither," answered Emma. "I'm the one who was looking at that photo. I noticed it on the wall in the hallway and bought it out to show Milo. I was curious about one of the men in the photo and wanted to ask Milo about him." She pointed to another man in the picture. "This one. I believe that's Jimmy Hoffa."

Foster bent forward to study the photo closer. Garby leaned forward and looked at it over his partner's shoulder. Garby was the first to look up at Milo. "Your mother knew Hoffa?"

"Are you also going to suggest Dolly had something to do with his disappearance?" Tracy, never one to like authority, was getting agitated.

Milo patted Tracy's knee. "The detectives are just doing their job." He turned his attention back to Foster and Garby. "I don't know if Dolly knew Hoffa personally. She's the showgirl on the right. She took a lot of photos with famous people when she was a dancer."

"There's even one in the hallway with her and Frank Sinatra," Emma added.

Milo nodded. "Yes, there is." He looked down at the photo. "From this picture, I think it's easier to assume that Mr. Morehouse knew Jimmy Hoffa rather than my mother and that she and the other woman in the picture were merely window dressing."

"Who is the other man? Do you know that?"

"Yes," said Milo with a nod. "I believe that's Moe Dalitz."

Foster took a closer look at the photo.

"Dalitz was known as the Father of Las Vegas," Milo added.

"I know who Dalitz was," said Foster, not looking up.

Again, Garby checked it out over Foster's shoulder. "Seems your mother kept some pretty fast company and with known criminals," he said.

"Those were publicity shots," Milo stressed. "As I told you, my mother posed with a lot of people when she was a showgirl. Men seem to like having their picture taken with pretty girls in feathers and fishnet stockings and not much else."

Ignoring the sarcasm, Foster tapped the photo again. "Who's the other woman? Do you know her?"

Milo nodded slowly. "That's Madeline

Kurtz, my mother's closest friend and business partner. She died last night."

At that announcement, Foster finally raised his eyes from the photo to look at Milo. "She died last night?"

"Yes," Emma told him. "She'd been ill and apparently died in her sleep."

Garby jotted something down in his notebook then motioned to a police officer to come over. "Check out this name," he told him as he tore the sheet out of his notebook and handed it to the officer. "Possibly died last night." The officer left.

"And how did you know Ms. Kurtz?" Foster asked Emma.

"I don't. When I stopped by Dolly's shop last night, Madeline's great-niece Megan was there and told me about Madeline's passing."

Foster studied Milo. "Two old people who knew your mother died on the same night. Very convenient."

"Convenient?" shot Tracy. "Are you suggesting Dolly had something to do with Madeline's death, too?"

"I'm just saying it seems odd." He looked over at Quinn. "And how do you know Dolly Meskiel?"

"I don't. I'm a friend of Emma's. I bumped into her on Fremont Street last night and tagged along because I'd been wanting to meet Milo and Tracy for some time."

Foster looked to Emma. "I understand from my wife that you're a bit of a TV personality, Mrs. Whitecastle. She told me about meeting you yesterday."

Garby showed interest. "You related to that Grant Whitecastle who's on the tube?"

"He's my ex-husband," Emma answered, her words cool and direct. "I have my own talk show on a cable channel."

"You deal with the paranormal, correct?" asked Foster. "In fact, both you and Mr. Ravenscroft here are pretty wrapped up in that creepy stuff, aren't you?"

"It ain't creepy," snapped Granny, who popped in at that very moment.

Milo's eyes went to Granny, then quickly to Foster. He straightened his shoulders. "Both Emma and I are practicing mediums, Detective," he answered with directness. "I came to town to give a presentation at the university. That was yesterday. As I told the police last night and you just a short while ago, the last time I saw my mother was at that event."

Garby consulted his notes. "And from there she went to the rest home to see Nemo Morehouse, who kicked the bucket either during or right after her visit."

"I honestly do not know where my mother went after my presentation," answered Milo. "She said she had an appointment. Later she was to meet Emma at her shop, The Raven's Craft, but she never showed up."

"According to Morehouse's caretaker" — Garby checked his notes again — "a Frankie Varga, Ms. Meskiel showed up and she and the deceased got into a heated discussion. This Varga guy said when he stepped in to see what the problem was, Ms. Meskiel said it was a family spat and promised to keep it down. Morehouse also confirmed it was nothing. But when Varga checked on them later, he found Meskiel gone and Morehouse dead."

"That doesn't mean my mother killed him," stressed Milo with an excited wave of his hands. "Wasn't he quite old and sick? Maybe whatever argument they had was too much stress on him."

"Pssst," whispered Granny to Emma, as if afraid the cops would hear her. "I need to talk to you. It's important."

"Did you ever meet Morehouse?" Garby asked Milo.

"I was a kid when that photo was taken and Dolly didn't mix her home life with her career."

"That wasn't an answer," Foster pointed out.

Milo amended his answer, "No, I don't recall ever meeting the man in that photo."

"Then how did you know he was old and sick?" prodded Garby.

"Come on," answered Quinn for Milo. He leaned forward in his chair and poked the index finger of his right hand into the palm of his left as he made each of his points. "In the picture this Nemo guy is already middle-aged. He'd have to be in his eighties or nineties by now and wasn't he in a rest home with nurses looking after him? Old and sick would be a natural assumption."

"Nice answer," noted Granny. She floated over to Emma and danced from foot to foot. "I really need to talk to you and Milo. I think I've found Dolly."

Both Emma and Milo snapped their heads in Granny's direction. Detective Foster noticed and turned to look in the same direction. He saw nothing. "Don't tell me, folks," he said with a half sneer. "Ghosts?"

"I thought I heard a car pull up," answered Milo.

"Me, too," added Emma. "Maybe it's Dolly."

"I told you, I found Dolly," insisted Granny.

Detective Garby looked out the front window and studied the street. Emma took the momentary distraction to try to signal to Granny to wait. The ghost got the message but wasn't happy about it.

"Humph," she groused, crossing her arms in front of her. She floated over to where Quinn sat and tapped her foot with impatience.

"Nothing out there," reported Garby.

"Does being a medium also give you special powers like super hearing?" joked Foster.

"Sometimes," answered Milo, being serious. "We are very sensitive to things the rest of you cannot sense."

"Ah, the famous sixth sense," Foster said, still sporting a smirk.

"Something like that, Detective."

Garby laughed. "Can you see dead people, Mr. Ravenscroft?"

"Yes. If they want to be seen."

Emma sensed Milo was entering shaky territory, but wasn't sure if she should stop him. Realizing he was serious, the two detectives exchanged glances.

Foster turned to Emma. "And how about you, Mrs. Whitecastle? Do you see dead people, too?"

"Yes," she admitted. "And hear them."

Out of the corner of her eye she saw Quinn lean forward even more. Even Granny waited to see where this was leading. Emma hated admitting her gifts to nonbelievers. She wasn't ashamed of them, but she knew most people didn't believe it possible to make contact with the dead, and exposing her gifts to people like that felt to her like she was cheapening both her talents and the spirits and holding them out to ridicule. "Both Milo and I are mediums who can see and speak to spirits. We told you that already."

Garby scratched his head with the nonwriting end of his pen, but his face displayed a wide grin. "I don't know. I thought you folks meant dabbled in scam séances and fortune telling."

"Speaking of fortune telling," said Foster. "Isn't that what your mother does, Mr. Ravenscroft?"

"Yes," Milo answered. "She gives readings to people in her shop downtown."

"Can she see ghosts?" asked Garby.

"No," Milo answered. "Dolly does not have that gift."

Next to Milo, Tracy fidgeted like an antsy kid.

"Is something the matter, Ms. Bass?" Foster asked her.

"Yes," she answered, being careful not to look at anyone but the detective. "I'm worried about Dolly. Shouldn't you be out looking for her instead of grilling Emma and Milo about their paranormal talents, which, by the way, are very real."

Emma stiffened, sensing the passionate Tracy was about to go on a rant.

"Can you see dead people, Ms. Bass?" asked Foster.

"No, I cannot, but I've been around these two long enough to know it's real and that they are honest people interested in helping others. The people who attended Milo's presentation yesterday know it's real, as do the people who buy his books and watch Emma's show. Instead of making fun of them, you should be out looking for Dolly. And I don't mean looking for her as a murder suspect." Tracy gave a final huff and puff, crossed her arm across her chest, and leaned back against the sofa with a scowl.

"Bravo, girlfriend!" said Granny, clapping.

Milo patted Tracy's knee then turned to Emma, his eyes meeting hers in communication. She gave him a single, short nod of consent. A few seconds later, he turned to the two cops, who were waiting, and announced, "The ghost of Nemo Morehouse came to us last night, Detectives."

"I thought you said you'd never met the man," said Foster, clearly getting annoyed.

"I hadn't, at least not when he was alive." Milo remembered that Nemo had called him *little Milo* the night before and added, "Unless I met him as a kid and don't remember. Growing up here, I certainly had heard the name."

Garby was scribbling in his notebook. "So let me get this straight," he said, looking at them all. "You're saying the ghost of Nelson Morehouse came to you last night in a dream?"

"Not in a dream, Detective," Emma responded. "But here, last night, while we were all awake. We had a lengthy conversation with him."

"And you all saw and spoke to this ghost?" Foster asked, again giving all four of them a wide sweep with his eyes.

"Not all of us," clarified Quinn. "Tracy and I cannot see or hear spirits, but we do believe he was here last night speaking with Milo and Emma."

"That's right," confirmed Tracy, still peeved at the police.

"I was here, too," said Granny, who didn't like being left out.

Emma leaned forward and looked John Foster directly in the eye. "I don't know why you're so skeptical, Detective Foster. A lot of police departments call on psychics to help solve crimes when they're stumped."

Foster leaned back in his chair, considering that for a few seconds. "So what did Nemo have to say?" His question still held a lot of sarcasm, but with more restraint. "Did he mention Dolly's visit?"

"Yes," answered Milo, "but he said nothing about her killing him. He told us his people were holding her."

The two detectives did a double take. "Ghosts of dead guys are holding your mother?" asked Garby, his voice laced with mockery.

"No, people who work for Nemo or know him are holding her," Milo clarified. "He showed up here looking for another spirit — the ghost of a man he had killed years ago. He said that spirit had information he wanted, and if he didn't get it, his people would kill my mother."

Garby stepped forward, waving his notepad at Milo. "And you expect us to believe that bull?"

"No, we don't." Outrage was starting to build inside Emma, each sarcastic comment a building block to an explosion, but she did her best to keep it tamped down. "But whether you do or not doesn't change the fact that they have Dolly and have threatened to kill her."

Granny jumped up and down. "I know where she is. She's still alive!"

The officer Garby had given orders to earlier returned. "That Kurtz woman did die last night," he reported. "Heart attack. Family said she was ill with a bad cold or flu, and had a bad ticker."

Milo hung his head in sadness. Tracy pulled him close and Emma patted his arm.

"Madeline was like an aunt to Milo," Emma told the police, her brows knitted in challenge. "He's lost her and possibly his mother in one day."

"I'm sorry for your loss," said Foster in a low, serious voice. After a short pause, Foster cleared his throat. "And who is this other ghost? The one Morehouse was looking for?"

"His name," Emma answered, "is Leonard Speidel. He was a friend of Dolly's and had some dealings years ago with Nemo."

At the name, Foster sat up straight. "Leonard Speidel? Are you sure?"

"Yes," Emma said. "Back in the sixties, Nemo's goons killed Lenny before they got the information they were after. Now other men working for Nemo are holding Dolly until they get that same information."

"Why now after all these years?" Foster asked.

"I really don't know."

"I don't either," Milo told them. "Dolly may be the only one who does."

"I wonder if this has something to do with the Lucky Buck robbery," said Foster, getting to his feet. He put his hands on his hips beneath his suit jacket and stared out the window lost in thought. His gun, tucked into a shoulder holster, could be clearly seen under the open jacket. "It was always believed that both Speidel and Morehouse pulled that off and that Morehouse killed Speidel afterward to shut him up. But nothing was ever proved, including Morehouse's involvement in the heist itself." He turned back around to face them, looking for more information.

"Nemo admitted to us last night that he had Lenny killed." Emma held hope that Foster was coming around at last.

"Aren't you a little young to remember that bank robbery?" Quinn asked Foster.

"Vegas history is a hobby of his," said Garby, jerking his head in the direction of his partner. "Especially the gangster end of it."

Granny was still fussing and fidgeting. Emma tried to give her a sign to hold on a minute. Admitting to Nemo's presence was one thing, She didn't want to tip her hand about Granny if she didn't have to.

"The ghost of Lenny Speidel has been hanging around Dolly for a long time," Emma told the police. "Possibly since his death. He expected Nemo to pull something."

John Foster stared at her. "Was he here last night, too?"

"No," answered Emma truthfully. "But he did show up at my hotel last night." Now it was Milo and Tracy's turn to be surprised. They looked at Emma with open mouths. "He was very disturbed. All I got out of him is that we're all in danger from Nemo."

"A dead guy?" asked Garby. "You're all in danger from a dead man?"

"Yes." Emma turned to Foster. "You know that game Dolly plays with Nicholas? The one about Lenny the Lightbulb?"

Foster said nothing, but nodded with caution.

"Leonard Speidel is Lenny the Lightbulb," Emma explained. "He was haunting that light fixture in the kitchen and entertaining your son on the days Dolly cared for Nicholas. Your son saw the ghost."

"My son?" Foster was in disbelief. "My son can see ghosts?" He didn't seem pleased.

"It's quite normal for children to see spirits when they are very young," Milo quickly explained. "But it doesn't necessarily mean they will be able to communicate with them later in life. Animals can usually see or sense spirits, too."

Granny was waving at Emma with determination, even distracting Milo. Police or not, Emma decided it was time to see what Granny had to say.

"Do you mind," Emma said to the cops, "if I visit the bathroom? It's right down the hall."

"No, Mrs. Whitecastle," Garby told her. "Go right ahead, but don't take forever." Foster said nothing. He had gone into the kitchen and was staring up at the light fixture, no doubt considering Lenny's attachment to his infant son.

CHAPTER SEVENTEEN

As soon as Emma entered the main bath-room off the hallway, Granny joined her. Emma used the toilet. "I really did need to go," she explained to Granny in a voice barely above a whisper. "I had a gallon of coffee at breakfast."

"Yeah, I know," snapped Granny, "multi-tasking. Never even heard that term in my day."

"So," Emma asked, "where's Dolly?"

"Some place in the desert."

"This whole place is in the desert. Can you be more specific?"

Granny pouted. "You want my help or not?"

"Of course we want your help." Emma washed her hands. "Do you have any idea where in the desert?"

"Not exactly. I was able to locate Dolly and pop in on her. She's safe and seems okay except that she's very fretful. They have her locked in a room, a tiny bedroom with a bed and TV and not much else. There's a small window but it has bars on it."

Looking in the mirror, Emma ran a hand through her hair. She hadn't slept well and looked a little pale in spite of her makeup. She wished she'd brought her purse into the bathroom so she could dab on a little more lipstick. Lipstick always improved everything. Too bad it couldn't help her find Dolly. "Were you able to go outside at all?"

"Yep, and it's desert, I tell ya. The building is small and isn't a house exactly. It sort of is, but not a fixed building like your house."

Emma gave that some thought and turned to the ghost. "Do you mean it's a trailer or a mobile home?"

Granny looked puzzled, so Emma tried to give her a reference point. "Remember when my mother and I went to visit Mother's friend Sarah? You came along."

Granny nodded. "She had that teeny, tiny dog named Crackers." Granny smiled. "I had fun with Crackers." Granny loved playing with animals, especially dogs.

"Yes, that's the one. Do you remember her house? It was long and set up a little high rather than set on the ground. It was also in a row with others like it in a park-like setting."

Granny's face brightened as she remembered. "Yes, like that one. Where Dolly is being kept is a lot like Sarah's home but kind of run down."

"That's called a mobile home or trailer because they can be moved. They're not fixed to the ground."

"Yes," Granny confirmed. "Like that, but it's not in a nice place with a lot of others close by like Sarah's. There are buildings like it around, but they're not close together. More like scattered around the desert like they've been thrown down instead of parked neatly."

"And you say it's in wide-open desert? Not where there are a lot of other buildings?"

"There are other buildings, but nothing close to it. It's in the real desert — open and dry and dangerous. But that's all I know."

A knock came on the door, followed by Detective Foster's voice. "Mrs. Whitecastle, are you okay?"

"I'll be right out," Emma said to him through the door.

Emma glanced into the mirror again.

"You look just dandy," Granny said, shaking her head. "You're dealing with gangster ghosts, not entering some beauty pageant."

Emma smiled into the mirror at the remark. She could always count on Granny to keep her focused. "You did great, Granny." She turned to the ghost. "Very helpful. Thanks."

The ghost smiled at the praise, then the smile faded. "A lot of good it will do if we don't find Dolly soon. Especially if you can't get any information out of Lenny."

"We'll do our best," Emma assured her. "In the meantime, do you think you can go back and keep an eye on Dolly? And try to find out as much as you can about where she's being held and who has her?"

"Sure. And one more thing," Granny said as Emma put her hand on the doorknob to leave. "I think I saw that girl there."

"What girl?" Emma asked, still keeping her voice barely audible.

"That Laura girl. You know the fortune-teller with the cute wagon."

Emma took her hand off the knob. "Are you sure?"

"Not a hundred percent, but I think it was her. She was at that mobile house, too, but not in the same room."

"Did she look like she was there on her own or being held like Dolly?"

"Not sure. She was sleeping when I saw her. At least, I think she was sleeping, but I know she wasn't dead."

"We'll talk more later, Granny, as soon as the police leave. I need to bring you, Milo, and Tracy up-to-date on Lenny and on what Quinn found out."

"Okay, but if you don't mind, I'm going to go back to Dolly now. I'd feel better sticking close to her just in case something happens."

Emma opened the door, lost in thoughts of Laura and Dolly being held in a mobile home, and nearly ran into Detective Foster, who was lingering outside the bathroom door.

"Afraid I'd escape out the bathroom window, Detective?"

"Just checking out these wall photos in the hallway, Mrs. Whitecastle."

"Please call me Emma. After all, I'm acquainted with your son and wife." She smiled, trying to butter him up. They needed to start looking for Dolly and they needed him as an ally, not an enemy.

"Who were you talking to in there?" he asked, looking at her hands. "Were you on the phone?"

"Nope. I was talking to a ghost." She answered with just enough bluntness to let him know she wasn't teasing. "Who else?"

Foster gave her his full attention. "Lenny or Nemo?"

"Neither. Another spirit who is trying to help us find Dolly."

Foster shook his head. "I honestly don't know whether to believe you or not."

"I'm used to that, trust me."

"So did this other ghost find Dolly?"

"Yes and she's alive, but the spirit isn't sure exactly where she is. Spirits don't see things and places like we do, Detective, but I'm pretty sure Dolly is being kept in a mobile home somewhere in open desert or at least someplace sparsely populated."

"That could be anywhere in Nevada. We have both trailers and desert in large supply around here."

"I'm afraid that's all she was able to tell me, except that a person by the name of Laura Crawford is also there. She's another fortune-teller on Fremont Street. Quinn can fill you in more about that."

Emma started past Foster to move down the hall toward the living room, but he stopped her. He indicated an empty spot on the wall in the midst of the other framed photos. "Do you know what went here?"

"Yes, that's where the photo with Jimmy Hoffa was hung before I removed it."

"And do you know who this is?" He pointed to a photo of Dolly, not in costume, standing with a man. The man had his arm around Dolly, holding her close, and both were smiling.

Emma studied the photo, then answered, "Yes. I believe that's Lenny Speidel."

"Lenny Speidel." Foster repeated, studying the photo. "Lenny the Lightbulb. My son's playmate." He shot Emma a wry smile.

"And here is another of him." Emma pointed to another picture with just Lenny as the subject.

Foster turned to her. He was a bit taller than Emma but their faces were close. He was in her personal space, but she didn't feel threatened. "You really did meet this Speidel guy, or rather his ghost, last night?"

"Yes," was all Emma said, not moving back. She looked into his eyes and felt something, a thought or maybe a premonition, slim and delicate like a cobweb, pass over her brain. "He's more to you than just an interesting piece of history, isn't he?"

For a brief moment, Foster's eyes darted away from Emma's, then they returned. "My grandfather grew up here. I was always fascinated by the stories he and his brother would tell us about the heyday of Las Vegas when the Mob ran things and famous movie stars came here to play."

"Famous people still come here to play," Emma noted. "Even royalty."

Foster scoffed. "Today we get spoiled rich kids, druggies, and gangsters disguised as musicians. Trailer trash in designer duds and fast cars with too much money." He touched the photo of Lenny as if memorizing it through his fingertips. "When an opportunity came up to join the LVPD, I jumped at it and moved my family here." He paused, then turned to her. "Tell me, Emma, are my wife and son in any danger?"

"Who would they be in danger from?"

The detective shrugged. "This ghost. Other ghosts. I don't want them visiting Nicholas and frightening him, seeing as you claim he can see them. Suzanne is already upset by Dolly's disappearance. Knowing about these ghosts would only disturb her more."

Emma gave the question serious consideration, calling on her intuition for advice. "My gut tells me no, Detective. Lenny displays real affection for Nicholas and doesn't appear to be a frightening or vindictive spirit. And we're all upset by Dolly's disappearance."

After giving her words quick thought, Foster said, "Just to be safe, I'll send Suzanne and Nicholas to her parents for a visit." He gave Emma a crooked grin. "I'm still not sure I believe you, Emma Whitecastle, but I don't take chances with my family."

CHAPTER EIGHTEEN

Returning from his hallway discussion with Emma, Foster announced, "We seem to have a lead on Ms. Meskiel."

Everyone turned to look at him with surprise, even Milo. He knew Granny had found out something, but he was startled that Emma had disclosed it to the detective.

"We have a source." Foster told everyone. He paused to look at Emma a second. "We have a source that believes she is in a mobile home in the desert."

"A source?" questioned Garby. "Did someone call you, John?"

"No," Foster answered his partner. "Emma here has received information from . . . well, in her own way . . . and I feel it's worth checking out."

Garby looked at Foster and shook his head. "You're really going to listen to that mumbo jumbo?"

"For now, yes. We don't have anything else

to go on at the moment."

"Well, while you were in the back ghost hunting, I got a call on the old lady's car." Garby shot a look at Milo, who was staring at him with indignation. "I mean Ms. Meskiel's car. It was found abandoned off of Red Rock Canyon Road. They're combing the area now for any signs of the woman."

"Oh boy," exclaimed Granny, who was hovering by Milo. "I wonder if it's like on TV. I'd love to meet that hunk Stokes."

Milo, usually patient with Granny, rolled his tired eyes at her comment. Detective Garby, misreading the gesture, told him, "I'm sorry, Mr. Ravenscroft. I meant no disrespect."

Rather than clarify his gesture, Milo just nodded at the cop. Granny, however, did catch Milo's intent and took off to reconnect with Dolly.

For nearly an hour and a half, Emma and Quinn filled the detectives in on what information Granny had provided and on Quinn's visit to Laura Crawford's wagon, as well as every detail Milo and Emma could remember of the conversations with the ghosts of Nemo and Lenny. They each went over their stories, answering question after question posed by Foster and the still skeptical Garby.

"I think we have enough now," announced Foster. "Mr. Ravenscroft provided us with a few recent photos of his mother. We'll have these circulated, as well as look into mobile homes in remote places."

"Which will be like locating a needle in a haystack out here," commented Garby, not looking too thrilled by the prospect.

Tracy still didn't look happy. "Are you looking for Dolly as a missing or abducted person, or as a suspect in Nemo's death?"

"Ms. Meskiel," answered Garby, "is still a person of interest in Mr. Moorehouse's demise."

"But we'll also be taking into account everything you folks told us today," added Foster, "about her possible abduction and whereabouts."

"True," said Garby with some reluctance. "Considering where her car was found, there is no way an elderly woman could have left it there and walked somewhere on her own. She either had a ride back from the location or someone took the car and left it there."

"In other words," said Quinn, piecing together the detective's meaning, "she either had help in the crime you allege she might have committed or was abducted as we think."

Garby sucked his front teeth as he glared at Quinn, then made his way to the front door without another word. The uniform cops had left long before. Just before he followed the surly Garby out the door, John Foster told them, "You folks sit tight. I know that's difficult at a time like this, but if anything comes up, we'll be in touch. If you hear from Ms. Meskiel, please give me a call." He produced a couple of business cards and stepped toward Emma and Quinn. "I've already left my number with Mr. Ravenscroft, but I'd like you two to have it, too."

After taking the card, Emma dug into her purse to produce her own. On the back she wrote her personal cell number. "And here's mine. I'm staying at the Venetian and will be there until this is over. Quinn is at Treasure Island if you need to reach him."

Quinn stepped forward and handed the detective his card. "If you can't reach Emma, please call me. Considering the threats made, ghosts or not, I'll be sticking around to watch her back."

"I thought they'd never leave," groused Tracy after the police had finally left.

They were all huddled around Dolly's

kitchen table. Tracy and Emma had pulled together a quick lunch from stuff they found in the fridge and pantry, primarily sandwiches of various cold cuts and cheeses, along with some crackers and raw vegetables.

"They did take forever," Emma said as she made herself a peanut butter and jelly sandwich.

"A couple of hours," noted Quinn, pouring glasses of iced tea.

"Oh, look," said Tracy, pulling a plastic container out of the fridge. "Hummus. This will go great with those crackers and veggies."

Settled around the table, they went over the information shared with the police and made plans of their own while they ate.

Tracy laughed, remembering what Foster had said. "He told us all to sit tight. Obviously, he doesn't know us very well, especially you, Emma."

"Yeah, I think Foster eventually took a shine to you," Quinn added. "Did you two bond in the hallway?"

"Sort of." She looked around the room. "Milo, are there any spirits around that you can feel?"

"No, not at the moment," Milo answered. "Why? Do you feel one?"

"No, I just want to be careful about what I say and when, considering the particular spirits hanging about. You see, I think there's something funny about John Foster. Something he revealed to me in the hallway."

"His pecker?" asked Tracy, laughing.

"Maybe he knows where Hoffa's buried," suggested Quinn.

"Nothing like that," answered Emma, laughing. It felt good to laugh in the middle of all the worry, and even Milo joined in on the joke.

"That he really believes in ghosts?" asked Milo, adding his own suggestion.

Emma shook her head and took a drink of her iced tea before speaking. "John Foster went right to the photo of Lenny Speidel. He asked me who it was, but I think he already knew. He told me his grandfather grew up here and told lots of stories about Las Vegas."

"That's probably where he got his interest in that time period," said Quinn right before taking a bite of his sandwich. "Didn't Garby say it's a hobby of Foster's?"

"Yes," admitted Emma, "but I think it's more than that. I kept getting a vibe that he has a personal interest here. Something he's not disclosing."

The table went silent, going from jovial to hushed as if the volume had been turned off with the flick of a switch.

"You know," said Milo, being the first to find his voice. "I thought he looked kind of funny when we first mentioned Lenny's name. It was kind of surprise mixed with excitement."

Emma recounted her private conversation with Foster.

"Maybe he's related to Lenny," suggested Tracy.

"What's more," Emma added, "I think Lenny was Dolly's boyfriend. He's in several of the photos hanging on the hallway wall, and they're not photos with Dolly in costume. And the poses seem too intimate for just being friends."

"Are you sure?" Milo asked.

Emma went to the hallway and retrieved the photo of Dolly and Lenny together. She showed it to Milo. "This is the man whose spirit came to me last night. This is Leonard Speidel aka Lenny the Lightbulb. Do you remember him at all from your childhood?"

Milo studied the photo closely. "Sorry, but I don't."

"Let me see that," said Tracy, holding out her hand. Emma passed her the framed photo. Tracy studied it. "Dolly was quite beautiful, wasn't she?"

"Yes, and full of piss and vinegar," said Milo. "I knew that even as a kid."

Tracy turned the photo over and started removing the back of the frame. "Sometimes people date the back of the photos."

"Good thinking, darling," said Milo.

When Tracy took the back off, there was a piece of paper folded in the back of the frame, holding the photo tight against the glass. She put that aside and looked at the back of the photo. "Bingo!" she said, pleased with herself. "There's a date scribbled here of April 1962."

"I would have been not quite two at the time," noted Milo, "so no wonder I don't remember him."

Emma raised an index finger as a thought crossed her mind. "Do you remember when that Lucky Buck Casino robbery was?"

"Didn't the information we found say the early 1960s?" asked Milo.

"Yes, but when in the sixties?" Emma went to her bag and pulled out her iPad. Quickly she researched the bank robbery. "This information on Nemo just says early sixties." There weren't many sites mentioning the robbery, but Emma checked them all. "Oh my God," she said as she read the information on another site. "This site says it was May of 1962."

"Right after this photo was taken," noted Quinn.

"Yes. And I'll bet Lenny was killed shortly after that. It's no wonder you don't remember him, Milo. He was killed when you were just a toddler."

"Get ready for another shocker," said Tracy. In her hand she was holding the paper that had been folded and stuck behind the photo. Without another word she held it out to Milo, who took it from her and quickly scanned it.

"This can't be right," he said, his words coming slow and stunned. He read it over several times. "I've seen my birth certificate. I even have the original. Dolly gave it to me years ago."

"What is it, Milo?" asked Emma. When he didn't respond, she reached over and took the paper from him and read it for herself. It was a birth certificate. Without a word, she handed it off to Quinn, who also read it.

"Are you sure you have the original?" Tracy asked Milo.

"Yes, it looks just like this one," he answered, staring down at the table in shock. "Exactly like this one — date of birth, date of issuance, official seal. Everything except for the name of the father. When I needed to get a passport, I wrote to the State of Nevada for a certified copy and that one also had no father listed."

Quinn looked again at the document in his hand and read, "Name of father, Leonard Joseph Speidel."

Tracy reached over and took one of Milo's hands. "We need to find Dolly for a lot of reasons."

Emma shook her head at the latest development. "Didn't you ever ask about the man in the photos or about your father?"

"Sure," Milo answered, "especially when I was young. Dolly just said my father was out of the picture permanently. And wouldn't discuss it further." He huffed out a sad chuckle. "Of course, in this case my father was right in the picture."

He took the photograph and looked at it again. "Dolly said this guy was one of her friends who left the area a long time ago. I had no reason not to believe her. When Dolly refused to talk about my father, I assumed he was someone who'd passed through Vegas. Maybe a married man she'd had a fling with, or something like that. Turns out my father was a criminal and a thief." He sighed deeply. "Maybe I'd been better off not knowing."

"Boo!" came from the light fixture above the counter. Milo and Emma jumped in their seats, causing Tracy and Quinn to be startled by their reaction.

"Darn it, Granny," Emma scolded in the direction of the light fixture, "that was uncalled for."

Granny materialized next to the table. "I should have known you folks would be sitting around jibber jabbering while I was doing all the work."

"We're not jibber jabbering, Granny," Emma told the ghost. "The police left just a few minutes ago."

Granny took in the somber mood blanketing the table. "What's going on? You all look like someone shot your dog."

In response, Milo pushed the photo of Lenny over toward Granny. She looked at it. "Emma, didn't you say this is Lenny? At least I thought you and that detective were talking about that earlier, right before I left."

"Yes, it's Lenny Speidel," Emma confirmed. "It also seems to be Milo's father."

Granny studied the photo closely, then looked up at Milo. "Hard to tell if there's any resemblance from this old photo."

"Tracy found a birth certificate hidden behind the photo," Emma explained. "It says Lenny is Milo's father of record, even though the birth certificate Milo has doesn't list a father."

"And you had no idea, Milo?" Granny asked.

"None, Granny, but when I find Dolly, you can be sure I'll be asking a lot of questions." He took a deep breath. "Providing we get her back safe and sound."

"How is Dolly doing?" asked Emma. All faces turned to where Emma's eyes were focused and waited.

"When I left her, she was watching soaps on TV. She seems okay, just very nervous."

Emma relayed the information to Quinn and Tracy before asking, "Have you figured out any more about where she's being kept?"

"Not really," answered Granny, still looking at the photo of Dolly and Lenny.

"The police said they were going to look into all rural areas with a lot of mobile homes," Milo told the ghost. "And they're going to look into the disappearance of Laura Crawford."

"That's one of the reasons why I popped in," Granny told them. "I think they're using Laura to communicate with that scoundrel Nemo."

"Are you sure?" asked Emma while Milo

translated for the others.

"I was hanging around Dolly and floating through the house, trying to figure out its location, when I heard Nemo's voice."

"Did Nemo know you were there?" Milo grew alarmed.

"I don't think so." Granny started moving around the kitchen. "I tried to stay away and just listen. He was trying to communicate with the men holding Dolly through Laura. It wasn't going well. So far I've only seen two men. Both are kind of on the young side and neither seem too bright." Granny looked a bit puzzled.

Milo looked at Quinn. "Didn't you say Laura left her wagon in the company of two men?"

Quinn nodded. "Yes, one young and one older. Of course, the woman who told me that could have been wrong." He turned to the space where he believed Granny was located. "Granny, can you describe the men with Dolly and Laura?"

Granny gave it more thought, screwing up her face in concentration. "One is a bit pudgy and kind of sloppy. The other one is slim and better groomed, but not by much." Emma conveyed Granny's description to Quinn and Tracy.

"The heavy one fits one of the descriptions the woman gave me," Quinn noted. "Granny, did you see an older man with these guys? Maybe someone in his late forties or early fifties and better dressed?"

"Granny is shaking her head," Milo reported.

"What is it, Granny?" asked Emma, noting Granny's confusion.

The ghost shrugged. "If I didn't know better, I'd think the bigger guy is the same guy who stood behind you in line at Laura's. You remember, you asked him to hold your place while you went to get something to drink."

Emma nodded. "When Quinn first described him to me, I thought the same thing."

"Are you talking about the guy reading the comic book?" asked Quinn.

"Yes," Emma told him. "Granny recognized him, too. He's one of the men holding Dolly and Laura."

"And," continued Granny, "there's something mighty familiar about the other guy, too, but I can't put my finger on it."

Emma went on alert. "So you think you've seen him before?"

"I'm not sure. I keep trying to place him, but can't. Give me time; I'm sure it will come to me."

Milo turned to Emma. "Didn't you say Laura wasn't aware of her gift to communicate?"

"It sure looked that way to me," Emma said. "She didn't seem at all aware that Lenny had spoken through her."

"Could she have been faking?" asked Quinn.

"Maybe," admitted Emma. "But if she was, she was very good at it. Scary good."

"I don't think she was faking," commented Granny. "From what I saw today, she does have the gift of being a medium, but isn't fully aware of it or how to control it."

In a low voice, Milo conveyed Granny's words to Tracy and Quinn as she spoke.

"It seemed," Granny continued, "that it was hit and miss between her and Nemo, like a bad electrical connection. Sometimes she was able to talk to his goons; other times she just stared into space while Nemo jumped up and down yelling at her."

"Was Laura hearing everything Nemo was saying to her?" asked Emma. "Or was that also spotty?"

"I think she heard him just fine," said Granny after giving it some thought. "But I'm not sure she knew where it was coming from or what she was supposed to do. Most of the time she sort of cowered in a half-frightened, half-trancelike state. Every now and then she'd say something to the two men that Nemo would tell her, but it was sort of jumbled."

"That poor girl," said Tracy after getting the scoop.

Granny screwed up her face in thought. "And there's something else. Something that might be important." When Emma and Milo turned their attention to her, she continued, "I think Laura knew I was there, or at least another spirit besides Nemo."

"But I thought you stayed out of the way," Milo said.

"I did and I'm sure Nemo didn't see me. But every now and then, especially when Laura was in a sort of trance, she'd lift her head and her eyes would scan the place. It was weird. She wouldn't turn her head, just her eyes, and her chin would come up like she was trying to smell something in the air. It reminded me of when Archie sniffs something on the wind. You know how he lifts his head but doesn't move."

"Yes," said Emma, "I know that look."

"Well, that's how Laura looked sometimes. Like she was trying to hone in on some sort of scent she was getting."

"Laura did know you were with me in the

wagon," Emma noted. "Did the men notice anything? Or did Nemo?"

"Not that I could see. They seemed really focused on getting her to be the go-between. They probably just thought it was her weird way of doing her thing."

Emma got up and started clearing the table, more to have something to do while she gave the situation consideration. "The police said they were going to look into locating the mobile home and will check out Laura Crawford to see if she's really missing. Of course, all of us know she is."

"So what are we going to do about it?" asked Granny, her hands on her narrow hips. "Sit around and drink tea like a bunch of old farts?"

As soon as Milo translated the words, Quinn nearly shot the iced tea in his mouth across the table. "Good God," he said, wiping the front of his shirt and his chin with a napkin, "that ghost has an attitude."

"You don't know the half of it," said Emma. "But Granny is right. We need to get out there and find Dolly and Laura."

CHAPTER NINETEEN

"You know," Quinn said, "the police are right. Looking for that mobile home will be like looking for a needle in a haystack. From Granny's description, it could be in a very small town or settlement. There are lots of those throughout the Southwest, mostly inhabited by people who want to be left alone."

Emma knew it was going to be a big task. "I keep hoping Granny will notice something that will give us a clue. I know she's trying very hard. I told her to snoop around for any mail and see if she could read an address."

"Granny can read?"

"Yes, but not very well. She had limited schooling as a girl. Then there's the whole ghost distortion thing. Often even words on paper won't make sense to a ghost, even if they are well educated." Emma smiled. "Granny actually practices her reading with my mother."

Quinn glanced over at Emma. They were in her SUV and he was driving. Emma wanted to be free to concentrate in case any ghosts popped up. "You're kidding?"

"Not at all. Sometimes when my mother is reading the paper or a magazine, Granny will ask to read along with her and help her sound out words. My mother can't see Granny, but she hears her plain as day."

"Granny's pretty amazing."

"That she is," Emma agreed. "According to Milo, it's very unusual for a ghost to integrate itself into a family's day-to-day life the way Granny does. He thinks that's why she's not as confused as most spirits who interact with the living. Still, she has her limitations. It's hard to imagine my life without her anymore. Even my father said that recently. He can't see or hear her, but he knows when she's around. Sometimes he'll carry on a conversation with her through my mother." Emma laughed. "My poor mother had to be the go between when Granny was first learning about football, which she loves dearly."

The GPS in the vehicle alerted them that their destination was just ahead on the right. Before leaving Dolly's, they had decided on a plan of action. Granny would stick with

Dolly and try to find more clues to her location. Emma and Quinn would check out the rest home where Nemo was living and anything else they could find to help them piece together the players.

Milo and Tracy would stay close to Dolly's house and research and contact other local mediums who might have been contacted by Nemo or his people to see if they could identify who was actually in charge of this scheme. The two young men watching Dolly and Laura were obviously not the brains of the outfit. Emma's money was on the well-dressed man who had showed up at Laura's wagon. Tracy was also going to do more research about the Lucky Buck Casino robbery and Nelson Morehouse. Milo decided to go through his mother's things looking for something that might connect her to Nemo.

"I'm very puzzled by Nemo's appearance here at Dolly's," Milo had said shortly before they each went off to their assignments.

"Why, darling?" Tracy had asked. "He knew Dolly."

"Yes, but generally ghosts cannot connect randomly to places they've never been or people they're never met or had close contact with," Milo explained. "But Nemo

222

showed up here like he owned the place."

"Milo's right," confirmed Emma. "If Lenny hadn't connected with me here when I arrived, he could not have found me at Laura's or my hotel. Lenny told me that Nemo had been in contact with Dolly over the years, but didn't say if he'd been to this house specifically."

Milo looked puzzled. "We know Nemo knew Dolly, but she wasn't here at the time he popped in. He must have been here before, to the house, when he was alive."

"How long has your mother lived here?" asked Quinn.

Milo did some math in his head. "I bought this place for her when I had my first big bestseller. That had to be about eight or nine years ago. No." He paused. "It was actually just over ten years ago. They had just built this complex. She'd been living in a small apartment near downtown for a number of years and I felt the area was getting unsafe."

"Depending on his health," said Emma, "Nemo might not have been incapacitated for the past ten years. He might have visited here during that time."

"As much as I hate to intrude on her privacy, I think I need to have a look through my mother's things. Who knows?

Maybe I'll find another birth certificate." Milo shook his head in frustration. "Maybe this one will say I'm Nemo's son."

When they pulled into the parking lot of the Desert Sun Nursing Home, Quinn asked Emma, "So do you have a plan, or are you hoping they will simply spill their guts to you about a possible murder victim?"

"Not sure yet," Emma told him.

After the police left, she'd written up her own notes using her iPad, jotting down key information that came out during the police questioning, before she forgot it. She consulted those notes before getting out of the SUV.

"I think I'll start by asking for Frankie Varga."

"That was Nemo's nurse, wasn't it?"

"Yes," she answered, "or caretaker. Either way, he might have been the last person to see Dolly. It might be best to focus on Dolly's disappearance rather than Nemo's death."

"Lead the way," Quinn told her.

The front door of Desert Sun opened onto a very large area with a couple of sofas and chairs. A few patients were in the lobby, some in wheelchairs, some using canes to shuffle around. Through a wide door just off the lobby, Emma spied a large room with tables and more chairs and sofas. Babble from a daytime talk show drifted into the lobby from the room, and Emma caught the voice of her ex-husband. She wrinkled her nose in distaste.

In spite of the facility being clean and cheerfully decorated, the smell of slow-moving time hung over it like a waiting shroud. It was a very nice and upscale place as rest homes went, but in the end it was still a place where people came to wait out the end of their lives. Its occupants were people who were no longer able to care for themselves, or who had no one able to care for them at home, whether due to the extent of their illnesses or by default. Several of the patients in the lobby eyed them with interest. She and Quinn were new faces — two bright sparks to their otherwise dull day. Emma smiled at them and approached the large semicircular reception desk.

A thick brown woman with short salt-and-pepper hair manned the reception desk. She was dressed in maroon scrubs that were a little snug across her ample chest. Glasses perched precariously on the end of her nose as she paged through a magazine. Her name tag read *Gloria*.

"All visitors must sign in." Without looking up, Gloria tapped a clipboard resting on the counter.

"We're not here to see a patient," Emma told her. "We'd like to see Frankie Varga."

Gloria looked up, giving Emma her full attention. "Frankie isn't working today. Can someone else help you?"

"Is there someone here now who was on duty last night?" From the corner of her eye, Emma saw Quinn go over to one of the old men in a wheelchair who'd been watching them.

"Is there a problem?" asked Gloria.

"We're looking for a woman who was here visiting someone last night." From her bag, Emma produced a photo of Dolly. It was a recent photo similar to one of the ones Milo gave the police.

Gloria pushed her glasses farther up her nose and looked the photo over. "Isn't that the woman the police are looking for?"

"Yes, I'm a friend of her son's and we're double-checking every place she might have gone yesterday."

"They told us about it when we started the day shift this morning." Her eyes went from the photo to Emma's face and clouded with caution. "She was here visiting old man Morehouse, wasn't she?"

"Yes, she was," Emma answered, wondering how much the facility had disclosed to their staff. Had they mentioned they thought Nemo had been murdered, or that Dolly was a suspect? "Have you ever seen her before? Maybe visiting him another time?"

Gloria studied the photo again. "Can't say I have."

When Gloria made no move to ask someone else or to offer any further assistance, Emma asked, "Is there someone here now who was on duty last night? Maybe they remember seeing her."

"No one here now would have been here last night."

"I understand Mr. Morehouse passed away last night?" Emma hadn't wanted to bring up Nemo, but she needed to find a way to scale Gloria's formidable wall.

"Yes, he did."

Emma waited for more explanation, but got none. "I know he was very old and sick."

"Yes, he was. Like most of the guests here."

"Did he have many visitors?" Emma asked, not giving up. "Family members maybe or other friends like Dolly? Maybe one of them can help us find her."

"You really should talk to the police about this, Ms. . . . I didn't catch your name."

"Emma. Emma Whitecastle." Emma said

her name quickly, hoping it wouldn't be linked to the man's voice coming from the TV in the other room. "Like I said, I'm a friend of Ms. Meskiel's son and I'm helping search for her. Any help would be very, very appreciated."

"Well, Emma, you really should speak with our director. His name is Gene Garby. We were told any questions should be directed to him or to the police. He's not here right now, but will be back this afternoon." Gloria reached over and plucked a business card from a card holder on the desk. "Here's his card. But call and make an appointment first. He's in charge of a couple of facilities so he's very busy."

"Thank you," Emma told her, taking the card and looking at it. "Is Mr. Garby any relation to Detective Howard Garby? He's with the Las Vegas Police Department."

Gloria shrugged. "Don't know. But I do know that Mr. Garby is a local. He grew up in Boulder City." Gloria gave Emma a meaningful look from over the upper rim of her glasses, which had slipped down her nose again. "And I do hope you find that woman."

Emma wasn't sure if the look said, *Find her safe and sound,* or *Find her because she's a killer.* Either way, Emma was sure

Gloria knew more, much more, than she was letting on.

Emma pulled out one of her own business cards and jotted her cell number on the back. She placed it on the counter and pushed it toward Gloria. "If anything turns up, please give me a call."

Gloria started to pick it up. "I'll pass this along to Mr. Garby."

Emma gave Gloria her own significant look. "No, that's for *you.*"

Gloria picked up the card and read both the front and the back. She jerked her head in the direction of the other room. "You related to that buffoon on the TV?"

"Not anymore."

Emma's comment caused a sly smile to cross Gloria's face. She tucked the card into her pocket and went back to her magazine without another word.

Quinn was now chatting up an old woman sitting on one of the sofas by the front door. Emma went over to them. In front of the woman was a walker with yellow tennis balls on the back two legs. Dressed in a floral dress with her white hair impeccably done, the frail woman looked like a colorful and delicate hummingbird taking a break from a feeder. Quinn was all charm as he asked her questions and all ears as he listened.

"This is my friend Emma," Quinn told her in a break in the conversation. "Emma, this is my new friend Claudine Houser."

Claudine smiled at Emma, showing a very nice set of false teeth behind her pale pink lipstick. "Why, you're pretty as a picture."

Usually Emma took compliments about her looks in stride, but the genuine and old-fashioned comment from Claudine made Emma blush like a schoolgirl.

"Thank you, Claudine," Emma responded. "You're looking lovely yourself. Are you waiting for someone?"

"My son," she answered with a big smile. "Today's my ninety-third birthday. He's going to pick me up and take me to dinner."

"Why, happy birthday!" remarked Quinn. "But isn't it a little early for dinner?"

"Not when you're my age. Nor his. Edward is seventy himself. Wouldn't be surprised if one day soon he and I are sitting here side by side. If he ever got ill, that hussy wife of his would slap him in here without a second thought." Claudine closed one eye and gave them both a knowing nod. "She's his fourth, you know. And a lot younger. After his money, if you ask me. Frankly, my favorite was number two. Her name was Susan. They divorced after seven years because he couldn't keep it in his pants."

Emma raised a questioning brow in Quinn's direction. He winked at her in response.

"Claudine," Quinn said, guiding the woman back to their previous conversation. "Tell Emma what you told me about Nemo."

Emma sat in a chair next to Claudine and encouraged the woman with a warm smile.

Claudine leaned toward Emma and whispered, "Good riddance to bad rubbish is what I say. I remember Nemo when he was all high and mighty and running around with those mobsters back in the day. Quite the big shot. Thought he was still a big shot when he came here."

"Did you actually know Nemo back in the sixties or just through the news?" As Emma asked the question, a hazy apparition started to appear off to the side of Claudine.

Emma turned her head and saw a few more spirits materializing. They were hovering near various patients. She hadn't noticed them when she came in. It must have taken time for the ghosts to feel comfortable enough to show themselves to her. One old man, nearly as bent as the cane he was using, shuffled along mumbling. Next to him floated the spirit of an elderly woman. The woman looked at Emma and gave her a friendly wave.

"That's Edgar," Claudine told Emma, indicating the man with the cane. "Pay him no mind, he thinks he's talking to his dead wife. Poor thing."

Emma glanced over at Quinn, who was watching her with raised brows. Having no doubt he was asking about the presence of ghosts, Emma gave him a nod confirming his suspicions.

The spirit coming into focus near them was that of an older man, but not as old as Claudine. He didn't say anything, but hovered a hazy hand above Claudine's shoulder.

"You don't believe in ghosts?" Quinn asked Claudine.

She pursed her lips before answering. "Time was I would have given you a sound no to that question, but lately I've been feeling like my late husband, Bert, is close by." She chuckled. It sounded like the squeak of a baby mouse. "Maybe that's because I'm getting closer to the grave myself." She looked over at Edgar, still chatting away to his unseen wife. "I know thinking he's talking to Helen brings Edgar a lot of comfort. I almost envy him." The ghost by Claudine tried to squeeze her shoulder but she couldn't feel it and the ghost's hand slipped through her.

"I'm sure Bert is very close by," Emma said to Claudine. Claudine smiled at her and so did the ghost.

"Getting back to Nemo Morehouse," said Quinn. "Did you actually know him years ago?"

"Why yes, I did," answered Claudine. "Both Bert and I worked for the Lucky Buck, and Nemo was in there all the time. The Lucky Buck was a hotel and casino, but nothing grand like you see nowadays. It's gone now. It's been gone for many years."

Quinn and Emma exchanged looks. Emma turned to Burt's ghost and questioned him with her eyes.

The ghost confirmed the information with a nod of his head.

Quinn scooted a bit closer to Claudine. "I'd read somewhere that Nemo had something to do with a robbery at the Lucky Buck."

"He sure did," Claudine said, "although no one could pin it on him. Everyone thinks it was that other man, the one who disappeared. But sure as I'm sitting here, Nemo was behind it. For a short time they even suspected my Bert since he worked in accounting, but he was cleared."

"Do you remember who that other man was?" asked Emma.

"Speidel," answered the ghost of Bert Houser. "His name was Lenny Speidel."

Claudine, unable to hear the ghost, knit her brows as she gave thought to the question. "Oh dear, my memory isn't as good as it used to be."

Emma glanced up at the ghost then said to Claudine, "Was it maybe Lenny or Leonard Speidel?"

Claudine brightened and pointed a gnarled finger at Emma. "Yes. Yes. I think that was it. Speidel, like the watch company. He used to come into the casino with Nemo all the time, then after the robbery we never saw him again. Everyone was sure he disappeared with the money." She looked around, then leaned forward, indicating for Quinn and Emma to come closer. "I've always thought Nemo was behind it, though, and killed Lenny so he could have all the money."

Emma took out the photo of Dolly and held it out to Claudine. "Have you ever seen this woman?"

She peered at it, then brought it up closer to her face. Over her shoulder, Bert looked at the photo. "No. I don't think so," Claudine answered. "Why?"

"She was here last night visiting Nemo shortly before he died."

Claudine shook her head. "I don't remember her, but I wasn't feeling that well last night. I went to bed right after supper so I'd have enough energy for today."

"Did Nemo have a lot of visitors?" asked Emma.

After careful thought, Claudine answered, "No. I don't recall him having any."

The ghost of Bert Houser came close to Emma. "That woman was here last night. I saw her."

Emma cast her eyes quickly up at Bert.

Quinn watched her. "Any luck with Frankie Varga?"

She shook her head and gave him her attention. "No. He's not in today."

"Humpf," snorted Claudine. "With any luck, Frankie won't be back now that his pet is gone."

Emma looked at the old woman with interest. "You don't like Frankie?"

"Not one bit. And not many others here do either, including the staff. The only resident he cared about or did anything for was Nemo Morehouse. He waited on him hand and foot like he was royalty."

"Do you know why?" asked Quinn.

"Not for sure, but it was rumored that he was being paid under the table to give Nemo special attention. He shirked a lot of his other duties, leaving them for the other aides and the nurses."

Quinn looked puzzled. "Did anyone complain?"

"I've heard there were complaints and I complained about him myself. What he did do for the rest of us was sloppy and careless. But nothing was ever done about it."

Emma glanced over at Gloria. She was watching them from behind her magazine.

"Claudine," Emma asked, "how do you like Gloria over there at the reception desk?"

Claudine's lined face lit up. "Gloria is so nice and very professional. She's been here a long time. But she's not the receptionist. That's Maria, who is probably on break right now." Again she indicated for Emma and Quinn to come closer. "There was a rumor a few months ago that Gloria almost lost her job when she complained about Frankie."

Quinn was about to ask something else when an older man came through the front door. Claudine started to rise. "There's my Edward now." Quinn gently helped her to her feet.

Bert Houser floated over to his son, a smile stretched across his ghostly face at the sight of him. Side by side, Emma could see the strong resemblance.

"Are you ready to go, Mom?" Edward asked.

"Yes, of course I'm ready. These nice people were keeping me company while I waited."

Emma and Quinn made their way out the front door along with Edward and Claudine. Edward's car was parked in front. While Edward helped his mother into the front seat, Bert sidled up to Emma.

"We need to talk," the ghost said to her.

CHAPTER TWENTY

"I knew it!" Quinn exclaimed as soon as they were back in Emma's SUV. "I knew there was a ghost there while we were with Claudine."

"Quinn," Emma said to him as she buckled up her seat belt. "Meet Bert Houser, Claudine's dead husband. He's in the backseat right now."

Quinn glanced in the rearview mirror but saw nothing. He was getting used to addressing empty space. "You're the guy who worked at the Lucky Buck, right?"

"Yes, I am," the ghost answered. He turned to Emma. "Can he hear me?"

"No, and he can't see you either, but we manage."

Emma tapped Quinn on the arm. "Drive somewhere, Quinn, before we start talking to him. I don't want to raise any suspicion by sitting in this parking lot."

While Quinn maneuvered the vehicle out

of the parking lot of Desert Sun and down the street, Emma studied Bert Houser. "Your son is the spitting image of you."

"He's a regular chip off the old block." The ghost grinned. "Takes real good care of his mother, too."

"So you knew Nemo and Lenny?" Emma asked.

"Sure did. I worked behind the scenes at the Lucky Buck. Claudine tended bar. After work, I'd sit at the bar and unwind a bit before going home. With her odd hours, that was the best time for us to catch up. That's where I got to know Nemo and Lenny."

She relayed the conversation to Quinn.

"This is going to be awkward and time-consuming in the car," noted Quinn. He made a right-hand turn onto a busy street. "Why don't you question him and catch me up later? I'll throw out questions as they come to mind."

"Sounds good," Emma agreed. She turned back to Bert. "Do you believe they robbed the casino?"

"I don't believe it, I know it. They approached me to help them."

"And did you?"

Bert looked away. "Yes, I did." He turned back. "You have to understand, they were very persuasive, and I don't mean just with money."

"They threatened you?"

"They threatened my family. If I didn't cooperative, Claudine and Eddie would have paid the price. I didn't have to do much, just make it easy for them to slip into the back office early Sunday morning when we were counting up our biggest take of the week. Hell, of the year." Bert paused and turned to watch the scenery slide by out the window. "It was a big holiday weekend. There were several conventions in town. And there was a glitch in making our deposit the night before, so our safe had a lot more money than usual."

"The glitch," Emma asked, "was that also arranged?"

"Yes. Between the two weekend nights and the extra action, they took just over a million dollars."

"Lenny and Nemo did?"

"Nemo was behind it but he'd never get his hands dirty. Lenny and a couple other goons came into the back room where we were counting the money from Saturday's haul and robbed us at gunpoint, taking that money and the money already in the safe from the day before."

"Claudine said you were a suspect."

Bert nodded. "Yes, all of us who worked

in accounting were, but to steer the attention from me, one of Nemo's guys plugged me during the heist."

"You were shot? Is that how you died?"

"No, he shot me in the leg. You see, Claudine and Eddie did end up paying for the robbery, but it was me who dished out the punishment. After what happened at the Lucky Buck, I felt so guilty I started drinking heavily. And I never stopped until I ran my car off the road one night and straight into a wall."

"Poor Claudine," Emma said with sadness.

"Claudine stood by me through everything," Bert told her. "She's the best, and in the end I gave her the worst of myself. I've never forgiven myself."

"And the money?"

Bert shrugged. "I never saw any of it. Not even the payment I was promised. Neither did Nemo. Lenny Speidel took off with it."

"Is it safe to assume from what I'm hearing," chimed in Quinn, "that Bert here had something to do with the casino robbery?"

"Yes, he did."

Quinn stopped the SUV for a red light. "This town was run by the Mob back then. Wasn't Nemo afraid of robbing them? Seems to me that's a death sentence. I'm surprised he lived so long."

"Your friend makes a very good point," Bert said to Emma. "The Lucky Buck was one of the few remaining independent casinos not in bed with organized crime. It was family owned and a stubborn holdout right until the end. By robbing it, Nemo was actually doing his well-connected friends a favor, and they could say with a straight face they had nothing to do with it."

"What happened to the casino?" Emma asked.

"In time it went under, helped along by the robbery and the competition from the bigger hotels and casinos, not to mention the continued pressure from the Mob. The Foster family sold it for next to nothing and left town. The new owners bulldozed it and put up something fancier. Shame, too, because it was one of the first real casinos in Las Vegas. It opened back when the Boulder Dam was being built and the workers from Boulder City needed someplace to blow off steam and spend their cash on payday."

Emma sat up straight in her seat as the name pricked her like a pin. "Foster?"

"Yes," answered Bert. "The Lucky Buck was started by Gerald Foster in the thirties, and his family owned and operated it until it closed in the mid- to late sixties. Both Claudine and I lost our jobs. She managed to get back on her feet. I never did."

Emma relayed the answer to his question to Quinn.

"Foster?" parroted Quinn. "As in Detective Foster?

"It's not an unusual name," Emma pointed out, "but who knows? He did say his family was originally from Las Vegas, and he does have a strong interest in the history of the place. And here's another surprise for you," she said to Quinn. "Garby is the last name of the rest home director. Does that ring a bell?"

Quinn glanced over at her, his tongue pushing though the right side of his cheek as he mulled over the implications. "So," he finally said, "we have one detective possibly related to the guy who runs the home where Nemo died, and the other detective possibly related to the folks who owned the casino Nemo robbed."

Emma turned back to Bert. "Do you know what happened to the Fosters? Did they stay in the area after they closed the casino?"

"No, they didn't," Bert answered. "I heard they moved back East somewhere, but I'm not sure where. Gerald died of a heart attack before the robbery. I think that's why Nemo thought it might be a good time to strike. At the time of the robbery the casino was run by his two sons, Edgar and Nicky, who weren't nearly as savvy as their father. Edgar had a family, Nicky didn't, but I think they all moved to the East together."

Emma had a long-shot question on the tip of her tongue. "Was Nicky's real name Nicholas?" As she asked the question, she saw Quinn glancing at her again.

"Yes, it was, but no one ever called him that." When Bert answered, Emma nodded to Quinn.

"This is interesting and all," Quinn said, "but how can we use it to find Dolly and get her back safe?"

"Bert," Emma said to the ghost. "You said you saw Dolly Meskiel at Desert Sun last night."

"That the woman in the picture you showed Claudine?"

"Yes. She went missing right after she visited Nemo, possibly about the time Nemo died. The police think she might have had something to do with his death."

"I don't know where the lady is," Bert answered, scratching his head with his right hand, "but I do know when she left Nemo, he was still alive. I was sitting in the lobby

244

with Claudine. She likes to sit on the sofa and watch everyone. And the lady you're asking about walked right by us and out the door."

"How did Nemo die? Did you see that?"

"I didn't see it happen, but I know it was after the lady left. Not long after, but after. Claudine decided to go to bed early. I accompanied her to her room. We passed Nemo's room just as he was being moved from his wheelchair into his bed. I know he was alive because he was talking to the people with him."

Emma noticed Bert starting to fade, so she quickened her questioning. "Who was with him?"

"That Frankie, the fellow no one likes, and Mr. Garby, the man who runs the home."

Emma immediately told Quinn, who shook his head in disbelief. "So who's lying — the rest home or the police?"

"Or both?" suggested Emma. She turned back to the ghost, who was barely more than a haze. "Before you go, Bert, one last question. By any chance did you see Nemo's spirit leave his body?"

"No, I didn't." And he was gone.

Emma immediately called Milo and Tracy, and brought them up-to-date.

"Unbelievable," said Milo. "We'd thought we struck out with the local mediums, but finally hit one that was contacted with an odd request that might be what we're looking for."

"Only one?" Emma was surprised. "Do you think the others told you the truth, or that Nemo's people didn't do much shopping around?"

Milo paused long enough to think about it. "Could be either. I'm ashamed to admit it, but I used my celebrity status to get them to talk to me at all."

"I made him!" Tracy said over the speaker feature.

"The one that had been contacted," Milo continued, "had actually been at my presentation yesterday. Tracy and I drove over there and met with her. Her name is Helena and I remembered her in the audience. She said a middle-aged man in a business suit visited her about two weeks ago asking questions about contacting the recently dead and communication between spirits, as well as between the dead and the living. He explained that he had two relatives who were dead that he felt had unresolved issues and he wanted them to iron them out so they could rest in peace."

"That could fit Lenny and Nemo," agreed

Emma with a short laugh.

"The man asked if she would be available to work for him full-time until the matter was resolved. She said he offered her a nice sum of cash for her time."

"That must have been tempting," Quinn commented. "But she didn't take the offer?"

"No," Milo said. "Helena kept sensing something off about him, an aura of danger and death surrounding him. She said he called himself Mr. Charles, but she also sensed he was lying about his name. She told me she kept getting an intertwined N and M whenever she looked at him, like a fancy brand. When she asked if those initials had any meaning, he ended the conversation and left."

"Could stand for Nemo Morehouse," suggested Emma. "Maybe she was picking up that the spirit he was asking about was Nemo."

"Anyway, that's all we uncovered, except that Tracy and I did ask Helena if she knew Lady Laura and my mother. She said she'd heard of Laura and had met my mother a couple of times."

"Did you tell her Dolly was missing?"

"Yes, and asked her to try and get a bead on where she might be. All she could tell us was that Dolly was alive but in grave danger."

"Interesting thing, though," Tracy added. "This Helena also said a spirit was watching over Dolly. The spirit of a woman in a long skirt."

Emma smiled as she thought of Granny keeping guard over Dolly. "I'd say this Helena is a real and accurate medium."

"Yes," agreed Milo. "She seems very talented and apologized that she couldn't help us more."

"I want to know more about that Gene Garby," said Tracy. "If he is related to Detective Garby, do you think he lied to him about how Nemo died or do you think the detectives knew all along that Dolly had nothing to do with it and were using that as leverage to get us to talk?"

"Good theory about the leverage," Quinn said. He pulled the SUV into the drive-thru line of a fast-food restaurant. "I'm dying for an iced coffee," he said to Emma. "Do you want anything?"

"That sounds great," she said, glancing across Quinn at the posted menu. "Make mine a medium without whipped cream."

"So what's next?" asked Milo. "Do we go to Detective Garby and cry foul?"

"And tell him what?" asked Quinn after

placing their coffee orders and pulling the vehicle forward in line. "That a ghost related to one of the residents told us that Nemo didn't die by Dolly's hand. Oh, and by the way, a possible relative of yours was present and are you in on this conspiracy?"

"It's a start," said Tracy. "And while we're at it, maybe we should be questioning John Foster, too. Like maybe talk to them separately."

"Not a bad idea," said Quinn. He pulled up to the take-out window, paid for their drinks, and took them from a teenage girl in a uniform. After handing them off to Emma, he pulled the SUV forward into traffic.

Emma unwrapped straws and placed them in the tall, cold drinks. "Claudine said Nemo never had visitors, so how could he communicate with anyone about grabbing and holding Dolly, unless it was set up totally by phone."

"I think," said Tracy, "that Nemo is after the money Lenny took in the casino robbery. Didn't you say it had never turned up?"

"Yes," answered Emma, handing Quinn his drink. "Even Bert said both Lenny and the money went missing, but it sounded like Bert didn't know Nemo killed Lenny."

"If it is the money Nemo's after," said Milo, his voice faltering with worry, "then we'll have to get Lenny to tell us where he hid it. We need to find it and trade it for my mother."

"Any sign of Lenny there at the house?" asked Quinn.

"Nothing," Milo told them. "But Nemo showed up."

"He did?" Emma had just taken a drink of her iced coffee and nearly choked.

"Yes, about an hour ago, but it was just for a minute," Milo reported. "He wanted to know if we were making any progress and said we were running out of time. He also asked where you were, Emma."

"Aww," said Quinn with a smirk. "He's got a crush on you."

"I'm just thankful," said Emma with relief, "that he didn't hone in on us at the rest home."

"Did Nemo give you any indication of a deadline?" asked Quinn.

"No," answered Milo. "He just said we were running out of time."

"Keep trying to locate Lenny, Milo," Emma encouraged. "Appeal to his affection for Dolly. Let him know you know you're his son and you need his help to find her." She paused. "How about Granny, any sign of her?"

"Nothing lately."

"Milo," Emma said into the phone, "let's you and I concentrate on trying to contact both Granny and Lenny. I want to see how Granny's doing with things. I know she'll check in if she finds something, but I also want to ask her about Gene Garby. She might have noticed him last night."

"What about the detectives?" asked Quinn. "I think one of us should contact them. Maybe tackle Foster first, since he seems the least antagonistic."

"I have a question," said Tracy. "If Foster is related to the casino people, do you think he might have come to Las Vegas to find that money? I mean he might have heard stories all his life about the missing money, so why not look for it?"

Emma sighed. "We have two detectives and we probably can't trust either of them, at least for now. Maybe I'll call Foster and just sound him out. Meanwhile, you try to contact Lenny and Granny."

"Will do," answered Milo.

CHAPTER TWENTY-ONE

"I really want to find that Frankie," Emma said, going to work on her iPad.

"What are you looking for?" Quinn asked. He pulled into the parking lot of a grocery store and parked at the far end and left the engine running.

"It's an online people search engine. I'm going to see if there's an address for him." A few minutes later, she located something that looked promising. She pulled a credit card out of her wallet and punched the numbers into the purchase area. "It gave me a couple of listings."

"Where are you going to print them?"

"They'll pop up here, but will also be sent to my e-mail account. The accuracy will depend on whether or not he's moved around a lot."

Just as Emma was reviewing the two addresses provided for Frankie Varga, her cell phone rang. She answered. After the initial greeting, Emma listened to the caller and asked for an address. While on the call, she punched the address she was given into the SUV's GPS. When the call ended, she said to Quinn, "Head to that address." She picked up her iced coffee and sucked down a third of it without realizing it.

Following orders, Quinn put the SUV in gear and pulled out of the parking lot. "Who was that? You hardly said a word on the call, but you're about to suck an entire coffee, plastic cup and all, through that straw."

"That was Gloria Youngblood, the woman at the reception desk at Desert Sun. She said she wants to talk, but we need to come right this minute. It just might be the break we need."

"That's not the address for the rest home."

"It's a restaurant. She said she'd be there, but only for the next fifteen to twenty minutes."

They burned up ten minutes of Gloria's time getting to the address she'd given Emma — a hole-in-the-wall Mexican restaurant not far from the rest home. The restaurant was long and dark, its front windows painted over with fading and scratched pictures of desert scenery — the sort of place only locals would go to and even then only those who knew the owner.

Emma and Quinn walked in and let their eyes adjust before looking around for Gloria. They located her in a booth at the back by the kitchen. Without a word, Emma slid across red cracked vinyl and faced Gloria. Quinn slid in next to Emma.

"I don't have much time," Gloria said in a rush of words. Her glasses were pushed high on her nose and sweat beaded on her upper lip. In front of her was a half cup of black coffee in a thick, heavy mug. From the kitchen came the smell of hot lard, corn tortillas, and braised meat. An old woman, her doughy body wrapped in a dirty flowered apron, approached the table, refilled Gloria's coffee, and stood ready to take their orders. Gloria waved her away with a half smile and a few words in Spanish.

"Why'd you call, Gloria?" Emma asked as soon as the woman left the table.

"You were right," Gloria started. "Gene Garby and that detective are related. I think they are brothers."

"You could have told me that over the phone." Emma paused. "Unless there's more."

"Much more." Gloria's eyes darted around the dark restaurant, which was empty except for one table near the front door occupied by an old man eating and reading a newspaper.

"What about Frankie?" Quinn prodded. "We heard someone was paying him to take special care of Nemo Morehouse."

"Yes," Gloria confirmed.

"We also heard that you were almost fired when you complained about Frankie."

Gloria nodded. "Now I keep my mouth shut to keep my job."

"So why are you talking to us?" Emma asked.

"I don't want that lady hurt — the one you're looking for. They said she killed Mr. Morehouse, but I don't believe it."

Emma sat up straight, her whole body on edge with both caffeine and adrenaline. "Who do you think killed him?"

"Frankie. Frankie Varga killed Mr. Morehouse. Mr. Garby paid him to do it." Gloria tapped the side of her head, by her right eye, with an index finger. "I know. I saw money change hands and heard them speak. They were in the big supply closet just before the shift change. I was in there, too. I'd made a call, a private call about another job. They came in right when I finished and didn't know I was in the back listening."

"When was this?" asked Emma.

"A couple of days ago." Gloria shifted in her seat and looked into her coffee.

Emma waited until Gloria made eye contact again. "Who claimed Nemo's body?"

Gloria shrugged. "It was picked up by a local mortuary is all I know."

Emma sensed Gloria knew a lot more than that. "What about Nemo's family? Weren't they notified? Do you know where we can find them?"

Gloria glanced at her watch. It had a big easy-to-read face and was strapped to her wrist by a thick red vinyl strap. "I have to go." She started to say something else, but changed her mind and began to slide out of the booth. "I've said too much. Please don't leave right after me," she begged. Fear, hot and dry, wafted off her, mingling with the cooking smells. "I don't want anyone to see us together."

Emma reached across the table and put a hand on Gloria's arm, stopping her. "Then tell me this. We're trying to find Frankie Varga. I have two possible addresses — one on Gowan Street and one on Walnut. Do you know which is his current address?" When Gloria hesitated, Emma added, "It could mean life or death to Dolly Meskiel."

"Last I heard, he lived on Walnut." She slipped out of the booth and headed for the door. Right before exiting the restaurant,

Gloria turned on her heel and slipped back to the booth. She leaned down and whispered in a torrent, "Mr. Garby, he killed his own father."

Without giving Emma and Quinn a chance to respond, Gloria Youngblood crossed herself and ran out of the restaurant on rubber-soled shoes that squeaked on the old scarred linoleum.

Stunned, Emma and Quinn sat in the booth for a full minute after Gloria's departure without saying a word. Finally, Quinn said, "Did she just say what I think she said?"

Emma nodded. "That Gene Garby had Nemo Morehouse killed and that Nemo is Garby's father. At least that's what I heard."

"Wow. Didn't see that coming, did you?"

"Not for a second," Emma admitted. "I feel like I've been punched in the gut." Emma took a deep breath and exhaled. A crumpled paper napkin on Gloria's side of the table wiggled from the draft. "That means . . ." She paused, sensing Quinn was thinking the same thing, but saying it out loud would make it true and solid, like set concrete, and she wasn't sure she wanted to go there even though she knew she had to make the trip.

Quinn finished the thought, "That Nemo

is Detective Garby's father, too." He slid out of the booth, reached into his pocket, and pulled out some cash. He tossed a five-dollar bill onto the table. "We've got work to do." He held out a hand to Emma. She took it and let him help her out of the booth.

"That's right, Milo," Emma said, her cell phone on speaker once again. "Don't speak to the police about anything until we sort this all out. Who knows how much Detective Garby is involved. We need to confirm what we were just told. We need to find out if Nemo had sons, and if so, are they the Garbys."

"We can research that," said Tracy. "If there are records and references online, we'll find them."

"Too bad we can't ask Foster," quipped Quinn. "Isn't that his hobby?"

Emma nodded in agreement. "If I can think of a tactful way to broach it with him, I will, but we still have to be careful about Foster's personal motives. And finding Dolly is still our first priority."

"Do you think Foster even knows?" asked Tracy.

"That's a good question," said Quinn, "but considering who he is and how much interest he has in old Vegas, we should work on the assumption he does."

"In the meantime," said Emma, punching the Walnut address into the GPS while she talked, "we're off to track down Frankie Varga."

"By the way, guys," Milo said. "Unless something major breaks, we're going to swing by Madeline's nephew's house tonight and pay our respects. But we'll let you know if we learn anything about the Garby brothers before we go."

"And we'll text you if we learn anything," Emma assured him.

CHAPTER TWENTY-TWO

The address on Walnut took them to a tidy two-level apartment complex the color of dry clay. The complex consisted of three small buildings, huddled together in a U-shape, with all apartments facing a large courtyard with a pool.

After parking the SUV curbside, Emma and Quinn proceeded to Unit 103. It was downstairs at the far end of the building on the left side of the pool area. They knocked several times but got no answer. Quinn tried to peer through the window, but the blinds were drawn.

"You looking for Frankie?" asked a grizzly guy cleaning the pool with a long-handled net. He was wearing cutoff jeans and a white tank top, his long brown hair secured into a ponytail. A half-smoked cigarette dangled precariously from one corner of his mouth.

"Yes," answered Quinn. "Do you know

where we can find him? It's important."
Quinn noticed two young women sunbath-
ing nude on chaises on the far side of the
pool. He did a double take followed by a
quick recovery. Emma grinned and elbowed
him.

"Funny thing," the guy said, scratching
his narrow chest through his sweat-soaked
T-shirt, "hardly a peep out of the guy for
two years, now everyone's looking for him."

Quinn looked around. "You the manager
here?"

"Yep. Been here a long time — manager,
handyman, cleaning crew, security — you
name it, I do it. I've even pulled cats out of
trees and wrangled drunk boyfriends for
tenants." He took a drag off the cigarette
and blew the smoke in the opposite direction. "Don't tell me Frankie's one of those
serial killers. You know, one of those weird
little guys who keeps body parts in a stor-
age locker somewhere." He shook his head
and took another drag of tobacco. "Didn't
seem the type, but you never know. It's
always the quiet ones."

"Who else is looking for Frankie?" asked
Quinn.

"The cops. But you two don't look like no
police." When he stepped closer, Quinn and
Emma caught the scent of stale booze, rank

and sour, possibly from the night before.

Emma tried not to wrinkle her nose when answering. "No, we're not. We just need to find him."

The guy went back to trolling for debris in the water. "Well, good luck with that. Like I told the cops, Frankie moved out a couple of days ago. Said he was taking some time off work and moving in with friends for a while." The guy coughed and took another drag of his cigarette.

The two women got up from the chaises and wrapped towels around themselves. They waved at the guy. "Catch you later, Wyatt," they called to him before disappearing into one of the apartments on two sets of impossibly long legs.

"Exotic dancers," Wyatt explained. "They like that allover tan so I let them go bare-assed, as long as it's not on the weekend when most tenants are home. Not that I'm complaining." He winked at Quinn.

"Did Frankie say where he was going?" Emma tried hard not to roll her eyes — a habit of both Kelly and Granny that she disliked.

"Nope. When I asked him where I should send his deposit refund, he told me to keep it. Called it *chump change*." The guy stopped working and looked at them. "Who knows, maybe he hit it big in one of the casinos."

"How about a girlfriend?" asked Quinn. "Or a boyfriend?"

"I saw one girl with him from time to time, but not recently. Maybe he moved in with her."

"Do you remember anything about the girl?" Quinn prodded.

"Not really. They were mostly going in and out, and his apartment is close to the parking in the back so it was just the odd glimpse. I just remember she was always covered up." He winked at Quinn again. "I mean, with the eye candy around here, what's the point in paying attention to that, right?"

Emma wasn't ready to give up. "When you rented to Frankie, did you get an emergency contact?"

"Maybe." Wyatt snuffed his cigarette butt out against a nearby trashcan while he looked them over, coming to a decision. "Only thing I remember was it was a guy's name. The address was in Dolan Springs."

"Where's Dolan Springs?" asked Quinn.

"Arizona. Just over an hour and a half from here, out in the middle of nowhere."

Emma and Quinn exchanged a look before Quinn asked, "Do you remember what the police looked like who questioned you?"

"Two detectives. A young one, clean cut, and an older one. The older one was kind of thick and cranky. I have the young one's card in my place if you want me to get it."

"That's okay, but thank you," said Emma. "You've been very helpful." She reached into her purse, pulled out a twenty-dollar bill, and held it out to Wyatt. "We were never here. Understand? To the police or to anyone."

Wyatt didn't take the money. He looked at it, then at Emma, sizing her up. "I never told the detectives about Dolan Springs," he said. "I don't like cops. They're not very *appreciative.*"

Emma got out two more twenties and held the sixty dollars out to him. This time he took the money.

"You two thinking of driving out to Dolan Springs?" Wyatt folded the cash and stuck it in one of his pockets.

"Maybe," answered Quinn.

"A bit of advice. Free advice. Don't go looking so fresh faced and fancy. They don't like strangers, especially that kind. And don't go at night. No streetlights. Easy to get lost or step on a rattler. Or be taken for an intruder. A lot of folks out that way answer their door with a shotgun in hand."

"Boy," said Quinn with a chuckle as they climbed back into the SUV. "I got off cheap with that fiver I left the waitress. Good thing that clown didn't know who you were — he might have held out for a few hundred."

"The price of doing business." Emma buckled up.

"So where to?"

Emma rubbed her eyes. "I've been here less than forty-eight hours and feel like I've been here a month."

"Maybe we should call it a night. We can't go running out to Dolan Springs tonight. It will be dark before we get there and I'm prone to listen to ole Wyatt's warning."

"I agree with you. Especially since it's just a contact lead. I can put the last name of Varga into the search engine and see if anyone by that name pops up in Dolan Springs. If we get a phone number, we can give it a call. Who knows?" She put her hands on her thighs and rubbed them back and forth. "Let's go back to my hotel and see if Granny or Lenny shows up."

"What about dinner?" Quinn asked as he pulled away from the curb. "What would you like?"

"Room service, served while I soak in the tub."

"I could arrange that." He flashed her a grin.

She laughed. "And an early bedtime."

"How about we order room service," he suggested, "and eat while we go over our notes, then I'll head to my hotel so you can get that bath and some rest. We can meet up again in the morning."

"Sounds like a plan, but not too early for breakfast. I want to get down to the gym first thing. I feel so logy and tense, and a workout should help. I also do some of my best thinking while on the elliptical."

"Whatever you want, Emma. Consider me your guy Friday."

Emma looked up at the roof of the SUV. "You hear that, Lenny and anyone else who's listening? If you've got something to say tonight, say it early or it'll have to wait."

"Does that go for me, too?" asked the spirit in the backseat.

For once, Emma didn't jump. She was too tired. "Granny, I'm so glad you popped in. It's been a very busy day. We're on our way back to my hotel."

"Glad yours was exciting. Mostly mine was dull as dirt," the ghost reported. "Except for one thing, which I came to tell you."

"Hi, Granny," Quinn said, looking in the rearview mirror at nothing.

"Hey, Indiana," Granny said with a smile. She turned to Emma. "Nice chauffer you've got."

"So what was that one thing, Granny?" Emma asked, her patience worn thin.

"Just now I finally figured out why the young guy holding Dolly looks familiar. I think he's the same guy who was taking care of Nemo at the old folks home."

With a surge of energy, Emma whipped her head around. "You mean he's Frankie Varga?"

Quinn went on alert. "What's going on?"

"Are you sure, Granny?" Emma asked.

"Not a hundred percent, but I think it's likely. He looks kind of the same, but he doesn't have his uniform on. I was hoping someone would call him by name, but he's been alone with Dolly most of the day. When he gave her medicine, that's when it clicked for me."

"He drugged her?"

"Yeah, not too long ago. He gave her something to calm her down and help her sleep. There was a report about Dolly being missing on the news tonight. She watched it and started crying. About broke my heart. That's when he gave her something. It looks like he's settled in for the night. He was eating pizza and drinking a beer when I left.

And by the way, he has a gun. First time I've seen one at the place, but he was armed tonight."

"What about Laura?"

"I'm not sure what happened to her. I saw her this morning, but when I went back after talking to you today, she was gone. Nemo didn't pop in later today either. Only the one I think might be Frankie was at the place watching Dolly."

Emma gave Granny's report to Quinn, then said, "I wonder if Laura is off with Nemo trying to find Lenny. Milo said Nemo popped in at Dolly's house, but only for a few minutes."

While they drove back to the Strip, Emma filled Granny in on the day's findings.

"Wow," Granny said, her eyes wide. "You did have a big day and I missed it. Next time send a different ghost to look after Dolly and I'll come with you."

"Granny, do you remember seeing anyone else with Nemo that night at the rest home?"

The ghost gave it some thought. "I remember seeing someone who could be that Garby man. At least a man in a suit kept looking in on Nemo during Dolly's visit, but I didn't know who he was. And now that you mention it, he and that surly detective do look a lot alike. Are you sure they're

268

related to Nemo?"

"As you would say, not a hundred percent. But it's likely." Emma gave Quinn a quick summary of Granny's comments.

Granny narrowed her eyes. "That's pretty evil, killing off your own father then trying to pin it on an old woman."

"I agree, Granny. But I'm also wondering if that's part of the plan. Nemo was getting pretty weak. Maybe he planned his death with his son so he could come back as a spirit and track Lenny down."

Quinn glanced over at Emma. "You mean since he was dying anyway, he did it on his terms and with a master plan?"

"Yes, that's exactly what I'm getting at."

Granny wasn't so sure. "I've never heard of a spirit doing that before, have you?"

"No, Granny, I haven't, but as time goes on, I'm learning a lot more about spirits than I expected. It's pretty diabolical and the whole thing hinges on finding a medium to assist with the negotiations. Without that, there would be no way for Nemo to communicate with his son after he died."

"Or sons," added Quinn.

Emma looked over the seat at Granny. "You still don't know where Dolly is?"

The ghost shook her head. "I even did some surveillance. After Dolly fell asleep, the kid went out to get his pizza. I followed him. It only took him a few minutes because it was so close, but I wasn't able to see any street signs or much of anything except a bunch of homes and small businesses stuck in the desert. Even the pizza joint was all by itself, not bunched up with other businesses like at home." Granny laughed. "I'm telling ya, Julian is a busy metropolis compared to this place. Oh," added Granny, "the kid drives a black pickup truck. One of those small ones."

Emma turned to Quinn. "According to Granny, Frankie Varga is driving a compact black truck. We totally forgot to ask Wyatt what he drove."

"Great job, Granny," Quinn said to the ghost. "Glad you were on your toes with that since we weren't."

The ghost grinned, soaking in the appreciation.

"Yes, Granny," Emma agreed, "that's a big help. You didn't notice a sign on the pizza place while you were at it, did you?"

The spirit gave it considerable thought before answering. "It was very short, like just two initials. Nothing fancy. I'll keep trying to remember."

"How about the name *Dolan Springs*?" asked Quinn. "Does that ring a bell?"

Granny mulled the name over. "Nope, nothing like that."

Emma shook her head at Quinn, then turned back to Granny. "In the meantime, Granny, could you try to locate Lenny? Milo has been trying and hasn't been successful. If he wants to help us save Dolly, he needs to show up and now."

The diminutive ghost saluted. "You got it, Chief."

CHAPTER TWENTY-THREE

Once again Quinn pulled into valet parking at the Venetian and handed off the keys to the SUV to an attendant. And once again, Quinn walked Emma through the noisy lobby and casino toward the elevators leading to the tower that housed her suite.

In addition to being exhausted, Emma felt a bad headache coming on, made worse by the assault of slot machines, shouts of gamblers, and blaring music as they threaded their way toward the elevators. All Emma wanted was a hot bath, some simple food, and undisturbed sleep. She was about to ask Quinn if he'd mind waiting until breakfast to go over the information they'd gathered when a static flash nearby caught her eye. It wasn't bright or garish, but soft like a night-light being switched off and on just in front of her. No one else seemed to notice. She stopped in her tracks and stared straight ahead.

"What is it, Emma?" asked Quinn.

"I thought I saw something." She stayed rooted, while hotel and casino patrons went around them like a diversion in the road. Emma kept alert and saw the soft flicker again, followed by a hazy outline, but couldn't discern its identity.

"It's a spirit," she whispered to Quinn. "But it didn't stay. I'm not sure who it is." She started moving forward again. Quinn followed, keeping close to her.

They were in the elevator going up when another hazy flicker presented itself. Emma stiffened and Quinn noticed, but they weren't alone so Emma didn't speak. The entity soon disappeared without fully materializing. Emma's arms broke out in goose bumps. In silence, she showed them to Quinn.

When they reached her floor, they got out and started down the hall, taking it slow in case the ghost tried to appear again. She slipped her key card into the lock and opened the door to her suite. Inside, the lights were on and the TV was running. Without going in, she looked at Quinn, who understood her concern. He signaled for her to wait. He slipped into the suite just as the door to the bathroom opened and Phil Bowers came out wiping his face with a towel. The two men shouted in surprise while Emma gave off a short yelp. For several seconds the three of them stared at one another, until Emma entered the suite and closed the door behind her.

Phil was the first to speak. "Well, isn't this cozy?" He eyed the two of them, his lips a tight line of anger.

"What are you doing here, Phil?" Emma asked.

"I told you last night I would come. Obviously, you forgot."

Emma brushed past the two men and walked deeper into the suite. Locating the remote, she turned off the TV. After dropping her bag onto the coffee table, she plopped down on the large sofa, totally worn out. "And I told you it wasn't necessary."

"And I thought it was, considering how we left things and your refusal to answer my calls or texts."

Quinn and Phil followed Emma into the living room area. Quinn took a seat at the small table, stretching out his long legs in front of him. Phil remained standing and stared at him. "And now I can see why."

"Hey, Phil," said Quinn, "back off. It's not what you think. I'm helping Emma. That's it." He rubbed a hand over his face, almost as tired as Emma. "And how did you get in here anyway?"

Phil picked up a card key from the credenza and waved it at Quinn. "Emma usually lists me on her hotel reservations just in case I decide to join her. And if she hadn't, I'd have been camped in front of that door waiting." He turned to Emma. "Emma, we have things to discuss." He shot a harsh look at Quinn. "In private."

But Emma wasn't listening. She was focused on a faint light just to the right of where Quinn was sitting. The men grew quiet, both sensing that she was seeing something they could not. The spirit moved closer, fading in and out, hesitant and unsure.

"Lenny, is that you?" The hazy light flickered and retreated to the window. "Please stay," Emma coaxed. "These men are here to help you, just like I am. We need you to get Dolly back safe. It's very important."

Granny materialized next to Emma and took in the three of them. She crossed her arms in disapproval. "This is an interesting little party."

"*Sh,* Granny," said Emma. "There's a spirit over by the window. It might be Lenny, but I'm not sure. Can you tell?"

Putting aside his anger, Phil moved over to the table and took a seat near Quinn, out of the way. Both men watched and waited.

The light stabilized and moved forward again but didn't become clear.

"I don't know who that is," answered Granny. "But it's not Lenny. He's right here. You told me to find him and I did. I think I also remember the name of that pizza place and there's something else that's a bit weird."

Emma glanced over her left shoulder toward Granny and saw the hazy outline of Lenny Speidel hovering nearby. She turned her attention back to the unknown ghost. "Nemo, is that you?" Emma's voice changed from coaxing to stern. "If it is, quit playing games."

In response, the light retreated like a frightened kitten.

"No, don't go," Emma told it, getting to her feet. "Please don't go."

The apparition grew stronger but didn't come near.

"Maybe it's Bert," suggested Quinn in a whisper.

Emma rubbed her arms. She had goose bumps again and it wasn't just because of the cold air in the room. "You came here for a reason," Emma said to the hazy light.

"Tell me why you came. Let me help."

Slowly the flickering light took shape and features began to emerge. It was a woman with long hair. Emma slapped a hand over her mouth to squelch the scream threatening to rise up like bile. She dropped down again onto the sofa and stared at the apparition in horror. Both Phil and Quinn jumped to her assistance, but when he saw Phil go to Emma's side, Quinn backed off and took his seat again.

"What is it, Emma?" asked Phil. He put an arm around her and brought her close.

"Who is it?" asked Quinn. He looked in the same direction as Emma.

"I don't know yet," she stammered. "But it could be Laura Crawford."

"The fortune-teller from Fremont Street?" asked Quinn.

Emma nodded as she fought back tears. "If it is, it means she's dead."

"That's not Laura," Granny said, "unless she died in the last couple of minutes." In fits and starts the spirit started materializing. "That's Madeline, Dolly's BFF."

Emma stared at Granny. "Are you sure?"

"Sure I'm sure. She's been visiting Dolly."

Like a runaway roller coaster, Emma's emotions went from horrified to shocked to exasperated in record time. "You never told me that!"

Granny edged away from Emma. "Oops. My bad."

As Emma watched the apparition, it began to come more into focus, showing not a young woman, but an older one, thick in build. She had long hair, but not as long and sleek as Laura's. Emma wanted to scream at Granny for not telling her about Madeline, but she was so relieved at not seeing the ghost of Laura Crawford, she let it slide.

While Madeline materialized, Emma asked Granny, "Anything else you haven't told us that might be important?"

"No need to get all uppity with me," barked Granny. "You're not the only one who's tired and worried, ya know."

"What's going on?" asked Quinn.

It was Phil who answered him. "I think Granny and Emma are having a little tiff. It happens a lot. Just roll with it."

Emma looked at the two men. "This new ghost is Madeline Kurtz, Dolly's friend who recently died. Granny is here with Lenny. Apparently, Madeline has been visiting Dolly wherever she's being held and" — she shot a look at Granny — "Granny forgot to tell us."

"I've been busy trying to figure out where

Dolly is," Granny snapped. "Or is that not important to you anymore?"

Emma took several deep breaths. "You want some water?" Phil asked her. "Or something from the minibar?"

"Water, please," she answered, "Trust me, I'll be hitting the minibar later."

Quinn got up and retrieved a bottle of water that stood with several others on the credenza. He twisted the cap off. "You want me to get some ice for this?"

Emma shook her head and held out her hand for the water. She took several gulps from the bottle.

Lenny floated closer and watched with interest. "Who's the bald guy?" he asked Granny. "He wasn't here before, was he?"

"That's Phil, Emma's boyfriend," she answered.

"I thought the red-haired guy was her boyfriend."

"Nah, he's just a wannabe."

Emma snapped her head around and glared at both ghosts, who backed away with caution. "Seems Emma's a bit testy," Granny explained to Lenny. "She always gets that way when her blood sugar's low. She's a vegetarian. I keep telling her she needs to eat meat."

Emma's shoulders sagged in resignation.

Quinn leaned down to Phil and whispered. "I'd kill to know what's going down right now."

"Whatever it is," whispered Phil back, "I guarantee it's entertaining, or at least it would be to us."

Emma put the water bottle down on the table with a sound thud and stood up. She took a few cautious steps toward the ghost of Madeline Kurtz. "Welcome, Madeline. I'm Emma Whitecastle, a good friend of Milo Ravenscroft's. This is Phil Bowers and that's Quinn Keenan. They are friends of mine and cannot see or hear you."

Madeline looked the men over and nodded hello to them anyway.

"I am very sorry about your passing," Emma added. "Milo is with your family right now."

Madeline gave Emma a tenuous smile. "Not good timing for my heart to give out. Not with Dolly needing me." Madeline looked over at Granny and Lenny with surprise. "Is that you, Lenny? After all these years?"

"Yes, Mad, it's me. How's Doll?"

"Not too bad. Sleeping like a baby right now."

"A drugged baby," Granny added.

"Madeline," Emma asked, "do you have

any idea where they're holding Dolly?"

Madeline shook her head. "No, it's just out in the desert somewhere. Nothing looked familiar, but I'm still getting the hang of this being dead thing. Sometimes I'm confused. Other times I feel almost normal."

"But I have a clue." Granny raised her hand. "That's one of the things I came to tell ya. Or aren't you interested anymore?"

Emma turned to Granny, "Of course I'm interested. Tell me what you found out."

"It's not so much what I found out as what I remember," answered the ghost. "The pizza place, I think it was called B&B."

"Are you sure?"

Granny screwed up her face. "Not a hundred percent, but close enough for horseshoes."

Emma turned to the men. Phil was still on the sofa. Quinn was leaning against the credenza. "Will one of you fire up my iPad. It's in my bag. Look up B&B Pizza."

Quinn grabbed Emma's bag from the table and took out her iPad.

"And while you're at it," Emma added, "the charger is on the desk. Plug it in somewhere in case we need it fully charged later."

Quinn got the charger and returned to the

table. He plugged everything in, sat down, and got to work.

Phil asked, "What can I do?"

"Just sit tight," she told him. She hesitated, then added in a low voice, "And I am very glad you're here, but we do need to talk." They exchanged a sad smile.

"Enough of the mushy stuff," snapped Granny. "You can moon over each other later, when Dolly's safe."

"Who knew," Quinn said without looking up from the computer, "that so many pizza joints would be named B&B. But so far none are in Nevada."

Phil got up and went to look over Quinn's shoulder. "Try going on Yelp. If it's a small place, it might not have a website but might have reviews."

"Good idea."

"And there's something else," added Granny. "I think Laura was trying to tell me something."

Emma gave Granny her full attention. "But I thought you said Laura was gone."

"She was earlier, but just before we popped in here, the sloppy guy brought her back to the house. They fed her some pizza, then locked her in her room. I went in to look after her. She was crying, but I know she knew a spirit was in the room with her."

"What did she say, Granny?" Emma moved closed. "Please try to remember everything."

Granny furrowed her brows. "She called me *friendly spirit,* like she did in her wagon, and said she knew I was there. She kept asking me for help."

"Were you able to communicate with her?"

"A little. I told her who I was. It took several tries before she heard me but once she remembered, she stopped crying and said, 'Emma. Get Emma.' Then she started crying again and said, 'They're going to kill us.' "

Emma put her face in her hands and squeezed with frustration. "We have to help her and Dolly." When she looked up, her face was red. "Anything else?

"I kept asking her where we were, but she didn't seem to know. But she kept saying something over and over: *Ironwood.*"

"Look to see if there's an Ironwood anywhere nearby," Emma shot over her shoulder to Quinn and Phil.

While the men researched, Emma turned her attention to Lenny. "Is Nemo after the money you stole from the Lucky Buck Casino? Or is there something else we don't know about?"

"It's the money, but I'm not going to give it to him." Lenny stuck out his chin.

"Not even if it means saving Dolly's life?"

"You don't know these guys, Emma. They're probably going to kill her anyway."

"Listen, you moron," said Madeline, coming closer to Lenny. She put her hands on her hips. "Isn't it bad enough you broke Dolly's heart, now you have to cause her death?"

"I didn't break Doll's heart," Lenny insisted, going nose to nose with Madeline. "I was going to return the money, like I promised her."

Lenny turned to Emma. "You have to believe me," he pleaded. "Doll needs to believe me. After we robbed the casino, I thought she'd be happy because we'd finally have the money to take Milo and start over somewhere else."

"So you know Milo is your son?" asked Emma.

"Of course I know that. But Doll wouldn't marry me unless I got a real job, a respectable job. She had my name taken off his birth certificate and said he'd never know unless I went straight. When Nemo approached me about the heist, I figured it would be a good way to get the money I needed. One last score before going

284

straight." Lenny paced the hotel suite. "I robbed the place and stashed the money until things cooled down. That was the plan with Nemo. But when I told Doll, she kicked me out and said I was dead to her unless I gave the money back to the casino. I was going to get it to return it when Nemo's goons grabbed me and killed me. They beat me to death trying to find out where it was, but I never told them."

Granny stuck a finger in Lenny's face and shook it. "So now you need to tell us where the money is so we can use it to save Dolly."

Quickly, Emma told Quinn and Phil what was going on, then asked, "Any luck with Ironwood?"

"There's an Ironwood Homeowners' Association and an Ironwood Estates," Phil reported, reading over Quinn's shoulder. "They're close to Vegas. Someplace called Summerlin."

Madeline shook her head. "Those are expensive homes northwest of here. Certainly not in the wide-open desert."

"Keep looking," Emma told them. "Try anything you can."

Phil came to stand next to Emma. "Where's this Lenny?" he asked her.

Emma pointed straight ahead. Phil looked in that direction. "After all these years, maybe the money isn't still where you put it. There's been a lot of construction in this area since you were alive."

"It's there," assured Lenny. "I've checked. It's out in the desert in a place where nothing's been built yet." Emma relayed the words to Phil.

"Got it!" Quinn banged a fist on the table. "And you won't believe where."

Everyone, dead and living, turned to him, waiting.

"It's in Dolan Springs, Arizona," Quinn announced.

Lenny floated over to Quinn. "No, it's not!"

Emma went over to the table to check on Quinn's findings. "I don't think he means the money, Lenny."

"Remembering what that Wyatt guy said about Frankie?" Quinn explained. "I plugged in Dolan Springs, and guess what, there's a street there called Ironwood." He kept jabbing information into the search engine. "Hold on," said Quinn. "Bingo! There's also a B&B Pizza in Dolan Springs, and from the map, it's not that far from Ironwood."

"Good job, Quinn and Granny!" said Emma. "Although I wish we had more of an address."

"I don't think it will matter, Em." Quinn tapped the iPad screen. "Look at this Google map. There are not many structures on Ironwood. And we know what the creep drives."

Quinn was right — the map showed a small town with clearly marked streets and buildings. Ironwood wasn't very long and there were few homes or other buildings along it.

Emma left Quinn and started pacing while she thought through the angles. Granny paced alongside her. "What are you thinking, Emma?"

"We know where Frankie is and we know his vehicle," Emma said, wearing out the carpet. "If we go out there, we should be able to locate Laura and Dolly. Do we go tonight or tomorrow?" She looked at the two living men. "What do you guys think?"

Quinn, still hunched over Emma's iPad, straightened up and stretched. "That Wyatt guy said there are little to no outside lights out there, so it might be difficult tonight to see anything. But we could leave at first light or even before and surprise him in the morning."

"But that also means," added Phil, "that he'll see us sneaking up, especially if it's wide-open space." He turned to Emma.

"Shouldn't we call the police and let them know where we think Dolly is?"

"I just don't know how much to trust the police, Phil. Both Foster and Garby, the detectives on the case, have personal interests here. And Dolan Springs is in Arizona, not Nevada."

"Did you say Garby?" The ghost of Madeline Kurtz stepped forward.

"Yes," answered Emma. "There are two Garbys, Gene and Howard. They may be brothers and related to Nemo. One's a detective, the other runs the rest home where Nemo died."

"They are brothers," Madeline confirmed, "and Nemo's sons. If one of them is a cop, don't trust him."

"Hail, hail, the gang's all here."

Everyone but Phil and Quinn whipped around toward the door to the suite, the direction from where the voice came. In a matter of seconds, the ghost of Nemo Morehouse materialized.

CHAPTER TWENTY-FOUR

"Madeline, my dear, so nice to see you again." The ghost of the old criminal approached her. "I understand we died on the same day. How perfect is that?"

"Get away from me, Nemo," snapped Madeline.

Nemo smiled at Emma. "In our day, Maddy and I were quite the hot item. In fact, the four of us — Lenny, Dolly, Maddy, and I — made a cute foursome." He turned to Lenny. "At least until Lenny here went and spoiled it all by becoming a traitor."

"I was trying to do the right thing, Nemo," Lenny said. "You should try it sometime."

Emma walked over to the table. "Nemo's here," she whispered to Phil and Quinn. She tapped the iPad screen, making the information on it disappear. The two of them quickly understood, but Emma was worried about the ghosts, hoping none of them spilled the beans about knowing where

Dolly and Laura were being held.

"I thought it was getting cold in here," said Phil, keeping his voice low.

"Right now," Emma told them, "the dead outnumber the living, four to three. So just sit tight."

Nemo eyed Phil. "And who's this, Emma? Another suitor? Or a cop? He looks kind of like a cop."

"That's Emma boyfriend," Granny answered. "He's a lawyer."

"Ah, a mouthpiece," Nemo answered in an oily voice. "I used to own several."

Nemo wandered around the suite, looking at the other three ghosts. He dismissed Granny with a casual glance as he passed her. She lifted her upper lip in distaste.

"Yes, the gang's all here," Nemo said again. "Except for Dolly. And who knows, she might be joining us soon. Wouldn't that be nice?"

"Don't you dare hurt Doll!" Lenny charged Nemo but only ran through him. Lenny tried again, and again he only flew through the hazy image of the other ghost.

"You never were very bright, Lenny," Nemo sneered. "But now's the time to grow a brain and save Dolly. Where did you stash the money?"

"Your boys are going to kill her whether I

290

give it to you or not."

"Maybe, maybe not," said Nemo with hands outstretched. "You always liked the tables, Len. You willing to gamble with Dolly's life? You've got a fifty-fifty chance that she'll live if you give us the money. Zip chance if you don't."

Nemo's boys, Emma thought. She glanced at Lenny. He'd been saying that *Nemo's boys* were coming for her. It fell into place. Lenny had been trying to warn her about Nemo's sons but hadn't made himself clear. She looked at Nemo. "Both of your sons are involved, aren't they, Nemo? Even Howard."

"And what do you know about my sons?" Nemo set wary eyes on Emma.

"I know Gene is the director of Desert Sun, and Howard is a detective. The very detective assigned to this case."

"I knew you were smart when I met you, Emma." Nemo looked at Lenny and laughed. "Then again, motormouth there probably told you about them. Or even Dolly." Nemo stretched, a luxurious catlike stretch like he had all the time in the world and no place to go. "Who knew one of my boys would become a cop?" Nemo gave her a wide smile. "He's a good cop, too. Straight as an arrow. Above reproach, until now. Until his brother convinced him this whole cockamamie thing with ghosts and mediums could work."

Emma wondered about John Foster. "Is Howard's partner involved in this, too?"

"Foster?" Nemo laughed. "No. But he is an unwitting catalyst. I don't think Howard would have gone for the scheme, but the force brought that young upstart in from outside and promoted him over my boy. He's put his life on the line and this is how they repaid him. I've always told him only crime paid."

Emma stared at Nemo, wondering if he was telling the truth about John Foster and if she should have kept her mouth shut about knowing the identity of Nemo's sons. She turned to Madeline when another idea struck her. "Please don't tell me you're Howard and Gene's mother. Although I wouldn't be surprised at this point."

Madeline started to say something, but Nemo spoke up first. "She could have been, but she's not."

"No," Madeline confirmed, shooting daggers at Nemo. "After what this louse did to Lenny, I wanted nothing more to do with him. He'd already started running around with some tramp from Boulder City — a cocktail waitress named Lola — before then. She's the boys' mother. She popped them out one right after the other."

"So the boys didn't take your name?" Emma asked Nemo.

"I never married Lola," Nemo explained. "But I supported the boys and spent time with them. Lola married a guy name Garby, who adopted them. Considering the heat I was always under, we thought it best that their relationship to me was kept under wraps. When they were all grown up, Lola and her husband moved to Florida, but the boys and I got close again." He turned a stern eye on Lenny. "That money is my legacy to them."

"So close Gene murdered you?" Emma stepped forward. "And tried to stick that on Dolly?"

Nemo laughed. "Dolly wasn't under any real suspicion. In the end it would have been deemed natural causes. I was very old and going to die anyway, within two months according to the doc. It was all about timing. And by the way, Gene did not kill me."

"Not directly, but he hired Frankie Varga to do it. In the eyes of the law, it's still murder."

"You've been snooping around, my dear." Nemo tightened his lips, them relaxed them into a smile. "Frankie reminds me a lot of Lenny in his early days — none too bright but willing."

Before Lenny could process the dig, Emma said, "And by timing, you mean Laura Crawford or someone like her." Emma got even closer to the dead hood. "You couldn't die until you had a medium you could trust to be the communicator between you and your sons."

Nemo laughed. "You and your kind are amazingly ethical, Emma. At least the real ones are. We met up with a lot of crackpots who couldn't contact a ghost if they were one themselves. Others were wary of Gene's queries. It took us a while to find Laura. She's young and impressionable, and almost unaware of her gifts, which makes her both perfect and maddening. There's no quality control to her communication." He gave Emma a short jerk of his head. "What we need is someone like you."

"And you never knew about Milo?" Emma asked.

"Ah, yes, Milo." Nemo turned to Lenny. "Who knew you and Dolly would produce such a talent, but alas, Dolly insisted he was a scam and I never saw him enough to judge for myself. And when he was older, he moved away."

Lenny stepped forward, ready to charge Nemo again. "You keep Milo out of this."

"For years," continued Nemo, ignoring Lenny, "I believed her and even forgot about little Milo, then I read in the paper about his upcoming event at the university. Gene contacted Dolly and *strongly encouraged* her to set up a little meeting with us when he was in town to try and contact Lenny, but she insisted Milo wasn't capable of doing that, even though he was famous for it. That's why Dolly came to see me the night I died. She wanted to tell me she'd found someone better suited to help than Milo."

"Me," Emma said, pointing as herself.

Nemo winked his confirmation. "You."

Emma closed her eyes as more of the puzzle came together. It wasn't that Dolly hadn't believed in Milo's gifts all these years; she was trying to protect him. That was why she wanted someone else to look into Lenny's presence. She knew Nemo was about to make his move, and she wanted to be sure that Lenny was around and Emma could communicate with him. Not that Emma appreciated being thrown into the mix as a substitute, but she could see Dolly's motive from a mother's viewpoint.

"Over the years I kept in touch with Dolly," Nemo continued, "sure she knew where Lenny stashed the money, but if she did, she wasn't touching it."

"I never told her," Lenny insisted. "And I saw you hovering around her, watching her every move over the years. I just couldn't tell her anything." Lenny looked down at the floor. "If I could have, I would have told her so you would have left her alone."

"Maybe. Maybe not," sneered Nemo. "She was a good-looking woman. Who knows, maybe I could have picked up where you left off." Nemo was pushing Lenny's buttons and it was working. Once again he tried to charge Nemo and missed.

"He's provoking you on purpose, Lenny," Madeline said with disgust. "Didn't you learn anything working with him all those years?"

"For," Nemo corrected her. "Lenny worked for me, not with me."

"Stop the bickering," Granny said with impatience. "It's not getting us anywhere."

"Granny's right," added Emma. "Nemo, I want to talk to Lenny alone. Maybe I can learn more about the money." She stepped even closer to the ghost and pointed her right index finger in his face. "But if we do turn over that money, you have to promise to return both Dolly and Laura unharmed."

"You really think that creep is going to keep a promise?" Granny moved closer, but

Emma signaled her to stay where she was.

"And if I don't," goaded the ghostly criminal.

"Then you'll just have to wait and see what I have up my sleeve, won't you?"

Nemo locked eyes with Emma. "In return for the money and their safety, you have to promise not to turn in my boys. The money is exchanged. The women turned over. And my boys walk away without a hitch." He looked over at Quinn and Phil. "And that goes for them, too."

Emma stared at Nemo a long time, weighing the proposition. She nodded, agreeing to his terms.

"Say it," Nemo demanded as he started to fade.

"I agree," said Emma, her voice strong, her eyes latched on to the ghost. "Just return them without so much as a scratch or the deal is off."

"Tomorrow, Emma. You have until tomorrow to deliver the money. My boys will be in touch about the time and place."

When Nemo was gone, Emma updated Quinn and Phil.

"Talk about a deal with the devil." Quinn shook his head.

"What are we going to do about Dolly and Laura?" asked Phil. "Knowing you've learned about his sons might make Nemo concerned about you finding out about Dolan Springs and attempting a rescue."

"But there's no overt connection between the Garbys and Dolan Springs," Emma said.

"True," Phil said, "but he might be worried that somehow you'll stumble upon something to link them. If so, he may try to move them."

"Good point," Emma agreed, "but in order to do that, he'd have to communicate with his sons or with Frankie and that other guy. It sounds as if they had all this set up in advance of Nemo's death, but now communication is sketchy at best." She turned to Granny. "Granny, you and Madeline go back and keep watch on Dolly and Laura, and report back immediately if anything changes. Eavesdrop on everything as much as you can, but be careful and stay out of sight if Nemo is there. I don't want him knowing we know where they are. And Granny, try to communicate with Laura. If they do try to move them, I don't want her making it easier by being the go-between."

"Gotcha!" Granny said. "Come on, Madeline, let me show you how to be a ghost detective."

"If you don't mind, Granny, I'd like to move on to the other side." Madeline turned to Emma. "I can see that Dolly is in good hands. Keep her safe. It's not her time yet."

Emma nodded and assured the ghost they would do everything possible to save her friend.

Next, Madeline went to Lenny, who was looking confused and dejected. "Len, I know you love Dolly and Milo very much. And I know Dolly loved you. Now is your chance to make it all up to them. Listen to Emma and do exactly what she asks. It's Dolly's only chance to get out of this."

Lenny looked down at the floor and nodded. "You're right, Mad. As much as I hate the idea of Nemo and his sons getting that money, I know you're right."

As soon as Madeline and Granny left, Emma sat down on the sofa with a pen and notepad. "Okay, Lenny, where's the money?"

CHAPTER TWENTY-FIVE

Emma never got to the gym.

After Lenny gave Emma the directions to where he'd stashed the money, she, Quinn, and Phil put together a plan to retrieve it.

Quinn went back to the iPad and looked up the information. "He said Highway 95 south, right?"

"Yes," confirmed Emma. "It's a road named Jasper off of the 95 heading towards Boulder City." She consulted her notes. "Yes. Jasper will dead end. From there we have to go on foot."

"I see Rocky Point but nothing called Jasper intersecting with the 95."

Phil studied the map over Quinn's shoulder. "What's that road there?" He pointed at the screen. "Can you enlarge the map?"

"Sure." Quinn enlarged the map, then smiled. "Good catch, Phil."

"What is it?" asked Emma.

"There are two 95s," Quinn explained.

"An old road and the highway. I'll bet that highway was built after Lenny was killed."

"Let's see." Emma did some calculations. "Milo was around two when his father died, and he's fifty-three now, so if that highway was built in the last fifty years, it's not the highway Lenny's talking about."

"There's no Jasper intersecting the Old Highway 95 either," noted Phil, "but there are a couple of unnamed turn-offs. One of those is probably it."

"And like most everything else in Nevada, it's out in the middle of nowhere." Quinn looked at the two of them. "As much as I'd love to run out there tonight, I think we need to hold off until daybreak."

"Why can't we go now?" asked Emma. "The sooner the better."

Phil and Quinn exchanged looks. Phil said, "City folks." Quinn chuckled.

Phil turned to Emma. "That's the Mojave Desert, Emma. Lots of dangerous creatures roam the desert at night and I'm not talking about unhappy ghosts. Ever hear of the Mojave rattler?"

She shook her head.

"It's considered the most poisonous snake in all of North America. It's nocturnal and we'll be digging around smack in the middle of his home."

"He's right," agreed Quinn. "Not to mention burrow holes that can snap an ankle long before you ever see them. Trust me, I know about digging in the dirt in dangerous places. Our best bet is to get some rest and head out there as early as possible."

Emma wasn't happy about waiting, but running around in the desert in the dark with poisonous snakes wasn't something on her bucket list. "Okay," she agreed. "Daybreak it is."

"According to this map," said Quinn, "it will take about forty minutes to get there. Probably less at that time of day."

"Sunrise is around five thirty this time of year," noted Phil. "How about we hit the road no later than four forty-five or five." The other two nodded in agreement.

Quinn continued searching the Web. "One thing is for sure — we can't take Emma's SUV, even that time of day. The cops know it and might be keeping an eye out for it, especially Detective Garby."

Emma slapped her hands over her face. "Arghhh, you're right." She turned to Phil. "You didn't by any chance drive, did you?"

"No," Phil answered, "I white-knuckled it here in a plane. Now I wish I hadn't."

"No problem," announced Quinn as he got up from the table. "Consider me in charge of the motor pool and supplies." He started to leave. "I'll pick you guys up in the morning. I'll text you a place to meet me when I'm on my way." He was almost out the door when he shot back, "But you guys are in charge of breakfast. Something quick and portable — easy to eat while driving. And don't forget the coffee."

"Don't you want to stay for dinner?" asked Emma.

Quinn looked from Emma to Phil, then back to Emma. He shook his head. "Thanks, but I have things to do for tomorrow."

An awkwardness fell between Phil and Emma after Quinn left. Emma went to the closet and pulled out clothes for the morning. Phil started to turn on the TV, then stopped and put down the remote.

"Do you want to go out to eat or should I order room service?" he asked. When Emma didn't answer, Phil added, "Or should I go ask the front desk for a room of my own?"

Emma hugged the shirt in her hands to her chest and stared down at the carpet a long time before answering. "You can stay here, but . . ." Her voice trailed off.

"But sleep on the sofa," finished Phil. He pushed down on the cushions of the sofa, testing them. "I've slept on worse, and at

303

least I'll be with you."

They went quiet again, then Emma went to him, "I'm serious, Phil. We need to talk."

He sighed and passed a hand over his bald pate. "Yes, I know. I'm sorry I've been such an ass about Quinn. He's really a decent guy. I appreciate that he's been watching over you for the past couple of days. Really I do."

"This isn't about Quinn. At least not to me." Emma looked Phil in the eyes. "A little jealousy is fun in a boyfriend. It lets you know he cares. But when you get crazy jealous like you've been, you're telling me you don't trust me. That's what I have the issue with."

"I know. I —"

Emma put a hand gently to his lips. "Let me finish. I need to say this." She moved her hand so that it cupped the side of his face. "I've told you a hundred times that what happened in Pennsylvania with Quinn is over and that he and I are just friends. That's the truth and he knows it. If I had any feelings beyond that for him, you and I would not still be together. I'm not the sort of woman to tell one man I love him when I have possible feelings for another. And if you don't know that by now, Phil Bowers, you need to learn it fast or move on, because

I'm not giving up my male friends and I can't go on this way with you. Not if we're in this for the long haul."

Phil put a hand over Emma's and squeezed it against his face. "I want to marry you, Emma. You know that."

She nodded and pulled her hand away. "And I think about marrying you, but I can't if I feel you don't trust me. I don't plan on being divorced twice in my lifetime."

"Neither do I." He reached for her hand again, holding it in both of his. "You know, today was the first time since we've been together that you haven't greeted me with a kiss."

Emma started tearing up and looked away.

"Be honest with me, Emma. Have you already made up your mind?" When she didn't answer, he tried again. "Is it too late for us to fix this?"

In response, she leaned forward and planted a soft kiss on his lips. "No, Phil. It's not too late. Not by a long shot." She followed up with another kiss, this one a few seconds longer.

While Emma showered, Phil ordered their dinner through room service. Over dinner they discussed Dolly and the situation with Nemo and Lenny, steering clear of their personal problems. Not long after dinner, they turned in — Emma to her bed and Phil to the couch.

The text from Quinn came around four thirty, telling them to meet him in fifteen minutes on the third floor of the Venetian Hotel parking structure. They were ready and antsy to get moving. On their way out they made a quick detour to the food court to pick up breakfast and coffee for the road. They got to the designated spot just as Quinn pulled up in a shiny black Jeep Cherokee. Phil opened the front passenger door for Emma, then climbed into the back. Quinn started sucking down coffee before they were even on the road.

"It amazes me," said Emma, observing the brisk early morning traffic around the casinos as they made their way toward the highway, "how this town never sleeps."

"Many of these people probably haven't been to bed yet," laughed Quinn. "Or are coming to work at one of the hotels."

The ride out of town was uneventful with daylight just beginning to show itself. Emma dug into the bag they'd brought and handed Phil a wrapped item. She held one out to Quinn.

"What in the world is that?" he asked.

"A protein bar," Emma answered. "For

your breakfast."

"What? No egg and ham sandwiches? No cheesy croissants?"

"The coffee place didn't have anything like that ready yet. Besides, this is much better for you." She started unwrapping his for him.

Quinn glanced at it with a curled lip. "I eat those things when I'm tramping around out in the middle of nowhere. Doesn't mean I like them."

"As I recall," noted Emma, "we are tramping around in the middle of nowhere."

Phil leaned forward. "I'm with you on these things, pal. But you hang out with Emma, you eat protein bars." He chuckled and bit into his. "They're not bad with hot coffee."

Following the GPS, they traveled along a major highway shared by the 95, the 93, and Interstate 515 as it skirted the city of Henderson and made its way into the desert. To the left was a lone casino and hotel called Railroad Pass. Just past the hotel, the highway split off with the 95 going off to the right. Quinn followed it.

"Is this the Old Highway 95?" asked Emma.

"No. We're still on the newer road," he answered. "Since Lenny said if we hit Silver

Springs, we've gone too far and Silver Springs intersects both the old and new roads, I thought we'd turn at Silver Springs and backtrack on the old highway. Less chance of missing Jasper."

"Good idea," said Phil from the backseat.

"By the way," Quinn added, "back at that intersection, if we'd kept going on the highway, we'd be on our way to Dolan Springs."

"Really?" asked Emma, her voice swollen with interest.

"Yep. It's about an hour from here."

Phil leaned forward from the backseat. "You suggesting something, Quinn?"

Quinn shrugged. "Just throwing the information out there, seeing who salutes."

"It's very early," noted Emma. "We might be able to catch them by surprise."

"Armed with what," scoffed Phil, "our good looks?" He paused. "Then again, it might be worth a look."

"Let's shelve this until after we get the money," said Emma, her mind doing anything but letting the idea rest. "But it is something to consider."

Quinn glanced at Emma. "Did you tell Milo yet about Dolan Springs?"

"I texted him last night that we think we know where Dolly is and we're looking into it today." She took another drink of her coffee. "He texted back asking where, but I didn't tell him, just said we'd connect later today. I knew if I told him, he and Tracy would go running off to Dolan Springs with no thought to their safety."

"Or Dolly's," added Phil. "A surprise visit from any of us might backfire. We'll have to be very careful if we go."

Keeping her eyes on the landscape whizzing by, Emma nodded. "Granny did say last night that Frankie was armed."

Quinn looked in the rearview mirror at Phil "Phil, in the back right behind you, there should be a bag with some binoculars. Why don't you dig them out. They might be useful about now."

Phil undid his seatbelt and turned to reach in the back. When he faced forward again, he held a nice pair of binoculars. "Did you bring all that equipment with you to Las Vegas?"

"Survival store," Quinn answered. "There are a couple in Vegas and they're open late. Like I said, digging in the dirt is my specialty." Quinn turned to Emma. "I also bought something special for you."

"Bet I know which item that was." Phil turned around again and retrieved something else. He held it out to Emma. "Am I right?" he asked Quinn.

"You got it," answered Quinn.

Emma took the item, holding it carefully. "Is this what I think it is?"

"Sorry it's not pink," Quinn said with a chuckle. "They come in pink but survival stores aren't big on stocking pink anything."

"A Taser. More good thinking, Quinn." Phil looked at Emma. "I want you to keep that with you at all times, Emma. Especially when you make the exchange." He turned his attention back to Quinn. "You don't by chance have a handgun in there, do you?"

"Sorry," Quinn said with a shake of his head. "I'm not into guns myself, but I sure wouldn't mind having one right about now. Bet you could handle it."

"Been shooting all my life. I've even taken Emma here to the range a few times."

"Can we finish up the male bonding and get back to business?" Emma handed the Taser back to Phil. "Here, I don't want to even hold it. At least not until I know how to use it."

"Don't worry," Quinn said to her with a grin. "I'll show you. I bought one for my mother last year. Hers is pink."

It didn't take long before the Silver Springs turnoff came up. Quinn made a right-hand turn onto Silver Springs and almost immediately another right onto Old Highway 95, which almost joined at this point with the newer highway. With no other traffic around they were able to travel the older road slowly, keeping their eyes open for any sign of a road named Jasper or any unmarked road that might be it. Using the binoculars, Phil scanned the landscape for anything that might look promising.

"Okay," said Emma, pointing ahead. "This road here is Roger Ray."

They kept going. Soon after, they crossed an unmarked paved road. Quinn slowed down even more so Phil could take a good look at it through the binoculars. "That can't be it," said Phil. "It looks like it leads to some sort of business." Quinn moved the vehicle forward a little faster.

They passed another couple of unmarked but well-maintained short roads that also led to businesses of some kind. Two cars passed them going in the opposite direction and turned onto one of the roads. They continued on until they crossed Silver Line Road.

"I think we've gone too far," said Phil. "We're almost back to that casino."

"I think you're right." Quinn made a U-turn and they headed back south, taking it slower. When he got to the road where the cars had turned, he made a right. It appeared to be a quarry of some kind with a small parking lot. A man dressed in work clothes and carrying a lunch pail and Thermos was getting out of a beatup pickup truck. "When in doubt, ask a local."

Quinn pulled up next to the man. "Excuse me. We're trying to find Jasper Road. Do you know it?"

The guy was young but his face showed the wear and tear of working hard and out of doors. He nodded. "It's about a mile south on your right. Easy to miss because it's unmarked and nothing but dirt." He peered through the window at the three of them. "You hikers?"

"Sort of," answered Quinn. "I like to take photos of the desert in the morning and my friends here heard there's paranormal activity out that way."

"You mean like ghosts?"

"Yes, exactly that."

The guy shifted and glanced over his shoulder as if checking for nearby ghosts. "Yeah, I've heard the same. It's believed to be haunted by old Jasper Jenkins, a former construction worker on the Boulder Dam who holed up in a shack out there after the dam was finished. At least that's the local legend."

"So it's a dirt road a mile down on the right?" Quinn confirmed.

"Yep."

"Hey, thanks a lot."

The guy waved to them and started for the entrance to the quarry. Quinn headed down the drive back to Old Highway 95. "You ready to meet Jasper?" he asked Emma with a smile.

"Better than meeting a snake."

They drove down the old highway until they found a dirt road that was so little used it barely looked like a road at all. Quinn checked his odometer. "Just about a mile." He turned down it while Phil leaned forward and scanned the terrain for any sign of a structure. When the dirt road ended, Quinn kept the Jeep moving forwarded.

"There's something up ahead," Phil announced. "Just to our right."

They continued forward, stopping when they reached a pile of rubble. It was still too early for the sun, but a soft glow of daybreak spread over the desert and the hills beyond.

Emma got out of the Jeep and stretched while taking in the vast dry land spotted with cactuses and creosote. In the distance were brown craggy hills covered in the same type of vegetation. "It's so beautiful here. Not a peaceful beauty like in Julian with all the pine trees, but a stark, dangerous beauty." She scuffed the dirt with the toe of her sneaker. It felt like it hadn't seen water in decades. High above them two large black birds gracefully soared by.

Phil pointed at them. "They're looking for their breakfast. Lots of rodents in places like this." They watched for a few seconds, then walked to the back of the Jeep, where Quinn was pulling out small shovels. He handed one to Phil. "And here, I got us some work gloves, too."

Phil said thanks and slipped the gloves onto his hands.

"No gloves or shovel for me?" asked Emma.

"You won't need them," Quinn quipped. "The manual labor is our job. You just take care of the ghost stuff." He handed her a heavy-duty flashlight. "And be ready with this since we don't have good light yet."

When Emma looked to Phil for support, he said, "And I'm in total agreement with him. Just watch where you step and let us do the digging."

"Do you have Lenny's directions?" Quinn asked Emma.

"Yes, in my back pocket, but I also memorized them."

Quinn put on his own work gloves then

shut the back of the Jeep. "Then let's do this."

The rubble looked to be a wooden structure, or it had been at one time. The three of them looked it over. Phil poked around the base with his shovel, using it to push aside scraggly brush, being careful in case something was lurking underneath. "Doesn't look like much more than kindling now, does it?"

Quinn slowly walked around the perimeter of the dilapidated shack. "I sure hope Lenny didn't hide the money inside this pile of rubble."

Emma shook her head. "He told me it was buried under a rock at one of the corners."

"This looks to be what's left of the door frame," said Phil, still examining with his shovel. With the tip, he began tracing the fallen wood heading away from the door, going over the ground and around scrub brush, hoping to find a corner. "I think this is a corner, but there's no rock."

"There are two piles of rocks back here," Quinn told them. "Pretty evenly spaced, too."

Emma and Phil joined Quinn. Emma shined the flashlight along the base of the structure in the back so they would see it better.

"This was probably a single-room shanty," continued Quinn. "Old Jasper might have used the rocks to bolster the corners. At one time, he might have outlined the shack with them to discourage animals from digging under the wood and coming in."

Quinn put his shovel under one of the larger rocks at one corner. "Stand back," he told them, "in case something slithers out."

Emma didn't like the sound of that one bit. She took several steps back but kept the light trained on the area. As Quinn raised the rock, several lizards scattered in all directions.

Working together, Quinn and Phil used their shovels to move the rocks out of the way, then began digging where the pile had been.

"Any idea how far down he might have buried it?" Sweat beaded on Phil's bald forehead as he worked. The desert floor was hard and dry, making the digging difficult.

"I hope he had the sense to bury it a little deep or in something secure," said Quinn, scooping another shovel. "Otherwise rodents might have chewed through the money."

"It's at the other corner," came a voice to their left. "In a metal box."

Emma turned to see the hazy outline of

Lenny Speidel watching the men work.

"Lenny's here," Emma told them. "He said it's buried at the other corner in a metal box." She turned to the ghost. "I'm glad you're here, Lenny. It will make it easier to find it."

"I should have told you right off," the ghost said, its voice filled with remorse. "I should have told you the first day I met you at Doll's place. Maybe Nemo wouldn't have grabbed her."

Phil and Quinn stopped digging and went to the other back corner of the shack. Again, Quinn carefully started moving rocks out of the way and again there was a scurry of small reptiles.

"It's under the rock next to the biggest one," directed Lenny. Emma passed the direction along to Phil and Quinn. Phil stuck his shovel under the rock indicated and slowly pried it up and moved it away from the area. Then both he and Quinn took turns shoveling dirt.

"I hit something," announced Quinn when his shovel hit something hard. He tapped the end of his shovel downward and was rewarded with a metallic echo.

He and Phil worked until they uncovered a box the size and shape of a briefcase. Once they had it uncovered, Quinn got down on

317

his knees and started clearing the dirt from around the edges of the box with his gloved hands. "Dig here on this side," he directed Phil.

Phil stuck his shovel where Quinn indicated, removing dirt from around the edge of the box in several spots. "Okay," Quinn told him, "I think I can grab it now." Using both hands, Quinn started wiggling the box free. He stopped just long enough to wipe the sweat dripping from his forehead into his eyes, then went back to it until he could lift the box out of its longtime residence.

"There's a lock on it," Quinn noticed. He looked up, focusing near Emma. "Hey, Lenny, don't suppose you have the key?"

Phil laughed. "Stand back." When Quinn got to his feet and moved away, Phil took a couple of powerful stabs at the lock with the edge of his shovel. On the third thrust the old lock gave way. Quinn bent down again and opened it.

"So this is what a million dollars looks like?" he said, giving a long whistle. "It's almost tempting to hit the road with it, isn't it?"

"But you can't!" yelled Lenny, his image spinning like a whirling dervish. "You have to save Doll."

"Calm down, Lenny," Emma told the

ghost. "Quinn's just kidding. Of course we're going to use it to help Dolly."

"Nice work, Emma and friends."

Emma turned toward the voice she was learning to hate. It was Nemo. He'd not even been dead forty-eight hours and he was already giving ghosts a bad name. He drifted over to them. "Nemo's here," she told Phil and Quinn.

Phil looked around. Emma pointed to where Nemo was hovering. "So, Nemo," said Phil to the spirit, giving him a smirk. "Are you going to haul this away right this minute? If so, be our guest. Just leave Dolly and Laura with us and we can all go home happy."

"He makes a good point, Nemo," responded Emma. "Here's the money. Let's make the exchange."

"I'd love to." Nemo floated around, moving closer to Emma. "But you see, we have a little problem. The Lady Laura is not working out, so you'll have to handle the communication between me and my sons."

"There is no way I'm doing that, Nemo." Emma stepped closer to the ghost, showing him she was not afraid.

"Then we have no way to make the exchange. I can't very well tell them where to meet you, can I?"

"Tell me where Dolly is. We'll go there with the money and make the exchange. This cash for both Dolly and Laura." She hesitated as a cold vibration shot through her. "You haven't hurt Laura, have you?"

Nemo waved Emma's question away with his hand, as if swatting a fly. "No, the girl is fine for now, though we are growing very impatient with her." Nemo considered Emma's suggestion. "Your suggestion is reasonable, but I have no way to discuss it with my sons. I really should run it by them since they are the ones whose necks are on the line."

Lenny was agitated. "Tell them where Doll is."

Emma put out a hand toward Lenny, indicating for him to calm down. To Nemo, she said, "But I thought you were in charge."

A wide smile crossed Nemo's lips. "I am. But once the money is in Gene and Howard's hands, they'll be running the family business. Gene's always had a hand in it. Howard is just now seeing its value." He winked at her. "Maybe then I'll rest in peace. I've earned it, don't you think?"

"You deserve to rot in hell!" screamed Lenny.

"Lenny," Emma said to the disturbed

ghost, "why don't you come back later. I've got this."

Lenny wasn't so sure, so Emma added, "See if you can find Granny. Tell her we've found the money and let her know this will be over soon." She gave Lenny a knowing nod, hoping the slightly dim-witted ghost picked up on it.

"No need," said Granny, materializing next to Phil. "I'm right here."

"Granny," Emma said with relief. "Glad you're here. Nemo wants me to be his communicator with his sons. He tells me Laura isn't working out." She turned her head away from Nemo and looked at Granny, giving her a slow wink, hoping to convey she had a plan. Granny, unlike Lenny, was sharp as a tack and could hold her tongue when needed. "I've asked him to tell us where Dolly is so we can make the exchange."

"But —" Lenny started. Before he could spill the beans about them already knowing about Dolan Springs, Granny scooted over to him.

"I know you're upset, Lenny. But let Emma handle this. She's dealt with snakes in the spirit world before." Granny gave Nemo the stink eye, which only made him laugh.

"You really need better help, Emma," the

old hood said. "Stick with me and my boys and you'll be able to do amazing things with amazing people. Much more exciting than that little cable show you have and this relic of a sidekick."

Granny crossed her arms and growled at Nemo.

"What's going on, Emma?" asked Phil.

"Nemo just offered me a job," she said, not taking her eyes off the ghost. "And offended Granny."

"And," Nemo continued, "you'll meet men more worthy of your beauty and talents."

"And he just offended you," she said to Phil.

Phil stepped forward and pointed at himself with the hand not holding the shovel. "Me?"

"Well, both you and Quinn," she answered with a small smile. Quinn straightened up and stood shoulder to shoulder with Phil.

Granny fumed at Nemo. "Both of those men are honest and decent and dignified. Something you know nothing about."

"Simmer down, Granny," Emma said. "They're big boys, they can take it."

"If you're through posturing, Nemo," Emma told the ghost, "let's get back to business. The money in exchange for Laura

322

and Dolly and they must be unharmed. Just tell us where."

"Call Gene," Nemo finally said after a few seconds' thought. "He'll set up the meeting."

"I have his number."

"Not his office," said the ghost. "Call his cell."

Emma pulled her phone out of her pocket. As Nemo gave her the number, she punched in the digits to save for later. Done, she looked at Nemo. "And what if he doesn't believe we've had this little chat? Maybe he'll think it's a setup."

A slow, oily smile leaked out of Nemo's face. "You are so smart, Emma. Always thinking of everything." Nemo paused, then said, "Tell Gene you want waffles for dinner."

"Waffles for dinner?"

"That's what I said." And Nemo disappeared.

CHAPTER TWENTY-SIX

"Waffles for dinner?" Phil swiped an arm across this sweaty forehead. Even though the sun was still low, it was growing warmer in the desert. "What in the hell was that about?"

"Some sort of code," Emma explained. "Probably a family joke. I'm supposed to say it to Gene Garby so he'll know I've spoken to Nemo."

Emma looked around. Besides Granny and Lenny, she spotted another ghost standing several yards off from them. The spirit was difficult to make out at first in the growing light, then slowly it came into focus. It was the ghost of an old man with long hair and a beard; he was dressed in dirty old work clothes.

"Who do you suppose that is?" asked Granny.

"I'm betting that's Jasper Jenkins, Granny. The man who lived in this shack many years ago. We were told he once worked on the Boulder Dam." Emma gave the ghost a friendly wave. Phil and Quinn looked off in the same direction but saw nothing, something they were used to.

"Mr. Jenkins," Phil said, saluting the ghost he couldn't see. "Hello." Quinn followed suit and waved in the same direction.

"We've come in peace, Mr. Jenkins," Emma told the ghost. "We're taking something that belongs to someone else, but not disturbing your home. I hope that's all right."

The ghost gave them a single solemn nod, then disappeared.

"He's gone now," Emma told the men. "Let's get the box to the Jeep and cool off, especially you Phil. Neither of you brought hats."

"Yeah," Phil said. "I miss my cowboy hat. Didn't think I'd need it in Vegas." He laughed. "Who knew I'd end up digging around in the desert." Pulling off a glove, he retrieved a handkerchief from a pocket and swiped it over his bald head. "Can't imagine what it's like out here in the middle of the day and it's not even June. Much hotter than the high desert at home, I'm sure."

"I also brought a small case of water," said Quinn as he lifted the box for transport to the Jeep.

"You need a hand with that?" Phil offered.

"Nah, it's not that heavy, just bulky. But grab my shovel and get the hatch, will ya?"

The three of them, along with Granny and Lenny, made their way around the shack back to the Jeep, where Quinn stashed the metal box in the back. He took off his own gloves, grabbed bottles of water, and passed them around. After taking a big drink, Phil doused his handkerchief with water and mopped his head, face, and neck. Quinn grabbed a small towel from the backpack and did the same.

"You even bought a towel?" Phil asked. "I'm impressed."

"It's a hand towel I grabbed from the hotel. You just never know. I have a couple of others here, too, if you want one." He handed one to Phil.

Emma smiled to herself as she watched the two interact, knowing Phil was making a huge effort to put aside his natural instinct to compete with Quinn for the female of the species.

After stashing the equipment in the back of the Jeep with the box, Quinn asked, "Now what? Call Gene and set up a meeting? Or head to Dolan Springs?"

Not wanting to say too much in front of

Lenny, Emma turned to him. "Lenny, why don't you rest and recharge. We might need you later."

"But I need to help Doll."

"And you did by showing us where the money is," Emma assured him. "Right now we need to think about our next move. Why don't you try to connect back with me later? Or why don't you try to connect with Dolly and keep her company?"

"I've tried," Lenny said with frustration. "I just can't seem to locate her like Granny can. I only seem to find you and Doll's house."

Emma wasn't surprised. She'd learned long ago that most ghosts never develop keen instincts like Granny. As much as they try, they are very limited to who they can contact and where they show up. It's another reason why ghosts tend to haunt specific places. Sometimes they choose to remain in one place; other times it's their individual limitations that keep them bound to certain people and locations. Emma had a theory that it was relative to their intelligence when they were alive. Not education, but raw intelligence and the ability to think and concentrate. Lenny seemed well intentioned but definitely not overly bright, which surprised Emma, considering Milo's considerable intelligence. Nemo, on the other hand, was very smart and quick. Although just a baby ghost, he managed to make contact with her almost at will. Emma reminded herself to be careful about that.

"Why don't you go back to Dolly's, then," she suggested to Lenny, "and keep Milo and Tracy company. Milo's your son and needs comforting. I'm sure with some effort the two of you can communicate. Wouldn't you like that?"

Lenny nodded. "Yes. I would. I'd like to ask his forgiveness." He looked at Emma with deep sadness. "Do you think he can forgive me for everything?"

"Milo is a very kind and open-minded man," Emma said with an encouraging smile. "I think he will."

As soon as Lenny was gone, Emma turned to Granny. "Nemo seems adept already at being a spirit. I'm worried about him popping up when we're making our plans and overhearing."

"He has caught on quickly," Granny agreed. "But he doesn't seem to be able to control how long he stays. He uses up a lot of his energy quickly with all his gabbing and posturing."

Emma laughed. "He is quite a blowhard, isn't he?"

"Back at the house, he'll pop in, fade, pop in, fade. It takes him several tries before he sticks it. I think that's one of the reasons Laura is having so much trouble communicating. He sticks it better with you. I think that's because your energy is strong and keeps him grounded longer."

Emma pulled out her phone again and texted Milo.

"Who are you texting?" asked Phil. While Emma and Granny talked, he and Quinn had taken a seat on the edge of the Jeep's open hatch, drunk their water, and tried to keep up with Emma's half of the conversation.

"Milo. I just sent Lenny back to Dolly's to try to connect with him. I want Milo to know that so he'll try to make the contact. A little father-son bonding wouldn't hurt either of them, and it'll keep Lenny out of our hair."

"As well as keep Milo out of things?" asked Quinn.

She kept typing. "Yes, at least for the time being. I'm also letting Milo know we have the money and are trying to make the exchange."

"When you're done gabbing on that contraption," Granny said to Emma, "let me know what I can do."

Emma finished her text to Milo and turned to the ghost. "Continue to watch Dolly and Laura. If anything happens, find me. The three of us need to make a plan."

"Okay," Granny said, "but I'm staying away from Laura. She started babbling to me last night. I'm worried she might blow my cover."

"Use your best judgment, but stay close and let me know if you learn anything important. I'm hoping we can set up the exchange early today and get this over with."

"Gotcha." Granny disappeared.

"And what about us?" asked Quinn. "What are our marching orders?"

Emma started for the passenger door. "I say we head back to that casino. I need to use the ladies' room, and I'm not about to squat in the desert with a modern facility so close by."

By the time Emma came out of the ladies' room, she was ready to face whatever was thrown her way. She'd freshened up, even applying a little lipstick. As soon as they arrived at the casino, all three of them had ducked into the public restrooms, agreeing to meet afterward in the twenty-four-hour restaurant. Phil and Quinn were already seated when she came out. Mugs of hot coffee and glasses of orange juice were already on the table.

"Did you order my omelet?" she asked Phil as soon as she was seated.

"They didn't have a veggie one," he reported, "so I ordered you an omelet with tomatoes and mushrooms and no cheese. Sound good? And I asked for fruit instead of hash browns."

"Perfect. I'm starving." She took a sip of her juice. Before she could take another, the food was served and they fell upon it like a pack of hungry wolves, not stopping to talk until they were half done.

Quinn spoke first. "When I mentioned grabbing breakfast when we got here, I was afraid you'd toss me another protein bar." He cut another bite of his steak and eggs before pointing his fork at Emma. "If you had, I might have dumped you and driven off."

"Not without me you wouldn't have," added Phil, taking a bite of his ham steak. Emma eyed Phil's plate. "I know, I know," he said after swallowing. "Ham and whole real eggs." He jerked his chin at Quinn. "What can I say, he's a bad influence." He cut another piece of ham. "My cholesterol and sodium are spiking with every delicious bite."

Quinn laughed. "I may eat what I like, but I don't have a woman who cares enough about me to bitch about it. Eating sprouts and tofu is a small price to pay, I'd say."

"She has yet to shove tofu down my throat," answered Phil, sawing off another big bite of the grilled ham.

"Not that you know of," said Emma, giving Phil a sly look as she took a bite of toast. She was very pleased. Not only was Phil becoming more relaxed around Quinn, but they seemed to be forming a genuine friendship.

After a few more bites, Phil pushed aside his plate. "Quinn and I were talking. What's to stop Nemo from double-crossing you and killing off Dolly and Laura anyway? You should make sure they are at the exchange."

"I was wondering that myself," Emma said, looking down at her half-eaten omelet.

"Since we all know about the Garbys and Frankie," Quinn pointed out, "we're also sitting targets. The Garbys aren't going to let any of us walk away, knowing what we know."

With her fork, Emma played with a small pile of chopped tomatoes. "It's a major concern." She looked up at the men. "But the Garbys don't know we know about them. Or about Frankie. As far as Detective

Garby knows, we're concerned about Dolly and claim to have met Lenny Speidel's ghost. There's no way he or his brother can know we're on to them being Nemo's sons or involved in this." She took a drink of coffee before continuing. "They can't talk to Nemo directly, and it sounds like Laura isn't being much help. Nemo knows what we know, but he can't convey that to his sons and their hired goons."

"But if you call Gene Garby, then he'll know." Quinn leaned back in his chair. "Only that Gloria Youngblood knows we know, and I doubt she'll talk to anyone."

"Exactly," confirmed Emma. "If I make that call to set up the exchange, it will tip the Garbys off to what I know, especially if I give them that code phrase."

"Sounds like we're holding the better card hand at the moment." Phil snatched a strawberry from Emma's fruit bowl and popped it into his mouth. "They want the money. We want the hostages. They don't know we have the money. And Nemo can't tell them or give them the order to kill the women. The only fly in the ointment is if the Garbys get restless and kill them anyway because they know too much."

Emma looked at her watch. "It's almost seven thirty. Do you think it's too late to storm Dolan Springs?"

"It'll take an hour to get there," answered Quinn. "But it couldn't hurt to drive out there and see if we can find that mobile home."

Emma dabbed her mouth with a paper napkin. "I'm also wondering if it's time to bring in John Foster. Nemo told me he's not a part of this."

Phil wasn't so sure. "But he might have his own agenda, considering his personal connection."

"True, but I think we're at a point where we need help." She looked at Quinn. He stared at her a moment, then nodded his agreement.

She turned to Phil. He sighed and said, "You might be right. We can't go up against armed criminals with just a couple of shovels and a Taser. It would be suicide. Just be careful what you tell him."

Emma pulled out her cell phone and Detective Foster's card and placed the call to his cell phone. "Hi," she said when he answered. "It's Emma Whitecastle. I think I know where Dolly Meskiel is being held." She listened, then said, "No, don't call Howard Garby. I have reason to believe he's involved. Don't call anyone." Pause. "Yes, that's right. I'm asking you to trust me on this, Detective. I also know you're related to the people who once owned the Lucky Buck Casino, so while you're trusting me, I'll have to trust you. Meet me, but come alone and not in a police car." Emma told him where she was. "I'm out here following up on a tip from a spirit."

"I noticed you didn't say *we* in that conversation," said Quinn after she ended the call.

"I don't want him to know you two are with me. I'll initially meet him alone while you make sure he didn't bring company. Once it's clear, we can all get together."

"It's going to take him at least thirty minutes to get here, maybe longer," Quinn noted. He caught the attention of the waitress and waved his coffee mug at her. She came over and refilled all their mugs.

Emma held her warm mug and chuckled. "This is exactly the type of cloak-and-dagger stuff Granny loves. Too bad she's not here."

"Can you contact her?" asked Quinn.

"I'll try." Emma put down her coffee, closed her eyes, and concentrated. In seconds she forgot about where she was. The coffee shop ceased to exist as she floated, at peace and carefree.

I must be tired and falling asleep, she

thought, but didn't do anything to shake herself out of it. She went from floating to standing in the middle of a street. She didn't know how she got there. It didn't feel like she'd been dropped. One minute she was light and airy, and the next on solid ground standing in the middle of a narrow street in the desert. In front of her was a small house. No, it wasn't a house. It was a mobile home. An old double-wide, white with green shutters, with rust along its edges. Parked parallel to the street in front of the trailer was an old black pickup truck. Emma moved to her right to study the side of the trailer partially blocked by the tail of the truck. Near the back, she spotted a set of weathered wooden steps that led from the ground up to a door. Moving to the other side of the trailer, she took note of a silver Honda Accord parked in a carport under a canopy. Off to the left of the back of the carport was a small shed, or more of a lean-to, under which lidded garbage cans were kept. Another set of steps lead from the carport up to the mobile home. There was no sight of anyone, not driving on the street or stirring on foot. She looked around and saw no homes, mobile or otherwise nearby, except for a single structure far down the road on the left.

She walked up the steps on the side with the vehicle and entered without opening the door. Inside a fat man was snoring on the couch. In a recliner, a younger man was also asleep.

"Emma, what are you doing here?"

Emma turned and smiled. It was Granny. "I've come to fetch you, Granny. We need you. Is Dolly okay?" In answer, Granny took her into a room where Dolly was sound asleep.

"Emma." Someone shook her. "Emma, it's Phil. You nodded off."

Emma opened her eyes. She wasn't in the middle of a street or in a mobile home, but sitting in a coffee shop with Phil and Quinn. The sounds of slots machines drifted in through the door.

She looked at Phil and shook her head. "How long was I . . . how long was I out?"

"Just a couple of minutes," said Quinn.

"I wasn't sleeping," she told them. "I saw the mobile home. I saw where they're holding Dolly. Granny was there. *I was there.* I was inside and I saw Dolly."

"And now we're here," said the ghost, who was standing next to her. Granny studied Emma with concern. "That was pretty spooky. One minute I heard you calling to me. The next minute you were inside the trailer with me. You haven't done that before, have you?"

"No," Emma told her. She looked at Phil. "It was sort of like what happened with that ghost Addy. Remember?"

He nodded with great concern. "Yes, you became her in your mind and saw her past."

"Yes, but this time I was in the present. I wanted to find Granny and ended up going to her instead of calling her to me." She looked at Granny, fear and confusion bubbling up inside her along with the acid from the orange juice. "Granny, was I a spirit of some sort?"

"No, at least not like I am. I didn't really see you, Emma, I just knew you were there. Like your mind was there, but not your body."

Emma picked up her water glass and drained it, taking a minute to shake off the weird feeling in her body, like she'd passed through some door into another dimension. It was definitely something she'd have to ask Milo about.

She forced her mind to clear and stay focused. "We've got to get ready to meet John Foster." She turned to Granny. "He's coming here to help us. Or so I hope. When he arrives, I need you to spy on him and make sure he's alone and not up to something. Phil and Quinn will also be watching. Foster thinks I'm here alone."

"You got it, Chief," Granny said.

"And Laura and Dolly are okay, right?"

"Right as rain for now," the ghost reported, "except we need to end this as soon as possible."

"Why do you say that?"

Granny looked worried. "Just a feeling I get. If I were alive, I'd say I have the heebee-jeebees. I just think if we don't get them out of there soon, we never will."

Quickly, Emma told the men what Granny said, then replied, "It's the same feeling I'm getting, Granny. That we're all getting."

CHAPTER TWENTY-SEVEN

Emma read the text: *He's here. Blue Prius. Def. NOT a patrol car.* It came across the screen from Quinn's phone to both Phil and Emma. Quinn was in the far end of the parking lot in the rented Jeep with the binoculars, keeping a look out for Foster, checking out every vehicle that pulled into the casino lot. There weren't many at this early hour, he'd reported earlier — just one car and a Pink Jeep Tours van — before Foster came along. *Appears alone,* came the next text. The plan called for Quinn to stay in the parking lot, keeping a lookout for any vehicles that were following Foster as backup.

Phil was positioned near the front door, sitting on a bench, pretending to read the morning paper. On his head was a baseball cap with *Boulder Dam* embroidered across the front, which they'd bought in the gift shop. They didn't worry about Phil being seen by Foster. Foster hadn't met him yet, so didn't know his face. He appeared to be simply a middle-aged man waiting on his wife before they started their day of sight-seeing. Phil's job was to make sure Foster was alone and follow him into the casino when he entered to meet with Emma.

Granny was with Quinn in the Jeep. Even though he couldn't see or hear the spirit, as soon as he spotted Foster, he would point him out to Granny. Her job was to go to him and eavesdrop, just in case he was communicating with backup. She would stick to him like glue all the way to Emma, reporting to her anything out of order. Granny had tried to get a bead on Foster earlier, hoping to be in the car with him the entire drive. Not being able to make the connection, she had to settle for limited sleuth time. The crime drama–loving ghost was beside herself with excitement at being included.

This was Emma's backup. Her posse. The people who had her back, front, and sides, and who would make sure Foster did what he promised — come alone. Emma herself was seated in the coffee shop. She'd moved from their table to one by an emergency exit, just in case she needed to make a hasty one. In that event, Quinn would run the

Jeep to the back of the building and pick her up. She'd avoided the booths, considering them awkward to get in and out of if she needed to make that quick getaway. It wasn't a foolproof plan, but it was all they had.

Foster coming, Quinn texted. *No gun spotted but he's wearing his shirt loose.*

A minute later Emma saw John Foster enter the restaurant. She didn't wave to him, but let him find her. He wasn't wearing a suit, but jeans and a light blue golf shirt, worn loose as Quinn had said. He was unshaved. Dressed as he was, he looked younger than he had the day before. His walk was confident but not cocky. He spotted Emma and made his way to her, threading between tables to reach her. Only two other tables were occupied, both by older couples. They were across the room in front of the large window facing the highway.

"Emma," he said, coming to a stop in front of her. "You made a serious accusation about my partner. I hope it's not unfounded."

"Have a seat, Detective." Emma indicated the chair opposite her. "We have a lot to discuss and not a lot of time to do it."

Before he was situated, Phil showed up, politely removing his cap before taking his seat. "This is my friend Phil Bowers," Emma told Foster. "He'll be joining us. He's a lawyer."

"Do you need a lawyer, Emma?" Foster asked, his mouth tight as he said the words.

"No, but they're always handy to have around, don't you think?"

"Did Dr. Keenan go home?"

Emma didn't answer the question, but instead glanced at Granny. "He's clean as a whistle," the ghost reported. "No calls to or from anyone. Not even one of those text thingies."

Satisfied, Emma began the meeting. Without going into all the details, she told Foster about Gene and Howard Garby.

"Yeah," Foster said with a shrug. "I know they're brothers." A waitress came over and Foster ordered coffee. Emma had had enough coffee and asked for some water. Phil ordered nothing.

"Did you know that they are also the sons of Nelson Morehouse?"

From the genuine surprise on Foster's face, Emma could tell Foster didn't have a clue about that.

"Nemo's sons?"

"Yes," Emma told him. "Nemo told me himself."

"His ghost told you they were his sons."

Foster shifted in his seat. From his posture, Emma could tell he wasn't taking her seriously. "I know my partner's life story," Foster told her. "He was raised right here in Boulder City. His father was Elmore Garby. His parents retired to Florida a few years ago."

Emma nodded. "They were adopted by a man named Garby when their mother married him, but they are Nemo's sons and are in contact with him."

"You mean *were* in contact with him." Foster leaned forward. "As you'll recall, Nemo died."

"They are still in contact with him, or at least trying to be. Just this morning, Nemo tried to hire me to be the medium between them."

Foster looked at Phil, who only nodded.

"I know this sounds fantastic, Detective," Emma said, keeping her voice low, "but hear me out."

After giving it several seconds of thought, Foster indicated for her to continue.

"Nemo and his sons are trying to locate the money stolen from the Lucky Buck Casino. You know, the casino once owned by your family." Her last words were laced with accusation.

"I know the story."

344

"Lenny Speidel and Nemo worked together on the heist, but afterward, Lenny hid the money and wouldn't tell Nemo where. Nemo's goons killed him and got rid of the body. Nemo is a big believer in mediums like myself and so is his son Gene. They hatched a plan for Nemo to contact Lenny on the other side once he was dead."

"Nemo was quite sick," Foster noted, "but he could have lingered for months."

"With Nemo's permission, they had Frankie Varga kill him. The plan was for Nemo to get Lenny to tell him where the money was and then use a medium to communicate the information to his sons. That's where Laura Crawford comes in."

"That's the girl with the fortune-telling wagon on Fremont Street, right?"

"Yes."

Foster poured milk into his coffee. "We followed up on your story. She did go missing in the last day or two, just like you said."

"Nemo has her. Or rather his people do. We know he's working with Frankie Varga. There's another guy, too. Kind of a sloppy, dumpy guy, but we don't know who he is."

Foster fiddled with his mug but didn't drink from it. "Frankie seems to be MIA also. He took a few days off after Nemo died, but no one can find him."

"He's with Dolly and Laura," Phil chimed in. "Armed and holding them."

Foster started to raise his mug to drink, but halted it halfway. "Where?"

"Dolan Springs, Arizona," answered Emma.

"In one of them movable houses," added Granny. "Tell him that."

"They're stashed in a mobile home in Dolan Springs," Emma clarified.

"Did Nemo tell you this, too?" ask Foster.

Emma couldn't tell if Foster was believing her or humoring her. "No, he didn't. He doesn't know we know. We figured it out just by asking questions and putting the pieces together. But Nemo did say that unless Lenny gave up the Lucky Buck cash, they would die. Laura isn't working out as planned, so I'm supposed to call Gene Garby and set up the exchange."

Foster nearly dropped his coffee. "You have the money stolen from the Lucky Buck?"

Under the table, Phil squeezed Emma's knee, which she took for a proceed-with-caution signal. "No, I don't have it, but I know where it is."

"We don't think," added Phil, "that Nemo and his boys will release Dolly and Laura unharmed even if they get the money."

"Nemo even taunted Lenny about it," Emma added. "Said there was a fifty-fifty chance Dolly would live even if he got the money, but a hundred percent chance she wouldn't if he didn't get it."

"That's one of the reasons we called you, Detective," Phil continued. "We need to figure this out and rescue the women. We didn't feel we had the best chance on our own."

"I'm glad you did call," Foster told them, his eyes fixed on the window and the view of the highway in the distance. "To be honest, Howard has been acting odd lately, even for him." He looked back at Emma. "But why would he do something like this? Why would he throw away a solid career?"

"According to Nemo," Emma explained, "Howard is upset because you were brought in from the outside in a position above him."

Foster sighed and took a drink of his coffee. "Yeah, I know he resents that. He hasn't even tried to hide it. But that wasn't my fault. They were never going to promote him. If it wasn't me, it would have been someone else. Police departments now are looking for college graduates with backgrounds in computers and forensic science, even psychology. Howard's good at his job but stuck in time and with bad people skills.

He's been so belligerent lately, he's even picked a few fights with other cops."

Emma believed that after meeting Detective Garby. "Right now the Garbys do not know that we're on to them or that we know about Dolan Springs. Nemo wants me to call Gene to set up the exchange, but if I do, then he'll know for sure that I know who he is and it will put not only those women, but me and my friends, in jeopardy." She leaned forward, arms on the table to get closer to Foster. "Frankly, I don't give a damn about the money," she hissed, "but I'm not about to let two women go to their deaths without trying to do something."

Phil also leaned forward. "Question for you, Detective: Are you also on the hunt for the casino money?"

Foster leaned back in his seat and rubbed a hand over his face. "I heard the story of the robbery many times growing up. It's what started my interest in that era of Vegas as a kid, but I always thought Speidel double-crossed Morehouse and took off with the cash, which is what everyone thought." He looked Emma in the eye. "I never considered Speidel being murdered by Nemo until you mentioned his ghost yesterday."

Foster leaned forward again. "You say

there's another guy with them, a kind of slobby young guy? Kind of fat?"

Emma looked to Granny and she nodded. "At first I thought he was older, but now I'm of a mind he's closer in age to Frankie. He has brown thinning hair and a skimpy mustache." Emma relayed the description to the detective as if it were her own observation.

"That could be Lloyd Garby, Gene's son," said Foster, again playing with his mug. "I've met him a few times. Not a very bright kid. Can't keep a job. He's been arrested a few times on minor drug charges." Foster scoffed. "Howard calls his nephew Baby Huey, you know like the old cartoon character. Lloyd is one of those fanatic comic book collectors. Spends all his money on them."

"My first night here I went to see Laura at her wagon. There was a young man standing behind me reading a comic book. He fits the description to a T and was probably Lloyd Garby. That was right before Laura went missing. Of course, at that time I didn't know yet who he was or anything about Nemo, except that Lenny's ghost was trying to warn me about him."

Foster looked at her with suspicion. "Then how did you know about him?"

Granny put her hands on her hips and

squared off with Foster. "Because I told her, copper."

"Granny told me," Emma confessed. "She's been keeping an eye on Dolly and Laura at the place where they're being held. She described them and I remembered seeing that guy at Laura's."

"What a minute," said Foster, his tone changing. "You said you pieced together information, but it was really a ghost who told you about Dolan Springs?"

"Granny didn't know about Dolan Springs," answered Phil. "Not specifically. Emma told you the truth. We did piece it together from information she and Quinn gathered."

"But I remembered the pizza place," squawked Granny, not pleased that her efforts were being omitted.

"Granny was simply keeping watch on the women," Emma reiterated. "She kept us posted on how they were doing. We found the town, but she told us it was a mobile home and she identified Frankie Varga and described the other guy. Granny was at Desert Sun while Dolly was visiting Nemo. When Dolly left, Nemo was still alive."

"But how do you know Varga killed him?"

Emma squirmed. She couldn't give up Gloria Youngblood but needed Foster to

350

believe the information was authentic. "Someone at the home overheard Gene and Frankie talking about killing Nemo and told me."

"Someone?" inquired Foster. "As in another ghost?"

Then Emma thought about Bert. No harm could come to him. She'd simply imply he'd told her everything. "Someone saw Nemo alive when Dolly left and Nemo dead shortly after with Gene and Frankie in the room with him. That coupled with what was overheard indicates they killed Nemo. And Nemo himself told me he was close to death, so he and Gene cooked up a plan to end his life sooner so he could go after Lenny and the money."

Foster looked at Phil. "You know testimony from ghosts will not hold up in a courtroom, don't you?"

"You'd probably need a confession," Phil agreed. "But our concern is the safety of those women. You're the one who is going to have to figure out how to put those creeps away for good."

"So you believe us?" asked Emma.

Foster scratched his morning beard. "I don't know what I believe. My son sees ghosts. You see ghosts. Ghosts are telling tales of murder and stolen money." He drained his coffee. "But I do believe Dolly Meskiel and Laura Crawford are missing and that you are hell-bent on finding them. And if I don't at least look into what you're saying and they come to harm, I'd never forgive myself." He studied Emma. "After we met yesterday, I looked you up, Emma Whitecastle. You're famous, well connected, and well respected. Except for some footage of a public brawl with your ex-husband, you have a spotless reputation."

"That wasn't a public brawl," Emma insisted, getting defensive. "It took place in the driveway of my parents' home and Grant got rough with me first. It was caught on tape by a sleazeball photographer following Grant."

For the first time since arriving, a small smile crept across Foster's lips. "I also looked up Dr. Quinn Keenan. Interesting guy — archeologist who travels all over the world and sometimes lectures. Kind of like a modern Indiana Jones."

"See," said Granny with a smirk. "I'm not the only one who thinks that."

Foster turned to Phil. "And what will I find if I look you up, Mr. Bowers?"

"I'm a rancher turned lawyer with long-time roots in Julian, California, and a thriving law practice in San Diego. Look all you want, Detective, I've got nothing to hide. Not even a parking ticket."

Foster laughed. "The three of you are like that old TV show *The Mod Squad,* just with better educations and a higher-income tax bracket."

Phil stabbed the table with an index finger, making a sound thud with each jab. "Julie, Linc, and Pete always solved the crime, and so will we, with or without your help."

Foster picked up the menu the waitress had left on the table. "Fair enough. But do you mind if I eat while we hash out a plan? I was up at dawn taking my wife and son to the airport."

While Foster ordered breakfast, Emma texted Quinn to join them.

CHAPTER TWENTY-EIGHT

"Police service for Dolan Springs is provided by the Mohave Sheriff's Department out of Kingman," Foster told them as he salted his over-easy eggs. "That's about twenty miles from there. I could give them a call but it might put the ladies in greater danger."

"Yeah," agreed Quinn. "They'd surround the trailer with drawn guns and we'd find ourselves in a standoff and the women with guns to their heads?"

"I think this is something we need to do on our own," said Emma. She turned to Granny. "Go back out there, Granny, and see if it's still just Lloyd and Frankie on watch."

Emma pulled out her iPad as Granny took off.

"If it's just them," said Quinn, "maybe we can devise a plan to divert their attention long enough to get the women out of there."

Emma pulled up a map of Dolan Springs and showed it to Foster. "Laura told Granny they are on Ironwood." She pointed to a street on the enlarged map. "As you can see, there aren't many buildings along Ironwood. Frankie drives an old black compact pickup and the trailer is white with green trim. It shouldn't be too hard to spot."

"Problem is," noted Phil, "with so few buildings around, it will be difficult to sneak up on them."

"Phil's right," agreed Foster. "There's no place to take cover."

"As I said, we need a diversion," noted Quinn. "Something that might draw the guys out of the trailer without their guns. Or at least if they have them, they're not aiming them at anyone." Everyone nodded in agreement, their heads bobbing over the map like bobbleheads while they thought about it.

"How about running along the streets on either side," said Phil. "They don't look that far apart."

"No, they don't," agreed Foster. Using a finger, he measured the distance. "According to the legend, they're only about five to six hundred feet apart."

"I have an idea." The men all looked at Emma. She turned to Quinn. "I hope you have good insurance on that rental."

The drive to Dolan Springs would take about an hour. Emma would go with Foster in his Prius. Phil and Quinn would follow in the Jeep.

"I don't like this," Phil said, taking Emma aside as they filed into the parking lot to start the journey. "I'd rather one of us go with him, not you."

"You don't trust Detective Foster?" Emma asked.

"I want to, but you never know. He could still be hiding something."

She considered his words. "You might be right, but my gut says to trust him."

As they joined Foster at his vehicle, Quinn trotted up to them. He handed Emma the binoculars. "Take these. You'll need them to watch us. And take this." In his other hand was the Taser. He quickly showed her how it worked.

Foster checked out the Taser. "Not a bad idea."

Foster reached under his car seat and retrieved a square metal box.

"A gun safe in a Prius?" Phil asked.

Foster smiled as he worked the combination lock. "The Prius is my wife's car. Mine is in the shop, but I couldn't leave this with it." He opened the lid exposing a good-size handgun. "Any of you know how to shoot a gun?"

"Phil," answered both Emma and Quinn almost at the same time.

Foster looked at Phil and he nodded. "Own a couple, including rifles."

"Good." Foster handed Phil the weapon. "I have my service revolver. You take this. I'd feel better if both vehicles were armed going out there."

Foster made a call to his station and asked to speak to his captain. Emma started to protest, but he stopped her. "Trust me." He walked away. When the call ended, he paused and gave each of them a long hard look. "I just asked my captain to bring in both Gene and Howard Garby on suspicion of murder and kidnapping. I may not want a showdown in the desert, but we need to keep both of them under wraps until this is over. This will do it, providing they find them. Cap said Howard called in sick, which makes me suspicious."

"And your captain agreed?" Phil was incredulous.

"Like I said, Howard's not an easy guy to get along with, especially these days, and Cap is one of the people he's been rubbing the wrong way. If Howard's involved in this,

357

it might explain a few things. I asked my captain to give me a couple of hours before explaining further. He knows I like Howard and wouldn't be doing this without good reason." Emma started to move away to get into the car, but Foster grabbed her arm. "Not only is Arizona not in my jurisdiction, but I just put my entire career on the line. If you're playing me, I'll go down in flames."

Emma locked eyes with Foster. "I understand."

They stared at each other a few seconds longer before Foster said, "Let's roll."

Emma sidled up to Phil. "Do you feel better now about Foster?"

He checked out the gun in his hand and gave her a quick wink. "Much. But you still be careful and don't hesitate to use that zapper . . . on anyone. You hear?"

Phil escorted Emma to the front passenger's side of the Prius and opened the door for her. She started to climb into the car, then stopped. She straightened, wrapped an arm around his neck, and planted a long, hard kiss on Phil's lips. "You will *not* be sleeping on the sofa tonight, cowboy."

He chuckled. "Now that's what I call an incentive to get this wrapped up and quickly."

The road to Dolan Springs took them back down the 93 and through Boulder City. Foster pointed out Hoover Dam as they passed it. "Ever see it up close?" he asked. "It's a wonder. I brought Suzanne out here shortly after we moved to Vegas."

"Yes," Emma said. "When my daughter was around fourteen, she and I took the full tour of it."

"You were married to Grant Whitecastle then, weren't you?"

She nodded. "But he stayed in Vegas and hit the tables. That was his thing. The next day Kelly and I took a Grand Canyon tour, including a helicopter ride. We had a lot of fun."

"You just have the one kid?"

"Yes. She's a junior at Harvard. Hard to believe." She pulled her eyes away from the desert landscape and glanced at Foster. "Before you know it, Nicholas will be off to college, so savor each moment."

"I do. I love being with him. Kids are messy but fun."

"They're even messy when they're older; it's just a different kind of mess."

Emma's phone rang. It was Milo. "Hey, Milo. No," she lied, "nothing new to report. What are you doing?" Pause. "Okay, stay close to the phone, just in case."

"You haven't told Dolly's son any of this?" Foster seemed surprised.

"No. I'm not sure if that makes me a good friend or a bad friend."

Foster was silent for a bit, then said, "In this case, probably a good friend. He doesn't seem as equipped as you for handling emergencies."

"Milo's usually pretty calm and collected, but this thing with his mother has him pretty rattled. Finding out about his father hasn't helped. I was afraid he'd call the police or come to Dolan Springs himself."

"But you called the police," Foster pointed out.

"No, I called you. You called the police."

They exchanged looks.

"Reporting in, Chief." Granny materialized in the backseat. She looked around.

"Hey, Granny," Emma said, turning around. "Phil and Quinn are right behind us."

The car swerved slightly. "There's a ghost in here with us?" asked Foster, glancing around as much as he dared while driving.

"Yes," Emma answered, "Granny's back."

He shook his head. "I'm still not sure if I believe this stuff."

"You don't have to believe it to help."

Granny buzzed with excitement. "We

gonna break into the trailer like a SWAT team?"

"No, Granny, not like SWAT. But we do have a plan. We're hoping to get them to come outside." Emma turned again in her seat to look at Granny. "What's going on at the trailer?"

"Those two gave Laura and Dolly bathroom visits and some cereal, then settled in front of the TV with their own bowls. They're watching cartoons. But I'm glad we're heading there. I don't think we have much time."

Emma grew alarmed. "Why do you say that?"

"What's going on?" asked Foster.

"Hold on," Emma said to him.

"That Lloyd got a phone call. I think it was Gene Garby because he called him *Dad*. They must have been fighting because he was yelling into the phone."

"Could you tell what they were fighting about?"

"I got the feeling his father wants him to do something and he doesn't want to do it. And whatever it is, it's supposed to be done today. Then Frankie told him to shut up because he couldn't hear the TV. When Lloyd didn't stop yelling into the phone, Frankie turned up the TV until it was

361

deafening. I couldn't hear a thing, but neither could Lloyd. He finally walked over to the TV and shut it off, making Frankie mad, but he didn't do anything about it. I think it's because it was Gene on the phone. Those boys are like a cat and a dog forced to share the same cage."

Emma turned to Foster. "Granny says Lloyd and Frankie are getting on each other's nerves."

"Good," he answered, not taking his eyes off the road. "We might be able to use that; pit them against each other."

Emma turned back to Granny. "Were you able to tell what it was Gene wanted them to do?"

Granny, her face screwed up like a dried apple doll, tried hard to remember. "It had something to do with gasoline, I think. Lloyd kept saying he had the gas."

"Gasoline? Maybe he meant he'd gassed up the car for the trip to Las Vegas."

Granny wasn't so sure. "Maybe, but I don't think so. He said the gas was in the trunk of the car. That I'm sure I heard."

"Think harder, Granny," Emma urged.

"I'm trying. I'm trying." The ghost concentrated. "Lloyd kept saying he didn't want to hurt them. I think he meant Laura and Dolly. He said a couple of times that he didn't want to kill them. That they didn't have to die. Then he gave the phone to Frankie and that's when I got scared."

Emma's gut turned. It sounded like they were going to kill the women no matter what happened to the money. "So Frankie talked to Gene. What then?"

"He listened mostly, then told Gene not to worry, that he'd take care of it. And that was it."

"Nothing else?"

"Then Frankie told Lloyd he'd light the torch if Lloyd was too much of a kitty cat to do it."

Kitty cat. If Emma hadn't been so terrified, she would have found Granny's misunderstanding of the vulgarity amusing.

"Light the torch or torch the place, Granny? Exactly what did Frankie say?"

Granny looked confused. "Ain't they the same thing?"

"No, not exactly."

For a minute Emma thought she'd stopped breathing. "Hurry," she said to Foster. "I think they're going to burn down the trailer with the women inside."

Before they got to Dolan Springs, Emma called Phil and Quinn and told them what Granny had said. They were even more determined to go through with the plan.

Granny left to go back to Dolly and keep watch in the trailer.

"Aim for the black pickup," Foster cautioned Quinn over the speaker phone, "not the other car, just in case Granny's right about gas stored in that vehicle."

When they rolled into town, Emma gave Phil and Quinn directions from the map on her iPad. "We're on Pierce Ferry now," she told them. "When we get to Seventh Street, we'll take a right. When you get to Ironwood, which is one block past Iron Drive, take another right. We'll continue another block before turning right onto Ivy."

"Wow," said Quinn, "this really is out in the middle of nowhere."

"As flat as it is out here," continued Emma, "you should be able to see us traveling along Ivy parallel to you. Go slow, give us time to get behind the trailer before starting the action. The trailer should be easy to spot. There's almost no other buildings out here." She put down her iPad and picked up the binoculars.

It didn't take long before Foster and Emma passed Ironwood and made the turn onto Ivy. Her cell phone was still connected to the Jeep. "Okay," she said. "Up ahead on your left is a white trailer. Hang back until we give you the signal."

When they reached the trailer, Foster eased the Prius off of the road and onto the desert floor. Being careful to dodge rocks and prickly shrubs, he moved the compact car directly behind the trailer so no one could see it approaching from a side front window where the men were mostly likely holed up. There were windows in the back but they were closed and covered. The arthritic groans of an old air conditioner could be heard from a window near the front.

"You can hear the TV from here," Emma whispered. "There's no way they're going to hear us coming between that and the AC."

"I agree," Foster whispered back. "I wish I had my SUV for this terrain, but at least this car is quiet."

When they were directly behind the trailer, they stopped and quietly opened their doors and eased out. Emma had her Taser. Foster his gun. Turning to their right, they could see the Jeep. It was on Ironwood, slowly getting closer. Emma glanced at Foster. He gave her a nod. She raised her left hand in the direction of Quinn and Phil. A second later, an arm was extended out of the Jeep's driver's side, letting her know they could see her. She dropped her left arm fast, slicing the air like a starter at a race. The Jeep's engine gunned and sped up the street, aiming for the black pickup truck, which was parked right where Emma had seen it in her vision.

Emma and Foster watched as the Jeep came up the street, then swerved to the left, heading for the pickup. At the last minute it swerved right, tires screeching, the side of the shiny vehicle clipping the pickup along its side with a loud crash that vibrated through the still warm air. Emma held her breath, sure the Jeep would tip and Phil and Quinn would be seriously hurt. But it didn't tip — it spun fully around and came to a stop in the middle of the road.

Emma and Foster ducked behind the trailer as Lloyd and Frankie piled down the steps next to Lloyd's car and spilled into the street.

Granny popped out next to Emma. "Lloyd has a gun, but I think Frankie left his on the kitchen table," she reported.

Emma told Foster in a whisper, "Granny thinks only Lloyd has a gun." He nodded his understanding.

"My truck!" screamed Frankie when he saw the damage. "My truck!"

Most of the action was taking place on the side with the carport. Foster started for that side, taking cover behind the lean-to. He motioned for Emma to go around the other side of the trailer.

She could hear Frankie screaming obscenities and Quinn's voice raised in excitement, telling them it was an accident and he'd take care of everything. Quinn sounded drunk, but of course he wasn't. Emma wondered where Phil was. She couldn't make out his voice in the mix. Was he in the fray, or lying low in the Jeep, protecting Quinn from behind with Foster's extra gun trained on one of the thugs?

"Look," she heard Quinn say, "my friend might be hurt. I need to call an ambulance."

Emma's blood ran cold, not knowing if it was part of the ruse or if Phil really was injured.

"You're not calling anyone," she heard someone say. It must have been Lloyd.

"Come on, man," Quinn said. Emma listened to the tone of Quinn's voice, which was pleading but with an undertone of lazy casualness. It was definitely not his usual take-charge voice. She decided it meant Phil was okay and Quinn was playing his part. She breathed easier and continued with the plan.

Quickly and quietly, Emma went up the back steps, which were out of view of the street activity, and tried the door. Finding it unlocked, she entered and was immediately hit with a blast of cold air. She'd been right — between the TV and the AC, anyone could have snuck up on these two. The door opened to the kitchen area. Emma tiptoed deeper into the main part of the mobile home and noticed the door to the carport was located in the living room. The inside was a pigsty of takeout containers and pizza boxes, and smelled of stale food and dirty clothes. On the table, right where Granny had said it would be, was a gun — Frankie's gun. Emma started past it then, having second thoughts, picked it up. She didn't like guns any more than Quinn did, but she was now glad Phil had insisted that she know how to use one. Making sure the safety was on, she stuck it in her waistband. Better she have it than someone else.

Peeking out the side window, she saw the men facing off. The thin one, who she guessed was Frankie, was still screaming at Quinn, who was in the middle of the street by the turned Jeep trying to apologize. He was offering money, telling Frankie he'd take care of all the damage in cash so as not to involve his insurance company. She still couldn't see Phil. Lloyd was at the end of the carport watching the entire drama but not participating. The only voices were coming from Frankie and Quinn. She strained to see more, being careful not to make any movements that might attract attention. Lloyd had a gun in his hand, but it was down at his side. Something caught her eye by the window. It was John Foster. He'd left the lean-to and was moving step by step toward the street, keeping low and using Lloyd's car as cover.

"How in the hell did you get here?"

She whipped around and saw Nemo's ghost. He was standing in the hallway, blocking her way, his hazy countenance screwed with anger.

Good, Emma thought. Nemo doesn't know about Foster and what's going on outside.

"Down here, Emma." From the end of the hall, Granny waved to her.

"It's over, Nemo. Your scheme is finished and so are your sons." She trotted down the hallway, passing a dirty bathroom, going through the ghost of Nemo to reach Granny.

The door to Dolly's room was flimsy and locked using an old-fashioned hook lock fastened near the top. It was pretty rickety security, but it would hold up against an old woman. Emma unlatched the lock and opened the door. Dolly was crouched on a

369

dirty double bed. The room was hot, with only a fan for circulation. Across from the bed was another TV. This one was turned on to a game show. Dolly looked up at Emma, but her gaze wasn't focused.

"It's me, Dolly, Emma Whitecastle. I'm getting you out of here. Can you get to your feet?"

"Emma," the elderly woman finally said, clearing her head. "Thank God."

"Stay with her, Granny. I'll get Laura, then come back to help."

Granny nodded and stayed next to Dolly, who was trying to get to her feet while Emma dashed to the door directly across the hall. It had the same hook lock and in seconds Emma was inside. Like Dolly's room, it was hot with only a small fan moving the close air. Laura was sitting on the edge of a single bed, her long hair pulled back away from her damp scarred face into a ponytail. She looked up at Emma and a small smile crossed her lips. "I knew you would come. I've been waiting."

Nemo stood beside the bed. "I won't let you do this." He made a dash at Emma but just passed through her, just as Lenny had done to him the night before. A cold chill passed through Emma, like a damp draft in her bones, but she shook it off and went to Laura.

"Come on, Laura. We have to get out of here."

Like an obedient child, Laura got to her feet. Just as she stood, Nemo charged her, but his spirit didn't go through Laura Crawford. It entered her and disappeared. Just as quickly Laura's scarred face changed from sweet and obedient to defiant. "I won't let you ruin everything," she said, but it wasn't Laura's voice but the voice of Nemo Morehouse.

Laura started for the door, but Emma stopped her. "You're not going anywhere, Nemo."

Laura started yelling, "Lloyd, it's a trap! The cops are here!"

Even with the AC and TV noise, Emma was worried the men outside would hear Nemo's warning. She grabbed Laura's arm, dragging her away from the door, and shoved her onto the bed. Quickly, Laura got to her feet and charged the older, stronger, and taller Emma, screaming as she aimed for her and the door. Emma again pushed the girl back, slapping her hard. "Come out of it, Laura. Fight him off."

Granny came in. "What's going on?"

"Nemo's inside Laura, using her body.

Stay with Dolly until I come for her."

"No problem. She's a bit dizzy and having trouble standing." Granny disappeared to follow the order.

Again Laura charged, surprisingly strong from Nemo's borrowed rage. She slammed Emma against the wall, knocking free the gun. Emma punched and slapped the possessed Laura, trying to knock clarity into her mind and free it from Nemo's grasp, but the tiny medium only fought harder. Seeing the gun on the ground, Laura made a lunge for it, but Emma kicked it away. When Laura followed the gun and stooped to pick it up, Emma zapped her with the Taser.

Laura let out a guttural cry and fell to the ground. She twitched and shivered in pain, then went limp. Emma retrieved the gun. While she watched, Nemo's ghost left Laura's body.

"It's over, Nemo," Emma said to the ghost. "The police have your sons and shortly Frankie and your grandson will be in custody, too."

Nemo glared at her. "I underestimated you, Emma Whitecastle. I won't do that again."

"Come, Nemo." In the corner of the room the ghost of Madeline Kurtz materialized.

"Come with me." She held out her hand to Nemo. "Come where there's no hate or greed or anger. Come with me and find peace."

"But my boys!" Nemo's voice was full of anguish. He pointed at Emma. "She did this. She's responsible."

"No, she's not, Nemo. You are. It's time to let go of all this and put it behind you. Gene and Howard will have to find their own way. You can't help them. And you can't hurt them or anyone else anymore."

The ghost lowered his head. "It was for them. All this was for them. That money was their legacy. A chance for them to have whatever they wanted. Howard was going to retire to Florida near his mother. Gene wanted his own business. They were both leaving Vegas to start over."

"Come with me," Madeline urged in a soft voice. "For you, it's over."

Nemo looked up at Emma. When their eyes locked, she said, "Madeline's right. You can't do anything to save them." She looked at the old gangster, knowing she should provide words of comfort like Madeline. She usually did when speaking with tragic spirits, but Emma couldn't. Not this time. Nemo hadn't acted out of pain and loss as most angry spirits did. He'd been motivated totally by greed. "Go, Nemo," Emma told the ghost with authority, "and do not come back."

From the floor, Laura moaned and moved. Emma sighed with relief. She looked up at the ghosts in time to see them fade together. She bent down and checked on Laura. She was still moaning, but was coming slowing back to herself. Emma helped her sit up and propped her against the wall of the bedroom. "I'm so sorry, Laura, but I had to do that."

Shots split the air, the sharp sound making its way through the TV and AC noise, and nearly stopping Emma's heart. After telling Laura to stay in the room, she retrieved the gun and stuck her head in Dolly's room. Milo's mother was curled up on the bed, her eyes wide with fear. "Stay put," Emma told Dolly, then jerked her head at Granny. "Go see what's going on, Granny. I'm right behind you."

"Me," Dolly said, not understanding that Emma was talking to a ghost. "You want me to go out there?"

"Dolly, you stay here and stay low," Emma clarified. "I'll be right back." She grasped the gun in one hand, and stuck the Taser in her pocket. With bullets flying, a Taser wasn't going to do her any good now.

More shots rang out as she made her way to the window she'd looked through earlier. Quinn was on the ground near the front of the Jeep. Frankie Varga was also down. Emma nearly collapsed but forced herself to stay strong.

Where's Phil? Where's Phil? The question went through her mind like a mantra on Red Bull.

"Quinn's down," Granny reported, popping up next to Emma. "He's shot in the leg."

"And Phil?"

"He's behind the Jeep. His gun is on the other guy."

"I can't see Lloyd, Granny." Emma's voice was frantic. "Where is he?"

"I'm not sure, but I think he's behind the truck, at the tail end. The cop is still between the trailer and the car with his gun on Lloyd, too. The kid is penned in, and if he runs, there's nowhere to go, just open desert. They've got him."

"Look, Granny." Emma pointed out the window. Quinn was moving, trying to crawl to safety behind the Jeep. Phil appeared, snagged him under the arms, and started to drag him. A shot was fired and hit the ground near the Jeep.

"Hold your fire, Garby," yelled Foster, "or

you're going down."

"Yeah, but I'm taking your friends with me." Lloyd fired again, this time hitting the ground near Quinn and Phil just as they disappeared behind the cover of the Jeep.

"Uh-oh," said Granny. "We've got company." Emma turned her attention down the road and spotted a car coming at them.

"Please let that be the police," Emma prayed under her breath.

Granny disappeared, returning in a flash. "That's the Garby boys."

"But the police were supposed to pick them up."

"It's them, I'm telling ya."

The car slowed down, stopping in a cloud of dust just before it reached the property. The passenger's door opened and a man in a suit stepped out. Emma guessed him to be Gene Garby since it wasn't Howard. In his hand was a gun, but it wasn't aimed at anyone in particular. "What's going on here?" he yelled.

"Dad!" screamed Lloyd. "They've got me pinned by the truck. Frankie's dead."

"Who are you?" asked Gene Garby. "Show yourselves."

No one answered.

Emma was relieved that Phil and Quinn were both out of sight.

"It's Foster," Lloyd yelled to his father. "Uncle Howard's partner."

The driver's side door opened. Howard Garby stepped out. Like his brother, he stayed behind the door for protection. A gun was in his hand. "John, is that you?" Howard called out. "I think this is all a big misunderstanding."

"No misunderstanding, Howard," John called. "I know what you've been up to. It's all over."

"John," Howard called in a friendly voice. "I'm sure we can work this all out."

Before Foster could answer, Gene Garby shot in the direction of Foster's voice. Emma paled at the sound but recovered when she spotted the top of Foster's head moving away from the street toward the back of the car.

Another shot rang out. This time from the direction of the Jeep. It hit Gene square in the shoulder. He howled in pain and dropped his gun.

Lloyd responded by firing several shots at the Jeep while Howard continued to pin Foster. Another shot came from the Jeep, this one hitting the front tire by Howard.

More gunfire came from near Lloyd's car. Foster was returning his partner's fire. Between the Jeep and John Foster, it was the Garbys who were now pinned down with only their vehicle for cover. Gene Garby tried to pick up his gun with his good arm, but another shot from Phil discouraged his plan. He crawled back into the car and ducked low. Lloyd tried shooting at Phil and Quinn, but his shots only hit the body of the Jeep.

Emma yanked open the door she'd entered and took the steps two at a time. In her hands, she still held the gun.

This side of the mobile home offered no cover. Pressing herself against the side of the structure to stay out of sight, Emma quickly made her way as close to the end of the trailer as she dared. The crash with the Jeep had pushed the front of the truck close to the front of the trailer. It was too small of an opening for Lloyd to squeeze through. He was trapped in the triangle created by the truck and the trailer. His only way out was past Foster.

Emma peeked around the corner and saw Lloyd edging for the far end of the truck, getting closer to the carport. His broad back was to her. Lloyd got ready to shoot again, not at Quinn and Phil this time, but at Foster.

Like Phil showed her, Emma took aim with the pistol.

"Lloyd," she shouted into the small space. When the startled young man turned, Emma fired.

CHAPTER TWENTY-NINE

Emma sidled up to John Foster. "Granny and Lenny want to know where Nicholas is. They want to play with him."

Foster laughed and looked at the empty air on both sides of Emma. "Sorry, guys, but I told my wife to stay at her parents' place awhile longer." Then he turned his attention back on Emma. "You did say he'd grow out of this ghost thing in time, right?"

"Most children do," Emma assured him. "Then there are those like Milo who never lose it and those like me who develop communication with spirits later in life."

"No offense, but let's hope my son is of the first variety."

"Humpf," groused Granny. "He's no fun."

It was Saturday evening. They were at Dolly Meskiel's home. She had wanted to have a combination going-away and thank-you party for everyone. The next morning Emma and Phil were driving back to California. Quinn was catching a plane home and they were giving him a lift to the airport on their way out of town. Milo and Tracy had decided to stay a couple more days. Milo was getting to know Lenny and acting as the conduit between him and Dolly. He was learning a lot about his father, and his spirit communication skills were no longer on the fritz.

Phil came up to Emma with a glass of wine and handed it to her. "Pretty fancy spread just to say good-bye to us, isn't it? And I've just seen the hors d'oeuvres. God only knows what's going on in the kitchen. They won't let anyone in there." He indicated the screens that had been placed across the entry to the dining area and kitchen to make his point.

"Smells good, though," said John. He lifted his nose and sniffed.

"It was Tracy's doing," answered Emma. "She hired a caterer so Dolly wouldn't have to fuss and went all out." Emma laughed and looked at Foster. "Tracy is an all-or-nothing person. Always has been."

"So, John," said Phil, "what's going to happen to the Garbys?"

"They've been charged with soliciting to commit murder and kidnapping. Lloyd Garby has been charged with kidnapping.

Howard cut a deal, which doesn't surprise me. He confessed and told us everything about the setup. It really does seem like it was all Gene's idea. Lloyd also confessed. It's just a matter of time before Gene does, too. There's too much evidence against him."

"I'm glad they're cooperating," said Phil. "I'd hate to see this ghost business and Emma in the limelight during a trial."

"Me, too," said Emma.

"Yeah," said Foster, "but it would make for an interesting trial and would certainly boost your show's ratings."

"Sensationalism is more my ex-husband's style," Emma answered, "not mine."

"You know," Foster told them, "that woman from Desert Sun came forward."

"Claudine?" Emma asked.

"No, Gloria Youngblood. She's the one who tipped you off to the Garbys, isn't she? At least that's what she told us in her statement."

Emma nodded. "But she was so frightened, there was no way I would have given you her name. She's really the one who changed the game for us. That and figuring out the Dolan Springs location."

Emma's face clouded over as she took a drink of her wine. "It's too bad about

Frankie Varga, though."

Foster shrugged. "He made his choices."

Granny's intel about the gun had been wrong. Frankie had more than one gun and had taken one with him when he left the trailer. He'd pulled it and fired at Quinn in anger over his truck, striking him in the thigh. He was about to fire again when Foster shot and killed him, kicking off the gunfight on Ironwood Drive.

"Still, a death is a death," Emma said with a half sigh. "But better him than any of you." They were all silent for a moment.

"What about Nemo?" Foster asked, breaking the silence. "Will he be causing any more problems?"

"I doubt it," Emma answered. "When he left with Madeline, I asked him not to come back. He may or he may not, but I don't think he'll be causing any mischief if he does."

"What about the money?" Phil asked Foster. "Will your family get it eventually?"

Foster shook his head. "The casino was insured, so it will go to the insurance company once it's released from evidence. I called my great-uncle and told him about it. He was quite excited. He said the insurance company initially didn't want to pay up because they were sure it was an inside job."

Emma thought about Bert. It had been an inside job, but she didn't say anything. There was no need.

"By the time they did," Foster continued, "the casino was sold. He wanted to call up the insurance company and give them a piece of his mind, but I think I talked him out of it." Foster laughed. "Uncle Nicky is quite a character."

Quinn hobbled over on crutches. "Hey, sports fans."

"Saw you talking to Laura," noted Phil. "How's she doing?"

"Seems okay," Quinn answered. "She's a pretty fascinating young woman and very resilient. I learned she's from Oklahoma and has been on her own since she was like thirteen or fourteen."

Emma studied the girl, who was sitting on the sofa with Dolly. The two were talking with their heads close together. Dolly was holding Laura's hand. "Did she say anything about how she got the scars on her face?"

"Her father did that," answered Foster. "According to her, he cut her up in a drunken rage when she was a young girl. She's had several surgeries. After the final one healed, she took off."

"What an awful thing to go through." Emma's mouth turned downward as she fought the tears threatening to well.

"Uh-oh," said Phil. "I know that look."

Emma turned to him. "What look?"

"That *here's another little chick to rescue* look."

Emma gently slapped Phil's shoulder, but didn't deny her tendency to help young people.

Phil turned to Foster. "Emma's the earth mother to all lost girls and boys, both living and dead."

Foster laughed and took a sip from his own drink. "I can see that, and it's not just boys and girls, I'm betting." He looked at Emma. "You went after Lloyd Garby like he was threatening your personal brood."

"He was." Emma's words held no humor. She'd shot Lloyd without so much as a second thought or shake of the hand. The bullet from her gun caught him in the shoulder just as he turned to face her. He now had an injury to match his father's. Soon after, they'd heard sirens approaching. Surrounded by Mohave County deputies, the Garbys surrendered. Foster had called the sheriff as soon as Frankie was down.

"That's my girl," Phil said with pride, putting an arm around her. "She's a dead shot on the range," he told Foster. "A natural." He gave Emma a squeeze. "And to think you fussed when I taught you about guns, saying you'd never need it."

She gave Phil a small smile. "That I did. But I hope I never need it again."

Phil gave her a quick kiss on the side of her forehead. "Me, too."

"Well, I don't think you'll need to worry about Laura," said Quinn. "Dolly's applying to be her mother figure." They looked back over at the sofa and saw the two fortune-tellers in an embrace. "And Milo is going to be her mentor."

"Yes," said Emma. "He seems quite eager to test her skills and see where she is with them. He'll be very good for her. He's already told me that Laura is a ball of raw talent that needs shaping." She looked around. "Speaking of Milo, I haven't seen either him or Tracy for a while."

Foster indicated the hallway. "I saw the two of them head that way a bit ago." He was about to say something else when he noticed Dolly waving him over to the sofa. "Excuse me," he said to them with a smile. "I'm being summoned."

Quinn adjusted himself on the crutches and looked at Phil. "So did you ask her?"

"Ask me what?" Emma looked at the two men with suspicion.

Phil cleared his throat. "I'm thinking that instead of sticking Quinn on a plane in the morning, he can ride back to Cali with us. He could stay at one of our places in Julian until his leg is better."

The surprise on Emma's face melted into a smile. "I think that's a great idea, but you don't need my permission to have a sleepover with your little friend."

The two grown men laughed, then Quinn said, "Please, Mom, please. I don't have school for at least three weeks."

"School?" Emma asked.

Quinn nodded. "I'm giving a short lecture series at a university in about a month. I can prepare while my leg mends."

Emma laughed. "Okay, but don't call me Mom. Save that for Phil's aunt Susan. It won't matter if you stay at my house or Phil's; she's going to fuss over you until you beg for mercy."

Quinn grinned. "Sounds great to me."

"Did I hear right?" Granny floated over. "Is Indiana coming to stay with us?"

"Yes, Granny, he is," Emma confirmed. "For a couple of weeks until his leg heals."

"Hot diggity!"

"Granny votes yes," Emma told the men.

387

Quinn looked around until Emma pointed him in the right direction. "Thanks, Granny."

"He can rock with me and my man Jacob on the porch. Does he like *CSI*? Old movies? We can watch TV together. I need someone to work the remote when you're not around."

Emma laughed. "Granny has plans of her own for you," she told Quinn.

"And I can teach you how to communicate with her," added Phil.

Quinn was surprised. "You understand Granny?"

"I don't hear her, but we've worked out a little routine."

Phil's demonstration was interrupted by an exclamation from Dolly. "Oh my!"

All eyes turned to Dolly, then to where her eyes were fixed. She was staring at the entrance to the hallway. Coming down it was Tracy and Milo, arm in arm. Milo was dressed in a dark suit and Tracy in a white tea-length lace dress. Her hair was pulled up. She was wearing makeup and holding a bouquet of sterling roses, which Emma knew were her favorite flowers. No one spoke, but gaped at the two of them with open mouths.

Tracy nudged Milo. "Welcome to our

wedding," he announced, his voice a little shaky.

"What?" exclaimed Emma, going to her friend. She turned to Dolly. "Did you know about this?"

Dolly shrugged. "I was sworn to secrecy."

Emma looked at Tracy with tears in her eyes. "You didn't tell me?"

"We wanted it to be a surprise," Tracy said with a big grin. "Surprise!"

"Can I hug you or will it mess you up? You look so beautiful."

"Emma Whitecastle, if you don't hug me right this minute, I'm going to smack you with my flowers."

The two women embraced, then Emma hugged Milo. "But what about your family in Chicago?" she asked Tracy.

"They can give us a big reception if they want," the bride answered. "But after what happened this week, we decided to get married now while we're all together safe and sound."

"And while Lenny is with us," added Milo. He looked over to his right, where the ghost of Lenny Speidel beamed with pride. Milo looked at Dolly. "What more can I ask for than to have both of my parents here on this special day."

Dolly touched a tissue to her eyes and smiled.

With her hands on her hips, Granny said to Emma, "Maybe this will give you and the cowboy the kick in the pants you need."

Emma frowned at the ghost, but Milo laughed out loud. Everyone else looked confused until Milo said one simple word of explanation: "Granny."

Emma touched Tracy's shoulder and grinned. "I can't believe you pulled this together in just two days. You usually need a week to decide which movie to see."

"It wasn't rocket science," the bride explained with a smile. "There are only eight guests and the dress is off the rack." She linked an arm through Emma's. "Now, come with me. There's a bouquet for you in the kitchen because you're my maid of honor."

Milo approached Phil. "I was hoping you'd be my best man."

Phil stuck out his right hand to Milo. "I'd be honored."

The ceremony was held on Dolly's patio under a trellis of flowers, performed by a justice of the peace who did not look like Elvis.

ABOUT THE AUTHOR

Sue Ann Jaffarian is the critically acclaimed author of three mystery series: the Ghost of Granny Apples Mysteries, the Odelia Grey Mysteries, and the Madison Rose Vampire Mysteries. In addition to being a writer, Sue Ann is a full-time paralegal for a Los Angeles law firm and a sought-after motivational speaker. Visit her website at sueannjaffarian.com.